"Annab _____ _____ ___ written a love story that is as laugh-out-loud funny as it is emotionally profound. Don't miss this perfect summer escape."

—Emily Giffin, #1 *New York Times* bestselling author of *The Summer Pact*

"Annabel Monaghan has a direct line to my heart—and my funny bone. With *It's a Love Story,* she's given us an enemies-to-lovers rom-com that's SO MUCH MORE. This is dopamine in book form. And don't we all need that right now?"

—Mary Kay Andrews, *New York Times* bestselling author of *Summers at the Saint*

"[A] bingeable, beachy contemporary . . . Monaghan mines a lot of joy out of [a] close-knit family dynamic and the scenic coastal setting, while creating a heroine readers will root for. This is an addictive romp."

—*Publishers Weekly* (starred review)

PRAISE FOR ANNABEL MONAGHAN

"Poignant, funny, and bingeable, Annabel Monaghan writes five-star reads."

—Abby Jimenez, #1 *New York Times* bestselling author of *Just for the Summer*

"Anything Annabel writes, I'm reading it."
—Carley Fortune, #1 *New York Times* bestselling author of
Every Summer After

"In Monaghan's charming mid-life romances, triumphant second acts, hilarity, and good vibes are guaranteed."
—*The Boston Globe*

"Annabel Monaghan is topping the list as our new favorite romance author."
—*Country Living*

"Perfectly captures the apprehension and excitement of infatuation blended with life's complications."
—*The Washington Post*

"The perfect escape."
—*USA Today*

"Filled with swoon-worthy moments and hilariously lovable characters."
—*Woman's World*

"Annabel Monaghan delights with her bright, sparkling, witty writing style that makes everyone want to be her best friend."
—Katie Couric Media

"Honestly, I will read every single thing that Annabel Monaghan writes until the end of time. . . . Add in Monaghan's sharp-shooting wit and writing, and just don't blame me if you neglect your work and family to turn page after page."
—The Nerd Daily

"Funny and smart, with a Nancy Meyers–movie quality."
—*Real Simple*

"Annabel Monaghan's writing is smart, snappy, and satisfying."

—Elin Hilderbrand, #1 *New York Times* bestselling author
of *Hotel Nantucket*

"Annabel Monaghan knows how to write romance, how to sweep you up and make you feel as though you, the reader, are falling in love. This is what romance books are all about."

—Sophie Cousens, *New York Times* bestselling author of
Just Haven't Met You Yet

"Annabel Monaghan has joined my shortlist of instant auto-buy authors. Her writing is packed full of chemistry and warmth."

—Paige Toon, internationally bestselling author of
Only Love Can Hurt Like This

"Annabel Monaghan is known for her breezy but substantive novels about marriage, divorce, motherhood, grief, and newfound love in the midst of it all." —*Elle*

IT'S A
Love
Story

ANNABEL MONAGHAN

G. P. PUTNAM'S SONS
New York

PUTNAM
— EST. 1838 —

G. P. PUTNAM'S SONS

Publishers Since 1838

An imprint of Penguin Random House LLC

1745 Broadway, New York, NY 10019

penguinrandomhouse.com

Book design by Ashley Tucker

Library of Congress has catalogued the G. P. Putnam's Sons
trade paperback edition as follows:

Names: Monaghan, Annabel, author.
Title: It's a love story / Annabel Monaghan.
Other titles: It is a love story
Description: New York : G. P. Putnam's Sons, 2025.
Identifiers: LCCN 2024050205 (print) | LCCN 2024050206 (ebook) |
ISBN 9780593714102 (trade paperback) | ISBN 9780593714119 (epub)
Subjects: LCGFT: Romance fiction. | Novels.
Classification: LCC PS3613.O52268 I87 2025 (print) |
LCC PS3613.O52268 (ebook) | DDC 813/.6—dc23/eng/20241028
LC record available at https://lccn.loc.gov/2024050205
LC ebook record available at https://lccn.loc.gov/2024050206

Hardcover edition ISBN: 9798217046577

Printed in the United States of America
1st Printing

The authorized representative in the EU for product safety and compliance is Penguin Random House Ireland, Morrison Chambers, 32 Nassau Street, Dublin D02 YH68, Ireland, https://eu-contact.penguin.ie.

For my beautiful friend Tiffany O'Toole,
now my lucky star

IT'S A
Love
Story

CHAPTER 1

FAKE IT TILL YOU MAKE IT IS A PHILOSOPHY THAT serves in literally every aspect of life. Slap a smile on your face and your brain will eventually think you're happy. That's not just me talking; it's science. Walk around in those Nikes until you feel like going for a run. Dress for the job you want. I was an actress for a big chunk of my adolescence, so you could say I am an expert in harnessing the power of imagination to get yourself where you want to be.

This morning I am also harnessing the power of my flat iron, a newly sharpened brow pencil, and a strawberry Pop-Tart. I need to show up for work looking like a winner, so I've been standing in front of my closet for ten minutes, re-ironing my hair and hoping the right outfit will reveal itself to me. I have a meeting with my boss to talk about next steps for my new project. If it's green-lit, *True Story* will be the first script I've brought to the studio that will actually be made into a movie. If it's made, it will make me. Today I need an outfit that whispers success really loudly. I don't miss much about being on TV, but on mornings like this I do miss the costume department. I want someone to tell me what scene I'll be walking through today and exactly how I should look.

I sort through my work clothes, blouses and skirts in shades of blue and gray. They're freshly pressed and definitely make me seem competent but make me look more like a flight attendant than an airline CEO. Next to them is my dating wardrobe, which I've chosen with more care than any costume department ever did. My first-date dress is green and white pin-striped and hits right below my knees. It's a dress you can't argue with. It's dignified and says I'm feminine but not trying too hard to be sexy. It says I'm a person you might consider kissing and then later introducing to your grandmother. When my future partner and I tell our kids about our first date, that's how I want him to describe me: kissable and Grandma-worthy. Think Reese Witherspoon in basically any movie.

The rest of the dresses also each have a specific purpose. Second date—show a little more skin. Third date—invite a kiss. And the all-important fourth date—Enter an Actual Relationship. I finish my Pop-Tart, wipe my hands on my pajamas, and pull out the fourth-date dress. It is, in a word, sensational. It's red and silk, not entirely appropriate for August in Los Angeles, but it's a deal-closer. The tags still dangle down the back because I haven't actually had a fourth date since I got serious about my Manifest a Solid Partner project last year. I bought it because I hoped it would bring new energy to the consistently disastrous fourth date. Sometimes it's the guy who blows it—he's rude to the waiter or admits to owning an accordion. Any mention of NASCAR and I'm out. More often than not, it's me. I get comfortable, I forget to be Reese Witherspoon, and he sees me for the B-teamer that I am. By the fourth date, I get impatient to just make it a thing already. I talk too much or too fast. A few times I've suggested plans way too far in the future, as in "My boss is getting married next spring, you should come!"

Oof!

I hold up the red dress and look in the mirror. *Yes,* I think. This is the kind of energy I want to bring to my meeting this morning. Today I'm going on a fourth date with my career. I love this thought so much that I take the dress off its hanger and rip off the tags. "Showtime," I say to my reflection.

I've been trying to get a script green-lit ever since I was promoted to creative executive two years ago. The scripts I've brought in have been low-stakes romantic comedies that I thought were pretty good, but none of them compare to *True Story*. This script is a total game changer. There's a tenderness to the writing and a truth to the humor that has its hooks in me. I even dreamed about it this morning, and I woke up laughing, chest vibrating from the force of it, tears in my eyes. I do that sometimes, laugh in my sleep. I don't know how I'll explain this to a partner if I find one.

I tie my sash in a careful square knot and take a second Pop-Tart and a mug of coffee onto the front porch just as the sky starts to brighten on Montana Avenue. Being a funny kid on TV got me the down payment on this little Spanish house. It has a big porch and a tile roof and a rounded front door painted a deep French blue. I am training bougainvillea to crawl up the porch and along the roofline. Bougainvillea feels like a kindergarten art project, little petals made out of fine pink paper that blow in the wind but are, oddly, fine in the rain.

I'm two miles from the beach, but if *Pop Rocks* had been picked up for more seasons or had been syndicated, I'd be down on Pacific Coast Highway listening to the waves with the cast of *Friends*. It's fine. Four years of my adolescence as barbecue-sauce-in-her-braces Janey Jakes was plenty. The thing I've learned about funny is that it can be a little reckless. To be laughing is to be a little out of control. And certainly, when trying to Manifest a Solid Partner, it is imperative that you keep funny in check. *You're funny, I'd like to procreate with you*, said exactly no man ever.

That's also science.

The teakettle whistles, and a minute later Clem joins me outside. "Wait. Fourth date?" she asks as she sits next to me on the porch swing.

"Well, sort of," I say and smooth the hem of my dress over my knees.

"There's no way you broke out the sacred dress if you're not a hundred percent sure there's a date. Who is it? I don't remember the third date." Clem raises her dark eyes to me. They're kind and tired. She moved in with me last year after the World's Shittiest Divorce. Of course I'm sorry about her terrible financial situation, but coming home to a house where another person lives has been the best change of my thirties. Clem was a godsend of a college roommate and is now a full-time geriatric nurse and a part-time bartender. She makes a living tending to human frailty.

"The date's not a who," I say. "It's a script. I've decided that today I'm having a fourth date with my career."

"Oh God, Jane. This sounds like YouTube self-help."

"No, this is coming from me. I have a meeting with Nathan this morning, and I am a hundred percent sure this script is the one that's finally going to get made. I can feel it." I don't say what I've been thinking: that this script is like an Aquarius or the number eight, just exactly right. I don't say that the universe has sent it to me to save me from the rumored round of fall layoffs. Which it totally has. I've lived in Los Angeles my whole life, and I know enough to know when I sound like it.

"And it's worthy of that dress? Wow. I hope you two will be very happy." She gives me a sideways smile and sips her tea.

"I swear I have a crush on this script," I say. "Like I might be madly in love with it." My voice cracks a tiny bit when I say this. I don't know what my problem is. There is something about this script that scares me a little. Just the heart of it. It's like I've swallowed the world's tiniest crowbar, and it's floating around inside me prying my closed bits open. To be clear, I don't actually believe in true love. I'm a grown-up. But if this script can affect me this way, then normal people are going to lose their minds.

"Is this the one where he puts his hand on his heart at the end?"

"Yes," I say. "And then she knows." I have my hand on my heart as I say it, and I swear I feel something move. "You'll see. This movie is going to make me legit."

I PULL OUT of my driveway, turn on the radio, and it's Jack Quinlan playing his number four single, "By My Side." I change the station, and it's Jack Quinlan playing his number two single, "Purple." I switch to a reliably country station and, you guessed it, Jack Quinlan. I turn off the radio. I knew Jack when we were teenagers. The whole thing was embarrassing. This wouldn't be such a big deal if we weren't two people who started our careers in the same spot and only one of us is a recently minted megastar. The other one, incidentally, is me. I have it in my head that by my age I should be doing whatever my forever is going to be. Making big career strides with a partner by my side. I should have a pet. I thought by now I'd know Spielberg and how to use my oven.

I arrive at the office before nine o'clock. The lobby is nearly empty, and I have the sense that this place is entirely mine. Pantheon Television, where I spent my adolescence on camera accidentally sitting on nachos, is a half mile away, but inside this building, I'm an executive, calling the shots. I am not told where to stand or how to act. I am a decision-maker. I check the integrity of the square knot on my dress and then say it out loud: "Decision-maker."

The elevator doors open, and no. No, no, not today. Not when I'm about to turn literally every single thing around.

"Good morning, Jane," he says.

"Don't jinx me. Just press twelve. No, I'll do it. Don't touch anything." I am supremely agitated. It's stupid Dan Finnegan, with his mop of black hair, presumably coming up from the underground parking where he's crushed his clove cigarette next to his unicycle. Of course it's freakin' Dan Finnegan. I have no proof that he travels by unicycle, but he's the kind of above-it-all, know-it-all jerk who probably pays up for cruelty-free cashew butter and then blogs about it. I've seen him around the studio, of course, since he called my last project "trash" and set in motion the events that would have it murdered, dead on the floor. He thinks I'm a little unhinged, so he puts his hands up when he sees me, in mock fear of an outburst. Oh, it's hilarious all right.

"I know not to make any sudden moves," he says, eyes straight ahead.

"Good one," I say.

"You're here early," he says. He's wearing khaki pants and a white shirt, untucked. Untucked and unbrushed are worse than unhinged, if you ask me.

"Yes, big day," I say and gesture to my dress. I don't know why I've done this. This small gesture with my hand has opened up the door for me to tell him that I have a new script. I don't want Dan anywhere near it, but I also want to rub it in his face. "I have a new project."

"Another think piece?" I refuse to look his way, but I can feel a little smile off of him.

Now I'm rolling my eyes. "It's going to be the film of the year."

"I'm sure." The elevator stops on the twelfth floor, and he steps forward and holds the door open for me. His navy blue eyes are disarming every time. All of his features are, as if a sixteenth-century sculptor with a too-sharp chisel arranged them on his face. But it's the eyes, wide under his black brows, that have the intensity to match his arrogance. "No one wants to watch two people who they don't care about fall in love for absolutely no reason."

He's just so superior with his omniscience about what everyone wants and doesn't want. He was so casual about crushing my first real project like it was a gas station receipt. So I step out of the elevator, turn back to him, and spill it. "It's funny and offbeat, with oddball characters. But more than that." I don't know why I'm selling this to him.

The elevator door starts to close and he stops it with his sneaker. "Wait. *True Story*?"

"No," I say. If you could throw a word at a person, I would have shot-putted this one at his chest.

"No, it's not *True Story*?"

"No. I mean yes. But not you." My hands ball up, all on their own accord, as Dan steps off the elevator and lets the doors close behind him.

"Yes, me," he says. "Jane, I'm meeting with Nathan about this at nine. He wants me as cinematographer, and I need it."

"You need it," I say. My voice has gone jagged. "This is about you now? Just trying to get all the facts straight."

"We both probably need it. But I don't hate this script. In fact, I can see it, in my mind, exactly how it should be."

The movie I've been imagining as I fall asleep is the same one he's been imagining, but probably with weird lighting and subtitles and whatever arty stuff wins awards and sells absolutely no tickets. He presses the button and the doors open. "If you can just act like a normal person, we can make this movie."

I am a normal person. In fact, I'm so normal that I don't scream those words at him. There's nothing that makes a person act more insane than trying to prove how sane they actually are. I have a little sweat beading up on my chest now and I really need to calm down. "This cannot be happening," I say as the elevator doors close between us.

CHAPTER 2

I SIT UNDER MY DESK WHERE IT'S SAFE. THERE'S NO place left to fall when I'm down here. It's where you'd sit in an earthquake. My office door is closed, and I just need a minute in this small space to regroup. The hard plastic mat that my chair rolls around on feels cool under me. My knees are pulled up to my chest, and I look up at the underside of my desk drawer where I've written the word "please" six times since my promotion. I can't say exactly why making it in this business means so much to me. Show business was a lifeline for my mom and me when I was a kid, and I mean that literally in the way a lifeline can be food and shelter. But it was also such a weird way to grow up, on television, always being a joke. I just want to be taken seriously for once, and preferably in the world I was raised in. I can't bear the thought of being part of the next round of layoffs, sent home with a cardboard box and a pity smile. I want Hollywood to give me a hug or a gold star, or at least a better table at the Ivy.

My current office has a view of the very top of Pantheon
Television and the soundstage where *Pop Rocks* was filmed.
The show followed four middle schoolers, unlikely friends,
who started an after-school band and became pop stars. If I
get a film made, there's a chance I will move to an office on
the other side of the building, where I won't have to look at
it. Inside that studio was our fake high school classroom,
fake recording studio, and fake auditorium where we were
discovered and given our own fake record contract.

My character, Janey Jakes, is immortalized as a meme,
the one you send your friends after they accidentally reply
all or pull out of a parking lot with a bag of groceries on
their car. *Oof!* I'm thirty-three now, and people seldom recognize me, but it happens. They see me at Starbucks making my famous *oof* face while trying to force open the cream
container, and they sing the familiar show ender: "*Poor
Janey, do do do do do do.*" I smile politely at their joke and
pose for their selfie, but honestly, it's a nightmare.

Hailey Soul, the lead singer, went on to be a soap opera
star and is now a Manhattan mom of three kids with a million Instagram followers (including me) who like to see what
she's wearing and harvesting in her urban garden. Hailey
has long legs. She has a dad who used to surprise her on set
and calls her Cricket. Hailey and her husband have a meet-
cute story that involves a horse. Hailey is the haver of good
things. Hailey is an eternal frontliner. Even in sweatpants
plucking leaves off her basil plant for the camera, she is a star.

Like Jack Quinlan, Hailey is a measuring stick for me.
It's not healthy, but I scroll her Instagram and keep score.

Me: one small house; Hailey: two large ones. Me: an awkward side hug after a third date with an orthodontist; Hailey: a surprise trip to Lake Como for her fifth wedding anniversary. My Manifest a Solid Partner project was born just after her third child, when she posted a photo of the baby in her arms, wrapped in cashmere and bathed in the soft light of her East Hampton firepit.

I reach on top of my desk for a pen and write "please" one more time on the bottom of the drawer before crawling out and standing up like a normal person.

I check my inbox, and Nathan's secretary is confirming our nine a.m. appointment. She's always very formal, like she works for the king. I pull my copy of the script out of my bag. "True Story," it says in the typewriter font that still makes me think something exciting is about to happen.

"You look pretty in red." Mandy, my assistant, is standing in my doorway with a pink smoothie.

"Thank you," I say. "Big day." I straighten up in my chair in case there's any part of my posture that would suggest I've recently been crouched on the floor.

She plops down on the sofa across from my desk. "So, Nathan at nine. In his office. With the director he's considering, some guy named Rodney Whistler."

"Yeah, I knew about him. But what I didn't know is that Nathan's also brought in Dan Finnegan as cinematographer." Besides this being a total disaster, it's weird that he invited a cinematographer to this meeting. Nathan has a little man-crush on Dan's last movie, which won some awards and which Dan probably calls a "film." I try to push away the thought that Nathan is looking for his opinion on this script.

"Dan with the man-bun who ruins everything?"

"The very one. Well, I made up the man-bun part." I don't really like the look on Mandy's face. There's pity there, as if we just opened a window and watched my big break fly away. I fold my hands on my desk in a vaguely presidential way to suggest the sort of calm and focus associated with a person who's got this.

"I'm sorry, this could have been a really good movie," she says. When I don't say anything, she goes on. "I mean, he might not shit all over it?"

I laugh a not-giving-up laugh.

When she's left, I bury my face in my hands and press my fingers into my forehead. I can feel the cog in my brain that's popped out and snagged my entire system. Dan is a giant loose cog in my life, out of nowhere. I have no idea why he has this effect on me. I have to go into this meeting calm and dignified. I have to reply to his criticisms with be-that-as-it-mays instead of shut-up-you-stupid-jerks. Dan gets under my skin. And honestly, the whole purpose of skin is to keep things out.

NATHAN HAS A huge corner office, which is supposed to convey his general importance, though I've never seen more than four people in there at a time. He normally likes to conduct meetings in the conference room next door with lots of food, specifically a large bowl of peanut M&M's and a platter of wrap sandwiches. There's always one of each kind—tuna, egg salad, turkey, ham, and one completely delicious grilled vegetable with mozzarella and the exact right amount of pesto. Unfortunately, today we are meeting in his office with four club chairs set around a coffee table and absolutely no snacks.

His assistant announces me at the door. "Jane Jackson, sir," she says.

He takes off his reading glasses. "Come, sit," he says and directs me to the club chair across from his. Behind him is a floor-to-ceiling window that almost perfectly frames the Hollywood sign in the distance. I think about this every time I go to his office, the almost of it. If this building were moved four yards to the right, that sign would be perfectly centered. I wonder if this drives Nathan mad.

"I'm excited about the script," I say.

"Yes. We paid less for the option than I thought we would."

"Good, that's good," I say. I smooth my dress over my knees and then squeeze my hands together. Calm, confident. Inexplicably, I think of Hailey Soul for the second time in an hour, and I mimic the way she rolls her shoulders back and looks just the right amount bored.

"Yes," he says, though it sounds like no, just as Dan and Rodney appear in the doorway.

I squeeze my hands together tighter as Dan takes the seat next to mine and Rodney sits across from him.

"Jane," Rodney says. "Nice to see you again. I think this script was a great find."

"Thank you," I say. And it's just what I needed. A compliment, an affirmation. This is a great script and I've brought it here. *Showtime, people.* I stop myself before I turn to Dan and smirk.

Nathan says, "I wanted to meet and hear your thoughts on casting and how and where this thing gets filmed, but I was talking to the head of the green light committee last night, and there's a little concern that this film won't be commercial enough to make sense for us."

"It's plenty commercial," I say without really thinking. "Super commercial."

"It's not, actually," says Dan. He's leaning forward in his chair with his forearms resting on his knees. He's rolled up the sleeves of his white shirt, and there's a thin bracelet around his wrist, just a piece of string. Literally everything about Dan is annoying.

"It is," I say and then force myself to take a breath. "I mean, why would you say that?" I turn my body toward him and rest my hands in my lap, trying for the gesture of someone who has just completed a delightful yoga class.

"The casting doesn't lend itself to big stars," he starts.

"Which is great because we don't have the budget for them," I say and turn back to Nathan. "This film is funny and different and irreverent. It's like spring break in movie form."

"Spring break?" asks Rodney.

"Yeah, like a big, great time," I say.

Dan lets out a breath. "I don't really know what script you read."

I'm not sure what's happening with this conversation right now, but there's something moving through my nervous system that is dangerously close to proving that Dan's right about my being completely unhinged. My challenge and best revenge is to stay hinged.

"The same one you did, Dan." I say his name like it's a joke.

He rolls his eyes at me and says to Nathan, "Of course this is a comedy, but what I love is the quiet romance that's growing in the background. When all the laughs and music die down, it ends with the two of them. And that's the beauty of this script and the thing people are going to connect to." He lifts his hand and almost places it on his heart, but doesn't.

"People want superheroes," Nathan says. "Explosions and disasters. They'll only go for this kind of film if it's got huge stars, like every big star. And I don't think we can pull that off."

Rodney nods.

Dan lets out a breath and sort of scrunches up his eyes as if he's not sure he should say what he's about to say. "That's all very loud," he says. "People want love. They want to feel connected and like they're okay."

"In real life, maybe," Nathan says. "But people aren't paying movie theater prices for that."

"I think they would pay for this one," Dan says. The balls on this guy. I mean all the balls in the world. But I agree. This script makes me feel like it's possible that even I could be connected and okay someday.

"I do too," I say. I'm surprised by the sound of my voice because it's calmer than I am currently feeling, and because I've agreed with Dan out loud. "It's a very funny script, but it's the love story that gives it weight. And if people don't want the weight, it still feels like a big, raucous comedy that will turn any cast into stars."

"Again, you might be missing the point," Dan says to me. "The bigness and the raucousness is ironic, Jane. It's in-your-face to hide the vulnerability of the characters."

"Oh, I'm sorry, Dan. I forgot this was our American lit seminar and that you're the guy with the man-bun who smells like weed."

And just like that, I have lost my cool.

Dan laughs. "Yes, the man-bun was huge at Brown ten years ago."

"You went to Brown?" asks Rodney.

"No." Dan laughs that annoying, smug at-you-not-with-you laugh. "Listen, Jane. I'm not going to let you turn *Casablanca* into *The Hangover*."

"Let me?" I say, too loudly.

"See! *The Hangover* had stars," says Nathan. "And a tiger. Jane. That's what this thing needs. A megastar and a tiger."

Dan leans back in his chair like he's given up. He's watching me as I sit stick straight, squeezing my hands together and listening to the roar of blood in my brain. I don't understand how the opinion of a glorified cameraman keeps derailing my career. Hailey has a beach house. Jack has a gold album. I can feel this moment slipping away. Nathan slaps his knees as if he's about to say, *Thanks for stopping by,* and shoo us all out. Rodney is looking at his phone, and Dan's watching me with that unnerving intensity. We might both be concerned that my head is about to explode.

"I know Jack Quinlan." I don't say it as much as I toss the words onto the table in front of us. Like it's the title of an essay I haven't written and I'm just floating the idea.

Nathan leans back in his chair. "Oh?"

All eyes are on me, and I can actually feel where the runaway train has clicked back onto its track. The roaring of blood in my head slows. "Yes, since I was a kid."

"Does he act?" asked Rodney. "He's plenty commercial." He laughs at his understatement.

I'm not entirely sure what I've started or where I'm going with this. But Nathan's countenance has changed from *No* to *I'm listening.*

"No, but he could write a song for the soundtrack," I say. Nathan and Rodney are looking at me like I am going to solve this problem, like they respect my leadership here. This is exactly the feeling I was hoping for when I walked in today.

Dan, however, rolls his eyes. "How are you going to pull that off?"

I have an image in my head of me trying to climb a ladder while a little raccoon is after me, gnawing on my shoe. I need to shake my foot to get free and maybe give that raccoon a black eye in the process.

"I talk to him all the time," I say. "He'll totally do it."

CHAPTER 3

I MANAGE A NEUTRAL FACE AS I WALK BACK TO MY OF-
fice. Nathan has assured me that Jack's involvement will
get this thing green-lit. And why wouldn't it? Jack singing a
song from our soundtrack to a packed arena would sell a
gazillion movie tickets.

Mandy follows me into my office. "Looks like that went
well?"

"It did!" I say, my voice too high. I sit at my desk and
straighten a pile of note cards. "Just a few details to work
out, and we'll be good to go."

"Need my help?"

"No, not now. I'm just going to make a few calls."

I smile the smile of a person who is being flushed down
the world's largest toilet but wants people to think she's enjoying the ride. When Mandy's gone and the door is closed,
I slide off my desk chair and sit on the floor. I don't know
what I was thinking. It wasn't even an exaggeration; it was
an outright lie. I haven't spoken to Jack Quinlan since I was

fourteen and he laughed at me. I wonder what he'd think about me now, trying to slide my desk drawer open from below to find candy.

Turns out this fourth date has gone like every other. The exuberance of my red dress mocks me as I take in the shoddy construction of my desk from below. "Made in Van Nuys," says the sticker next to all of my "pleases." I want to laugh this off. I want to stand up, go on with my day, and saunter— no, sashay!—into my next meeting. I want to call Clem and bust on Dan, who made this movie sound sleepier than it is. There is a thrum in my heart that this script has activated. I do not believe in love. I do not believe in finding The One. All of that is nonsense, but this script has given me this tiny ache, the sneaky kind that attaches itself to hope.

I had ached with hope on the day I auditioned for *Pop Rocks*. I remember being discovered in my middle school's production of *Little Shop of Horrors* and asked to audition. I couldn't believe it, being discovered. I'd just gotten braces and perfected a full metal smile that was like a cheat code to lifting my mom's mood, softening her tired face into a giggle. I was a young twelve and didn't know enough about Hollywood to be nervous. It all just felt fun. It was fun to make the stiff casting people laugh. I gave them something, and they gave me something back—an exact exchange of energy. *I love you*, followed by *I love you too*. I ended the audition with my full metal smile and got the job.

The studio found me an agent, and it all took off—the meetings, the contracts, the transition to on-set school and a life where I would only know three other kids: Hailey,

Will, and Dougie. As the awkward keyboardist, I was the punch line of almost every scene, but it was fun. My job was to show up at fake band rehearsals with a gooey rack of ribs in my hand. Intermittently, I'd be on the receiving end of a thrown milkshake, chucked right in my face. I'd walk into the student lounge and sit on someone's nachos and frown my *oof* into the camera while the rest of the fake band said, "Poor Janey," followed by that special guitar riff.

The irony was that this was the first time in my life I wasn't actually poor. My mom and I stayed in the Westwood apartment I grew up in, but we had new shoes and rotisserie chickens. It was a sharp change—a single mother and child living on welfare one day and then having money for new shoes and prepared food the next. This was a thing I'd been craving my whole life, and I luxuriated in being casual about the basics. *Oh, sure, let's grab lunch.* I still get a rush every time I put down my credit card and say, "I've got this." "I've got this" means I have this. I am not without.

The first time I ever saw my mother walk into a store, run her hand over a sweater, and then buy it, I felt actual joy. I do not exaggerate when I say that watching my mother purchase things that she didn't need was the great joy of my childhood. It was hope fulfilled.

And there it is, the thought that turns my tiny ache of hope into actual hope. I can figure this out. When I was twelve years old, I turned our lives around. I'm not going to squeeze an original song out of the biggest recording star in the country, but I have bought some time. I'm going to figure out how to catch this movie a tiger.

CHAPTER 4

I LEAVE WORK EARLY SO I CAN GET OUT OF THIS STU-
pid dress before falling into the comfort of Friday night
with my mom. There are no tigers to be caught on a summer Friday afternoon—they're all in traffic headed to Mal-
ibu or the Hamptons. I've painted myself into a corner, and
I could use some of my mom's trademarked brand of mis-
guided optimism. *Call George Clooney,* she'll suggest.

We're meeting outside the theater in Westwood, and I
see her before she sees me. She looks like anyone's mom,
but younger and prettier. Her hair is long and highlighted
back to the blond of her youth, stick straight and parted
down the middle. My dad had curly hair, which is where
mine comes from, and I have been fascinated my whole life
by the way my mom just wakes up with orderly hair. It's like
if someone was born with mascara on—what a time-saver.
She's smiling into her phone, and an old fear sparks behind
my chest.

"Jane!" she says when she sees me and pulls me into a hug.

"You look really good," I say. "What gives?"

She's reading another text. "Sorry, it's Gary." And there it is.

"Gary," I say. "Still?"

"Yes." She smiles and loops her arm in mine. When my mom falls for someone, she falls hard. And when it blows up, she is as tenuous as a sugar cookie in the rain. Gary is a guy she met at yoga who spends an outrageous amount of time reading magazines at the Coffee Bean next door to the real estate office where she works. Her usual type can best be described as "dashing," so Gary is a relief in a way. "Did you get tickets already?"

"I did," I say, and we walk in and line up for popcorn. My mom and I have been doing Friday night movie dates my entire life. When I was little, it was our one big extravagance. We'd smuggle home-popped popcorn and little bags of chocolate chips in our coat pockets and hold hands when the lights went low. Then, afterward, we'd get Chinese takeout and play spa day. As I got older, it changed and stayed the same. Always a movie, always Chinese. But now sometimes it happens on Saturday, if one of us has a date we're excited about. And we pay for our popcorn and Milk Duds.

We sit down on the aisle of the fifth row, per usual, just as the previews are starting. There's a remake of a World War II movie coming this fall. There's a Clearwater Studios

film called *Trauma Train*. What's more commercial than
that? There's a romantic comedy about a divorced couple
who are pretending to date so that their kids won't think
they're lonely, and then they fall back in love. My mom is
rapt. Her eyes are on the screen, maybe even a little wet.

"Mom. Come on," I whisper.

"What?" She reaches for my hand and gives it a little
squeeze. "It's sweet," she says.

I'm about to make a face, but the lights go all the way
low and our movie starts.

WHEN WE'RE BACK at her apartment and we've finished the
moo shu, we turn on the TV and do spa day. We don't call
it that anymore, but what started as my mom painting tiny
daisies on my nails before bed has morphed into her giving
me a smoky eye. A year ago she was experimenting with
false eyelashes and matte red lipstick. Now it's a neutral face
and a smoky eye. I almost always leave here looking like a
drag queen, but what I like about our Friday nights is what
I've always liked: the touchstone with my mom. As long as
we have Friday nights, I know she is okay.

She dabs a cotton ball on my eyelid. "You can just call
Jack and ask. You have nothing to lose."

I don't want to enumerate all the things I have to lose
here—my pride, my grown-up sense of self, my job. It
wasn't a small lie. "Even if I could, and I can't, there's no
way he'd do it. It's like I lost my mind for a minute. This
Dan guy makes me feel like a kid on the playground, stuff

comes out of my mouth and I swear I don't know where it's coming from. *I know Jack Quinlan.* Like why would I ever bring that up?"

She stops with the makeup and looks me in the eye. "Jane, you were fourteen. Let it go."

I let out a little laugh. "I know. Obviously. I have a 401(k) and a mortgage—I swear I've recovered. But there is no way in hell I'm calling him."

She continues the eyelid dabbing. "You can find another script."

"I really want to make this one. This was the one."

"You'll find the one," my mom says. She gives me the smile of a hopeless romantic, and I know we're not talking about the movie anymore.

I play along because that's what I do with her. "Sure," I say. "But this script—I don't know—I feel something. There's something different about the romance, it's believable."

"You'll figure out how to get it made," my mom says. "You have an exceptionally good eye for story because you have an exceptionally good heart. And I bet grown-up Jack Quinlan would love your script."

I smile because this is so my mom, putting the impossibly positive spin on everything. Even the great tragedy of her life, the story of my dad and her, has a happy feeling when she tells it. She told it to me regularly when I was growing up, my favorite bedtime story. They'd been young and fell madly in love and then had me, and they would have lived happily ever after, except he died when I was five.

The first time we saw *The Notebook*, I thought that if my dad had lived they would have died in each other's arms like Allie and Noah. I told my mom that, and she added it to the end of the story, an epilogue. I later learned that this story is a lie made of half-truths and my own gullibility, so I wince when she tells it now. But I let my mom think I still believe it because it feels like a betrayal not to. I'll eventually find a partner of some sort, and she'll keep looking for love, like the walking, talking version of that heart-eyed emoji. I can't protect her from this.

Tonight my mom perfects my smoky eyes and walks me to my car. "Get a good night's sleep," she says. "Everything will look better in the morning."

CHAPTER 5

~~~~

NOTHING LOOKS BETTER IN THE MORNING, ESPE-
cially since I fell asleep with smoky eyes. I find Clem's
cold cream and get to work unearthing my face from my
mom's handiwork. I wipe my eyes and watch the black kohl
smear across my face. I rinse the cloth and apply the cold
cream again. And there I am. Brown eyes, brown lashes.
Straightened hair curled right up again. The smoky eyes
were an illusion. The blockbuster movie was an illusion. I
can't seem to grab hold of any of yesterday's optimism. This
project is slipping through my fingers, and it's time to face
that reality.

"How'd the fourth date go?" Clem asks when she joins
me on the porch with her tea.

"Not so great."

She sips in silence, and I am grateful she's not a morning person. I've been out here for an hour, wrapped in my
duvet, watching the dew dry on the grass. There's a tiny
piece of raw cuticle on my pointer finger, and I am worrying

it with my thumb. I like the distraction of that quick wince of pain each time I touch it.

"How was your Friday?" I ask.

"The hospital was fine, then a guy passed out at happy hour and I taught his friends how to paint his nails."

"That sounds fun," I say with no fun in my voice.

"Are you sick?" Clem asks.

"No, why?"

"You're making a really weird face and you're wearing your bed."

"It'll be fine."

"Can I help?" she asks. And she probably could. If this were a solvable problem, Clem could tackle it. Rodents, oil changes, split ends—Clem can fix it. When we met, she kinda fixed me. She was my first friend at UCLA, and maybe my first real friend anywhere. We met in a little grove of trees when we both stopped to listen to a band practice through an open window. They were insanely bad. I liked how, when it got really, really bad, they all laughed. We both stood there, looking up, and laughed with them.

I kept going back to that spot. First because of the shaded benches, and then because of Clem and the laughter. Their laughter, our laughter. More than the spot itself, Clem was like a secret place I could go to tap into my inner underdog and feel like it was all going to be okay.

But of course she can't help with this.

"Nathan said Clearwater wouldn't green-light my movie because it's not commercial enough, and I told him that I was in close touch with—wait for it—Jack Quinlan and that I'm going to get him to write us a song."

"No." The horror on her face matches my own. "Oh God."

"Yep. So now I have to figure out how to get in touch with him and beg or get the screenwriter to add an alien invasion and a few superheroes to the second act." I shake my head. "Classic, right? Just peak Janey Jakes."

I swear I haven't thought about *Pop Rocks* this often in years. I don't really even Instagram-stalk Hailey that much. And I never google Jack Quinlan. I coexist with him the way everyone with a radio does. I haven't felt the shame of the whole thing in forever; in fact, burying shame might be my superpower. There's something particularly cutting about the shame of that day with Jack because I'm just mad at myself. I was the one. I said the thing. I want to rip off my skin and get out of my body so I don't have to sit with it. It's the tiny little nugget inside me that reminds me I used to be a person who wanted love too much.

She scoots closer to me on the swing and puts an arm around me. "This is just. Wow."

"Yep. All those Janey Jakes memes were a warm-up for this particular *oof* moment."

She laughs. "Temporary insanity. Just tell Nathan that Jack changed his mind and move on. Like today. Otherwise this is going to eat you alive."

"I could," I say. But I know that I won't. At least not today. I want to live for twenty-four more hours in a world where Nathan thinks this is happening. That I'm happening. "Working today?"

"Brunch shift."

"Bring home the extra bacon and I'll make BLTs for dinner."

"I'm also working the dinner shift." I rest my head on her shoulder. Truly no one works harder than Clem. She has been digging herself out of a hole since Nick quietly lost all of their savings betting on horses in Del Mar. She found out when she tried to withdraw some of that savings to throw him a birthday party. I am not a big Nick fan.

We sit in silence as a warm breeze rattles the bougainvillea. I let my mind drift into the final scene of the movie, when they know it's real and that they'll be together forever. My heart does that weird thing again, the thing it hasn't done since I was fourteen. The thing that tells me this movie will be a hit. I cannot let this project be trashed. There has to be another, better, easier way to make it commercial.

"You're doing it again," she says.

"What? Oh." I see my hand on my heart. Dan almost put his hand on his heart when he was talking about *True Story*. I'm sure he wants to turn this thing into something boring, but at least he gets it. He might have ideas. "As if things couldn't get worse, I think I'm going to have to call Dan Finnegan," I say, getting up.

"You hate Dan Finnegan."

"I'm sure everyone does," I say. "But it's easier than calling Jack Quinlan. At least I have his number."

I grab my phone and head into my bedroom. I type in his name to text him and see the last message he sent me, four months ago: Oh I get it. I like that. Tails

A fresh, hot embarrassment that I have absolutely no time for right now rushes up my face. How much shame can one woman bury in her heart? If I text him, he will see that prior conversation too, and no one needs to go back to that disaster. I go to delete the conversation, but don't. I open my closet door, sit down on the floor space that is exactly the right size for me, pull it closed so I'm completely in the dark, and I call him.

He picks up, groggy. It's nine thirty. "Hi, Dan? This is Jane Jackson."

"Why?" It's definitely the first word he's said today. An image flashes of all that black hair splayed out on a white pillowcase, the back of his hand shielding his eyes.

It's actually a great question. "I'm just thinking about the movie. If the whole soundtrack thing doesn't work out, I was wondering if you had any other ideas. Like to make it commercial."

"Mm, huh." Now I am picturing him sleeping in long johns and a nightcap, to be ironic while he sleeps.

"You liked it, right? I mean, you said it wouldn't be commercial and then a bunch of other stupid stuff. But you like the script?"

"I love the script." I can hear him moving around. He's awake now.

"I do too. So do you have any other ideas, like if it doesn't work out with the song? A way to make it glitzy. A tiger?" I cover my eyes, bracing myself for what comes next. The mocking. The catchphrase. Instead I hear a long stream of pee hitting the toilet. "Could you mute that?" I ask.

"Listen, I didn't ask you to call me first thing in the morning."

"It's nine thirty. It's like tenth thing in the morning."

"Not if you're between jobs," he says. "Oh, shit, is it Saturday?"

"What grown-up doesn't know it's Saturday when it's Saturday, Dan?" I'm not sure what it is about my exasperation with Dan that feels like a break. I lean into it like it's a safe space where I can stop berating myself.

"Me," he says. Something metal drops on the floor. "Look, I've gotta go. If you want to talk about this, call me later. I'm working by the pier all day."

"Like you sell cotton candy?"

"Yes, that's right, Jane. On Saturdays I put on a pin-striped suit and carry a snack box around selling cotton candy to tourists."

"I'm really surprised you don't have a goatee."

He laughs a little. "Yeah, I'm working on it. Listen, I've gotta go, but I'm off at five if you want to meet me down there."

"What?" I don't know what just happened, but it sounded like Dan asked me out. "Why?"

"I don't know, Jane. You called me." He puts his phone on speaker and turns his shower on. "To talk about the movie?"

"Oh, okay. Maybe," I say.

"See you maybe," he says and hangs up.

I reach for my Nike shoe box, orange with the white swoosh, and open it to find that Clem has refilled my candy supply. I grab a Snickers bar and tear it open. Dan is the only other person who seems to care if this movie gets made, but he is the least showbizzy person I've ever met in Hollywood. He's the guy who would turn this into a puppet show to make a point. But right now he's all I've got.

CHAPTER 6

CLEM'S LEFT FOR WORK, SO I MAKE HER BED THE WAY she likes it and clean the spaghetti pot from her dinner last night. To keep my brain from spiraling, I run to the beach and walk home. I manically clean the house, except my closet. It's still only two p.m., and the perfectly white grout between my kitchen tiles is offering me no solutions. I wash my hair and blow it stick straight.

When I have completely run out of things to do and ways to put it off, I decide to go to the Santa Monica Pier and talk it out with Dan.

I arrive a little before five o'clock. It's still hot out. I'm on the pier looking down onto the beach, and I'm not sure what I'm looking at. Dan is surrounded by women. He's in a red bathing suit and a white T-shirt like he's fresh off the set of *Baywatch*. The women are leaning in toward him, and there's something, even from this far away, that tells me he doesn't like it. It's the way he is taking tiny steps backward and smiling with his mouth closed. When the crowd breaks open, I see little kids too, grabbing small canvases and backpacks and leaving with their moms. After everyone else has left, I watch as the last little boy, maybe six, reaches into his backpack and gives Dan something. Dan plops onto the sand to examine it, so the boy does too. I'm not sure when I've ever been so focused on something in my life. I don't know what I'm watching, but it's possible that Dan has a child. The boy says something to make Dan laugh, really laugh, and I want to know what it was.

I text Clem: Breaking—man bun might have a kid

Dan looks up and sees me standing at the railing and points me out to the little boy. Dan says something and the little boy nods. The possibilities swirl around my mind—I decide to grab hold of *See that woman? She's about to make it in Hollywood.* I wave at them, and Dan pulls out his phone and texts me: The least you can do is give me a hand?

I make my way onto the beach as he's collecting towels and watercolor kits. "Grab those," he says by way of greeting. "This is Louis."

"Hi, Louis," I say and feel like I should say another thing. Not having siblings or cousins or friends with kids, I don't actually have a little-kid repertoire. "What's all this?"

"Art camp," Louis says and hands me his backpack. "My dad's always late."

"But he always comes," Dan says over his shoulder.

I pick up a few towels and fold them. "So you do this every week?" I ask.

"Mostly. It's a pop-up camp, for when I have time." He collects sandy paintbrushes into a canvas bag. "Which is a lot lately." It really is preposterous how little care Dan takes with his hair, I mean, comb it once. Just once. But on the beach, and now with Louis riding piggyback, it looks more normal. It's like if you first saw a cowboy in a ten-gallon hat at the mall, but then later you saw him out on the range and it sort of made sense.

"What?" Dan asks. I've been looking at his hair for too long.

"Have you ever come into contact with a hairbrush?"

"Was that a joke?" And over his shoulder to Louis, "Was it?"

"I think she thinks you're messy."

"Then maybe she'll help us clean up." He puts Louis down and points to three abandoned canvases down the beach. Louis runs to get them, and a man is waving at us from the pier.

"Always freakin' late," Dan mutters.

I pick up the stack of towels and follow Louis and Dan back up to the pier.

Louis hugs his dad, who's in a blue suit and a crisp shirt. I wonder where he's been today that's made him late.

He says hello to me, and Dan says, "This is Jane."

"She's his stalker," Louis tells him.

"I am not," I say just as Dan starts to laugh.

"She is a little. I mean, showing up at my place of business. In a dress," he says.

"It's a sundress. This is the beach. You said five." I can feel myself getting worked up. I turn to the late dad. "I'm his colleague, we have a scheduled meeting."

Louis's dad could not care less about me and my meeting. He just waits as Louis hugs Dan goodbye.

"See you, Peanut," Dan says. The intimacy of the nickname startles me. When I was a kid, I used to imagine that my dad would have had a nickname for me, maybe Doodle, something to do with the squiggly outline of my hair, our hair. Louis smiles a smile that matches one that's buried in my heart.

We watch them walk away, and the towels are heavy in my arms. "You okay?" he asks.

"Of course." We start walking. He's walking rudely faster than I, so I have to double step to keep up. "So can we brainstorm a little?"

"About what? You're the one who's got a soundtrack in the works."

"Well, sort of. I just want to talk the whole thing through. I think we're the only people who care if this movie gets made."

We get to his car, an old white BMW sedan. I mean old, with a little rust but pretty leather seats. "Get in," he says. "I'm starving."

We toss his stuff in the back seat and get in the car. I have *Dateline* vibes, and I can hear Keith Morrison telling the audience that I got into a car with the man I despised most in the world. *Why?* he'd say into the camera just before the commercial break. *Why would she get in that car?*

"Buckle up," he says, and it sounds chilling.

"Why?"

"Because we're in a car, Jane. And it's the law." He

shakes his head and pulls into traffic. We drive five minutes down to Venice Beach and park in front of a skate-rental store. We get out of the car and Dan still isn't talking to me. He's just walking toward the boardwalk as if we'd previously agreed that I would follow him anywhere. There's a hint of sand on the sidewalk, and I like the way it makes a sound under my sandals, like a crinoline under a big taffeta gown. We pass some artists selling paintings and sculpture and Dan stops to look. One of them, an older man, gets up out of a beach chair and slaps him on the shoulder.

"Is this new?" Dan asks. "It's great." They're standing in front of a small oil painting of a pile of feathers. It's actually beautiful, but what I'm really noticing is that Dan has his back completely to me, like I'm not here.

"And who's this?" the man with manners asks.

"Sorry. Pedro, this is Jane. We're trying to work together."

I say hello and shake his hand. "It's not easy," I say with a smile.

"Because she's insane," Dan says.

"Can you see why Dan never has a girlfriend?" Pedro asks me.

"Yes, no mystery there," I say.

Dan laughs like that's both true and fine. "We're going to Maud's real quick."

Pedro gives me yikes eyes. "Oh, he really does hate you."

"Wheatgrass," I say. "Tell me it's not wheatgrass."

"You'll be begging for wheatgrass," Pedro says.

I find out what he means when we are seated on opposite

sides of a picnic table with an order of potato skins and two lemonades between us.

"They're delicious," he says. "Try."

I pick one up and take a bite, and the grease rolls down my wrist. It is a celebration of starch and cheese and bacon the likes of which my mouth has never known.

My bliss must show on my face because he says, "See?"

"I see." I take a second napkin and wipe my face. "I had you pegged as a guy who would think cheese is murder."

"Yep, you've really got me all figured out." He leans toward me, gesturing with a potato skin. "So tell me why you're stalking me. You want ideas for Quinlan's song?"

I'm not ready to ask for help, so I take another bite of my greasy potato and use another napkin. "Are you a painter? Like is this the Bruce Wayne to your Batman?"

He laughs a little, a two on the Richter scale. "I paint, or I have painted. My degree is in photography. I sell prints online when I'm between jobs." I've never sat like this, across a table from him, and the navy blue of his eyes is deeper than I remember. His lashes are jet black like his hair—it's all so dramatic. He takes another potato skin and replaces a fallen piece of bacon on top. "I have a darkroom in my apartment, and the chemicals will probably kill me by the time I'm sixty, so there's no need to save for retirement. It's a pretty solid plan."

I laugh. I don't mean to. I want to take the laugh back, but it's gotten me. "Yes, death is a sure path to financial independence. You're a total catch."

The view of the ocean is behind him, beyond the

boardwalk. People are skating by. The sun is getting lower so his face is in shadow. He's completely still, and there's so much motion behind him, it's mesmerizing, like he's in time-lapse.

"Jane," he says, and I come to.

"Yeah, so can we talk about this movie?"

"I don't have a tiger," he says.

"I think the tiger thing was a joke," I say.

"When I said I didn't think it was commercial, I meant it in a good way."

"I bet you're terrible at breaking up with people."

"I am," he says. "How would you know that?"

"Just a hunch. How was it in a good way?"

He's quiet for a second, and the white noise of the boardwalk—rollerbladers, voices, gulls—intensifies. "The loud movies with the explosions and superheroes, they sell tickets because they're an escape. We don't have to think about our own lives when we watch them. We can hide in the noise. But it's the quiet movies that make room for us to look at ourselves. People cooking, teaching, gardening. They're quiet things, but they're the things that move us. And people, mostly, are afraid of the quiet."

"Yes." It just comes out.

"Wait, did you just agree with me?"

"Even a stopped clock is right twice a day, Dan."

"Wow, did you borrow my dad's joke book?" He smiles and sits up straighter. He has the posture of someone who's just won. "So, the movie."

"Yes, that. What you said about the quiet. I agree. And

I wonder, if the thing with Jack Quinlan for some reason didn't work out, how else could it be commercial?"

"I don't think it needs to be. I feel like this movie could be made really cheaply. It's so personal, it doesn't need to be big and sweeping. Like it could be one camera."

"I'm not letting you turn my movie into *The Blair Witch Project*."

He laughs. "That's big budget compared to what I'm thinking. The film I made with Wallflower Pictures—"

I interrupt him. "The one that won all the awards and sold exactly no tickets? That one?"

Dan leans in. "Yes, that one. We made it so cheap."

"That's impressive, but you're thinking of how to make this smaller, when Nathan wants to make it bigger. Clearwater doesn't make small films. We need to increase the wow factor without sacrificing the quiet of it all."

"Yes," he says.

"Did you just agree with me?" I smile at him behind my napkin.

"Which is why a pop star with a big song for the soundtrack is the right fix," he says. "It doesn't mess up the story."

And just then, Jack Quinlan's "Purple" comes on the radio. I want to say this was a coincidence or a sign, but that song comes on the radio three times an hour.

"What?" Dan asks.

"What, what?"

"I think you think you have a poker face, when I can seriously see every thought as it crosses your mind. You just had a sarcastic thought."

"Did not." My hand moves up to my face to hide whatever my next thought is going to be.

"Did too."

"Just, this song. It's on constantly."

"And?"

"It's just so weird that he's such a huge star. Like he's on TMZ every day and I'm still trying to get my first movie made."

He widens his eyes like he knows I've just overshared. I think he's going to pounce with some snarky comment about what a loser I am, but he says, "Well, I'm thirty-two and slowly dying of chemical inhalation in my apartment, so."

I don't say anything. I cannot fathom why I shared that with this man. It was an inside-the-house, under-a-blanket thought. The kind I'd only share with Clem.

"Your buddy Jack is actually performing next weekend at a music festival in Long Island. In my hometown. My brother's the electrician at the venue. It's supposed to be a big secret that he's showing up, but it seems like everyone knows. What kind of timeline is he on to write the song?"

"We've been pretty loose about the whole thing. Which is why I was sort of hoping you could help me with a backup plan?"

He gives me a long look, and I don't blink. "Nope. I think your plan's all we've got."

My plan is entirely made up, I don't say. I am sweating. It's hot and the sun is bright behind Dan's head. I am drunk on bacon grease and cheese. "I think we should go."

We don't talk on the way back to the car. I am not accustomed to not talking. I should be asking him what his plans are for the weekend; he should be asking where I live, if I have siblings or pets. But he's just walking next to me, taking in the sun on the water, stopping quietly to look at what people are selling. And I feel sort of ignored, like there's an arrogance to this quiet, like he's above the awkward silence. I also wonder if I'm one of those people who is afraid of the quiet.

"What?" he asks. He's caught me looking at him.

"What's with the string bracelets?" I ask.

He grabs his wrist. "Louis makes them. They're not very good."

"No," I say. "They're just pieces of string. Shouldn't there be some braiding or something?"

He stops walking and turns to me. "He's just trying to tell me something he doesn't know how to say. He's not trying to win design awards. Also, he's six."

"Of course," I say, and we walk toward his car. "And why 'Peanut'?"

"Just came to me one day and I said it. Won me these bracelets, so I guess it was a fit." He's casual about it, as if he doesn't understand the enormity of having given a well-received nickname to a kid who needs it.

CHAPTER 7

I WAKE UP TO A SUNDAY MORNING EMAIL FROM NA-
than's assistant. She wants to know when the details of
the soundtrack will be firmed up so she can schedule a
meeting with the green light committee.

I lie in bed imagining all the dramatic ways people walk
through fire to get the thing they want. Going to law school,
for example. Training for a marathon. Or actually walking
through the fiery shame of their adolescence to ask for a favor. I grab my phone and pull up Hailey's contact.

It takes me five minutes to compose this text: Hey Hailey! Hope you and the girls are good. I'm working on a new
project and the studio wants to get in touch with Jack Quinlan, any chance you're in touch with him still?

I cannot press send. I leave my phone on my bed and
grab a Pop-Tart and bring both it and my phone into my
closet. When the door is shut and it's mostly dark, I eat the
Pop-Tart and hit send.

Bubbles pop up immediately: Omg I just laughed out

loud. How great would it be if we were still in touch with him

My heart sinks. This is so stupid. Me: I know, right? Will or Dougie probably aren't either?

Hailey: Ha! Will's trying to get on one of those reality Realtor shows, and Dougie works at a restaurant in Anaheim, so probably not. I love that you're still trying to make it in the industry!

Oof. That hits like a sucker punch and a pat on the head all at once. And she didn't even break a sweat. This conversation is making me feel like I'm time traveling and losing twenty years of progress along the way. I need to change the subject, so I say: How are the girls?

Hailey: Loud, but good. Nelly screams all night and I actually think I've had some hearing loss because of it. I'm not complaining, enough hearing loss and I could sleep

That was her Instagram post this morning. I saw it just before I texted her. People thought it was funny and asked where her sweater was from (link in stories). I feel embarrassed for both of us that she's recycling a joke on me.

Me: Ha!

I refuse to lie and say *LOL.*

Hailey: You should reach out to Angelica's office, she might know how to reach Jack. I bet he's still managed by his weird uncle

When this conversation has come to its natural end (We should get together!), I get out of my closet and find Clem sitting on my bed with her tea and my coffee.

"What's going on?" she asks. I wipe a crumb from the corner of my mouth. "I heard the closet door close."

I accept the coffee and get into my bed, holding the quilt out for her to join me. I straighten the covers over our legs before I say, "Thank you. I was texting with Hailey." I close my eyes and brace for the blow.

"Jane."

"I just wanted to see if she could get in touch with Jack?"

"But let me guess, she can't, and you left the conversation feeling terrible about your life."

Hailey is a little bit like that black light they use to detect traces of blood at crime scenes. Just her presence shines a light on my less-than bits.

"She thinks I should ask Angelica how to get in touch with Jack. Which actually isn't a bad idea."

"Or maybe you could come clean to Nathan, find another script, and quit living in the nightmare of your early teens?"

I love the sound of that. Just come clean and move on. "I can't," I say.

"Because you're in a committed relationship with this script now?"

"Sort of," I say. It's the truth. Some part of my heart is weirdly attached to this story. "I'm going to call her."

Angelica was the showrunner on *Pop Rocks*, and calling her isn't such a huge emotional leap. I call her from my bed in the broad light of day and without the help of any additional sugar—that's how easy it is.

"Hello?" she says, hoarse. And it's then that I realize it's

Sunday morning and people don't call people on Sunday morning. "Janey?"

"I'm so sorry. I totally forgot it was Sunday. Go back to sleep." I shoot Clem my *oof* face and she takes my hand.

"What do you need? Say it fast."

"I need Jack Quinlan's manager's number. Or some way to get in touch with Jack."

"It's still the uncle, I think."

"Okay, great. Do you have that number?"

"I'll text it to you when I'm awake." She hangs up.

What adult doesn't know it's Sunday when it's Sunday?

I'VE GONE TO the store and dipped a batch of chocolate-covered pretzels for Clem to bring to the hospital tomorrow by the time Angelica texts me Lyle Anderson's number at ten o'clock. He's a stranger and should be easy to call, but the whole thing feels like the world's biggest can of worms. Clem comes out dressed for her hiking date.

"I feel weird leaving," she says. "Are you just hanging around stressing yourself out all day?"

"That's my current plan, yes. But I'd do that whether you were here or not," I say. "Go. Frolic. Make out in a cave." I usher her off the porch and down the front walkway.

When she's gone, I pace on my front porch. I need to make this call. I can't shake this feeling that I'm about to be exposed, filleted right open for all of Santa Monica to see. Wherever I've been burying this shame is well insulated because it's still red-hot.

"Jump-Start Love Song" didn't happen right away. In the first season of *Pop Rocks*, our characters were just four middle schoolers who started a band. We were twelve, and I was on the slower side in terms of puberty. My hair was short, a light brown version of Little Orphan Annie. I felt like a kid still, and I liked putting on my Janey Jakes costume and joking around. I liked the roar of the studio audience. I liked how there was always something to eat on set and how I didn't have to race to the grocery store on Tuesdays after school before the sale milk ran out. I liked the way Hailey, Will, Dougie, and I were a foursome—"the kids," as we were called on set. *Send in the kids. The tutor's here for the kids.*

The series plan was that we were going to get discovered by a record company at the end of that first season. This set us up for the second season, when I was thirteen, and we were traveling locally to perform in small venues. I was on the keyboards and was constantly birthing ideas that would make us dangerously close to missing our gig or booking us transportation in a wacky vehicle that would run out of gas. This all happened in a world where a bunch of thirteen-year-old recording artists were booking their own travel and managing logistics.

Recording a real song and releasing it as a single was a last-minute decision in the middle of the third season. In the first few seasons, our songs were just a few lines and a chorus—enough that we could end each episode with a performance and some applause. But then Angelica commissioned "Jump-Start Love Song."

The song was a duet between Hailey and Will, who had

just become a couple on the show. It was up-tempo in a way that would make you turn it all the way up in your car, but also romantic enough that you might tear up at the end. Or maybe that was just me. I really loved that song. Hailey and Will spent two full days at the recording studio before Angelica realized "Jump-Start Love Song" wasn't going to work. The song itself was a home run, but Hailey and Will's voices were wrong for it—Hailey's wasn't quite strong enough and Will's was too high. They sounded like two girls in a karaoke duet. The door to my dressing room was open the day Angelica passed by and heard me singing it. I'd just removed my prosthetic braces and had taken a second to look at myself. I was fourteen, close to fifteen, with perfectly straight teeth. My skin had cleared up and my face was thinning out. I made direct eye contact with myself and felt ripe and ready for something that I didn't quite know the name of. I knew that tomorrow I'd put the braces back on and contort myself into some comedically awkward position, but for that moment, the mirror and I had a secret: underneath Janey Jakes, there was someone else.

So I started to sing. I sang "Jump-Start Love Song" the way I heard it in my head. I sang as I brushed my hair, longer and falling around my face in a way that felt new. When I turned around and saw Angelica in the doorway, I wasn't embarrassed at all. I could see that she saw it too. I'd grown out of my embarrassing phase into this new, ripe self.

"Hi," I said. It was a one-word replacement for *Look at me, see this for the first time. Can you believe it? I might be beautiful.*

"I have an idea," she said. And then it all happened. I was going to record the song for Hailey along with someone who was going to sing for Will. I wouldn't get a recording credit, but I'd get a bonus and royalties and, more importantly, they were going to rewrite my character so that putting me behind the microphone would make sense going forward. I'd be a new version of Janey Jakes, all grown up and cool.

My duet partner was Jack Quinlan. He'd been trying to get a part on our show since it started. I still wonder if he thought recording this song would be his big break. If only he knew what was coming.

It's hard to explain the way I felt the first time I met him. You'd have to understand what it was like to only know three other kids. When Jack walked in, he wore jeans and a T-shirt with a California flag on it. His hair was cut short but longer on the top, and he had freckles on his cheeks that seemed like they were about to fade away. I had the sense looking at those freckles, and later running my finger over them, that they were a precious thing made for my eyes only.

We met at the recording studio. I'd come straight from home, so I was in my own clothes, jeans and a fitted black top my mother hadn't wanted me to buy. I was free of the braces and liked the way my lip gloss looked in the glass of the engineer's booth. Jack walked in and saw that person, Jane Jackson. I felt him see me, and it was like I was born right then.

He took one hand out of his jeans pocket and gave me a wave. "I'm Jack. We're singing together?"

"Yes. Jane," I said. I ran my hand through my hair, and he watched me do it. I'd later learn that he was sixteen, which didn't surprise me. He seemed like he was on the other side of something, and I wanted to go there with him.

The record producer came in and started talking to us, and I kept looking at Jack. We ran through the song once and then a second time. Jack was more comfortable in his skin than I was, like he'd spent a lifetime being cool and didn't know another way to be. I was still trying on this new skin, being a person who was not the punch line, a person who could be looked at the way he was looking at me.

On our third take, the producer told us to sing the entire song staring into each other's eyes. He wanted feeling, as if we were really jump-starting something. So we did. We sang face-to-face for three minutes and fifty-four seconds. And every second of that song, every word we sang, made the room smaller and smaller. I felt like he was singing directly to my heart. It is an understatement to say that I'd never felt this way before. My body was electrified, and I allowed it to take over. As I sang the last few words of the song, *"to be in love with you,"* and as my lips made the *u* in "you," he leaned in and kissed me. That was my first kiss.

We finished early, so I texted my mom that Hailey's housekeeper was taking us to the movies and would drop me home after dinner. It was the first lie I'd ever told my mom, though I'd soon find out she'd been lying to me forever. It was shocking how easy it was, how little it tugged at my heart. Jack wanted to hang out. With me.

He said, "Let's go to Beverly Hills," as if that was just a thing people did. I can still feel the crispness of the November air and then the oven-warm feeling of the inside of his car.

We walked around Beverly Hills and looked in the windows. No place was off-limits to him. He didn't hesitate when he spoke; he didn't pause before he walked through a door. I should have known then that Jack would be a star—the world really had no choice. We wandered through Neiman Marcus, where everything seemed foreign and one of a kind. We made our way to the little café on the top floor and ate fish tacos and popovers. He held my hand as we walked through the lobby of the Beverly Wilshire Hotel and kept holding my hand on the deepest, plushest lobby sofa.

"You think we'll be famous?" he asked.

"Yes," I said because it felt like the right answer.

It had been a day of firsts: the kiss, the feel of his hand in mine. I ran my fingers over the inside of his hand like it was a gift that had just been given to me and I wanted to learn how it worked.

He squeezed my hand, and my heart fluttered in my chest. I knew then that this was the thing my mom had been telling me about—this bigger-than-yourself feeling of true love. For the first time I could feel the thing my parents had, and I felt like I was part of it. He drove me home and kissed me in the car, and the windows fogged up like the air knew we needed our privacy.

The next day on set, everyone was excited about the song. Angelica was thrilled, and even Hailey was excited. The lie of it didn't bother her a bit—she was going to be an actual recording star. Jack and I sat offstage while Hailey and Will tried to get the lip sync right. We were supposed to be looking through the next song we would record, "Can't Find My You," but mostly we were pressing our legs together as we sat, entwining our hands under the sheet music. He stood and took my hand with him, leading me toward my dressing room, where he pulled me toward him and kissed me again. His hands on my neck, his chest up against mine. The magic I'd felt on my lips the day before spread throughout my body and I thought, *This. This is the thing they write love stories about.* Something in my heart told me this was forever, and because I was fourteen and only knew three other kids, I believed it.

"I love you," I said.

I know.

He pulled away immediately and said, "What?"

"I love you," and I leaned in to kiss him again, forever.

He removed my hands from around his waist and reached to turn the light on. "Jane, don't be weird. Gross." He wiped his mouth with the back of his hand, wiped me away. And I knew right then that I'd broken it. There was this thing starting to grow, and I'd smashed it before it even had a chance.

Weird and gross. Those words rang loudly in my head, unwinding the new version of myself I'd wanted to believe in. "Sorry," I said. "I mean. I didn't mean . . ." The shame started at my core and moved out toward my limbs. It made my heart speed up and my voice squeak. How could I be such an idiot.

He laughed an unkind laugh. "You're so embarrassing, God." He said this with a sprinkle of disgust that gave me the same thought I had the first time I saw him—that he saw me for exactly who I was. He opened the door to go but then turned back around. "And honestly, I don't think you get who you are on this show. They're all laughing at you. You're the joke."

Then he gave me a smile that sort of felt like *You're welcome*. Like I should be grateful that he shared this insight with me. I turned back to the mirror and saw exactly what he saw.

I knocked on Angelica's office door an hour later and told her in a too-chipper voice that I was thinking I'd like to sing "Can't Find My You" on my own rather than as a duet with Jack. Her expression held a little panic, and I had a difficult time convincing her that he hadn't done something horrible. I imagine my eyes held the expression of a person who had been irreparably hurt. I didn't know how to tell her that I was the one who'd misstepped. Jack's reaction was totally appropriate.

She leaned back in her chair. "Jane, maybe all this recording artist stuff is too much for you? How about you record 'Can't Find My You' on your own—I know you can do that. And then we'll get back to basics. You're brilliant as Janey Jakes. You're the heart of the show. We don't need to go turning you into Hailey Soul." I should have disagreed, but I couldn't make the words come out. She was right: there was no turning me into Hailey Soul.

WHEN I HAVE rearranged Clem's and my books alphabetically by the first name of the author, I know that I am out of places to hide. I grab a pair of sunglasses and bring them with me into the closet. When the door is shut and my knees are pulled up to my chest, I make the call.

It goes to voicemail. I panic and hang up. I hadn't planned for that, and now the hot shame burns and flickers. Of course no one picks up an unknown number. I catch my breath and call again. It goes straight to voicemail.

"Hi, this is Jane Jackson from Clearwater Studios in LA. Los Angeles." Okay, not a necessary clarification. I'm starting to sweat. "I called a second ago, but got disconnected, so, anyway, we're making a film. A great film, *True Story*? That's the title. And we'd love a chance to talk with Jack about writing an original song. I knew him when we were young. We worked together?" I hear desperation in my voice, and it bounces around my dark closet. I picture Jack's face when his uncle remembers me to him—he'll laugh and then roll his eyes. Maybe he'll tell the story; maybe he's been telling the story this whole time. "Anyway, if you would call back or maybe pass along the message. Again, this is Jane Jackson. Okay? Bye."

Honestly, someone should invent a way to take back a

voicemail once you've hung up. I could have written something out, a script. Instead I defined the little-known term
"LA." I run my fingers along the hem of a pair of pants that's
at eye level. I pull the pants from their hanger and wrap the
legs around my neck, like a shawl, and grab an Almond Joy.

I'VE SHOWERED, STRAIGHTENED the pillows on my made
bed, and cleaned Clem's room by the time my phone rings.
I answer just as the closet door shuts.

"Hey, it's Lyle Anderson. Jack's manager. You called
about that movie?"

"Yes, hi," I say. "Thanks for calling me back." Another
strike. It sounds like I am a person who is not accustomed to
being called back. Like I'm a cold-calling warranty salesman.

"Yeah, so, he's pretty sure he's not interested." He's
breathing heavily, and I have the sense that he's called me
from a treadmill.

"If I could just talk him through the story, or talk to you
actually—no need to bother him about it—"

He cuts me off. "Listen, Jane?" He says it like he wasn't
a hundred percent sure of my name. "I'm just calling back
to say no. We get a lot of calls like this. I mostly ignore
them, but you said you knew him, so I asked. And honestly,
he doesn't have any idea who you are. So."

I hesitate. The thing I could say: *We sang "Jump-Start
Love Song" together.*

And he would be intrigued. It would open up a whole

discussion, and of course Jack would remember me then. That was his first professionally released song.

Lyle hangs up.

I couldn't get the words out. I feel myself shrinking. "Okay, thanks," I say to the silence.

CHAPTER 8

I ALLOW MYSELF ONE MINUTE AND TWO KIT KATS BE-
fore I call Lyle again. I cannot believe I wimped out like
that. Of course I should have stepped up and owned it. I
sang that song with Jack, and his uncle would remember
that song. It rings and rings until I realize he's probably
blocked my number. *Oof.* I call Dan.

He picks up on the first ring. "Let's hear it." His voice
echoes. Not for the first time, I think of him as Batman, but
in his lair.

"Are you in a cave?"

"Darkroom."

"Ah, retirement planning."

"Don't use my joke," he says.

"So I'm wondering if your brother has seen Jack. Like
maybe he could talk to him?"

"Quinlan?"

"No, Jack Frost, Dan. Of course Jack Quinlan." I hate
the thing my voice does when I say his name. Like it wob-
bles on the way out.

Dan lets out a breath. "Okay? Why are we wanting an electrician involved in the negotiations? Jane, could you please start making sense."

"I sort of overstated where we are with Jack."

"Oh God," he says. "This is going to be good."

"It's not," I say.

He doesn't say anything, but I can hear him on the other end of the phone. "Are *you* in a cave?" he asks.

"I'm in my closet," I say. That hardly seems important now. "I haven't talked to Jack in nearly twenty years. It was just an idea I had on the spot. But it did buy us some time and another round with the green light committee?"

"You made it up." I hear him open and close a door, and it now sounds like he's in a bigger space. I hear his footsteps stop and water run.

"I did." I whisper it. "There are going to be layoffs. I was desperate. All we need to do is pitch the story to him. It's one song and he'll probably win an Oscar."

"Oh, is that all we need to do?" Dan lets out an infuriating little laugh.

I am crying. Just quiet tears rolling down my cheeks that tell me this is never going to happen. There's no song. There's no tiger.

"Jane? You there?"

"Yeah, sorry. I know you're right. There's no way."

"Yeah."

"Did you know that I used to be an actress?" I ask. I'm thinking about before I settled in to being Janey Jakes. I killed it in middle school as Audrey singing about a picket fence. I thought Angelica asked me to audition because of my singing voice rather than my flair for the awkward. I wipe my eyes on the hem of my first-date dress. Fresh and likeable rather than deceptive and sad.

"I didn't," he says. "Is that when you knew Jack Quinlan?"

"Sort of." I am obviously not going to elaborate. "It was when I was a kid. I really thought I was going to be famous. The joke was always on me, but I made it work. But then I grew up. I keep trying and failing to be taken seriously. Everyone else seems to be leveling up, you know? Joke's still on me."

"I'm sorry," he says.

"For what?"

"For screwing up *Star Crossed* for you, though I probably saved you."

"See, it's not an apology when you immediately take it back."

"Yeah, I'm sorry about that too."

We're quiet on the phone.

"Are you still in your closet?" he asks.

"Yes."

This is the spot for a zinger. *I'm wide open here, Dan. Sock it to me.* But he says, "You could go to Long Island. Jack plays Saturday night. Finn could get you into the Owl Barn. And you might even run into him in town—people say he's really friendly with fans."

The thought of this makes my stomach churn: running into Jack, who has taken his humiliation skills up ten notches by not remembering who I am, then refreshing his memory and waiting for the laughter. Something about this thought makes me angry. Everything about Jack makes me angry, not even what happened between us, but more the way he's tangled up in the memory of what came after and how quickly my understanding of the world and myself changed right then. The anger pulls me back from the ledge of my self-pity. It feels like action. I could go. "I could check in to a hotel and sort of stake out the town."

"There are no hotels in Oak Shore."

I've stopped crying, and I wipe my eyes with the sleeve of my sweatshirt. "Okay, then I'll rent a house."

He laughs. "I'm guessing every rental was booked a year ago. Listen, I can put you up at my parents' house."

"Seriously?" I'm trying to picture this. Dan's parents are definitely rich. You don't study photography and joke about your long-term plan being an early death without some kind of a trust fund. I bet he keeps saying he's broke just to keep up his die-for-my-art vibe. He'll be sheepish as we pull up in front of his parents' stately brick home on the water. The kind with wings that need to be aired out when guests come. White trim, black shutters, and a matching set of English bulldogs by the door.

"Seriously. It's my parents' fortieth wedding anniversary Friday, and my brothers are doing a whole anniversary-week thing. Everyone's going to be there. I wasn't sure I was going, but now that I'm a hundred percent sure you're paying for my flight, let's go."

"To Long Island. For a week." With the most annoying man alive. I'm picturing ascots and riding crops. Readings from Chaucer in a worn but thoughtfully arranged drawing room. So much tweed. They'll want to know about my people, where we're from.

"Yes. It's August seventeenth, Jane. Nothing's happening here anyway. Take the week, clear your head, and maybe catch the tiger."

I sit up rod straight. "Okay. Let's try. We'll leave in the morning. Text me your full name and birthday."

I AM A terrible liar. I am an okay actress, but that hits a different register emotionally. Acting feels fun, like dressing up at Halloween and going trick-or-treating. Lying feels like breaking into someone's house and stealing their candy. My heart races; my nose goes red. I add extra words to my explanation; details spill out of my mouth that are sure to trip me up later. So I decide to email Nathan instead of call:

Hey! Had a quick call with Jack Quinlan's people. I am headed to New York tomorrow to meet with him and finalize things. I'm staying with friends so I'll take the week. Back in the office Monday the twenty-fifth. Mandy (cc'd) can always reach me.

This email took me an hour to write and in its longest iteration was over six hundred words. The fact that I got it down to forty-five makes me feel like I've won something. Plus, none of it is really a lie besides Dan being my friend.

I call my mom. "So I'm going to Long Island for the

week. That guy Dan says that Jack is going to be at a music festival there, so hopefully I can talk to him." When she doesn't reply, I add, "About the script?"

"Yes," she says. "And that feels okay for you?"

I let out a huff. "Well, none of this feels okay since I've screwed up so badly, but I have to at least try."

"I mean about Jack. Two days ago you seemed pretty iffy about contacting him."

"I still am," I say. I can feel the dread, the way my heart rate quickens just talking about it. "But I'm going to do it anyway. I really want to make this movie."

"Of course, but—" She stops. "You're right. You're a tough cookie, Jane. You'll be fine. Wait till he sees how gorgeous you are now."

"Mom."

"Well, you are. Gorgeous and successful and funny and warm."

"Okay, thank you."

"And you give the best hugs."

"I'll be sure to tell him."

"Do. He's the one who's missed out all these years."

I laugh. It feels good to see myself through my mom's heart-eyes every once in a while. "Yeah, I'll brag about the hugs first and then get to the movie. I leave in the morning, call you when I land."

"Okay, I'm going up to Santa Barbara with Gary, back Tuesday."

"Overnight?"

"Yes, Jane, I'm fifty-six. I'm allowed a sleepover."

"Okay." A trip gets him one step closer to breaking her heart.

CLEM IS MORE vocal about her Jack concerns as she sits cross-legged on my bed and watches me pack. "This is a flat-out disaster in the making."

"He can only say no."

"You're going to spend a week hunting down a guy who you're terrified to see while shacking up with another guy you can't stand? At a minimum, I think this is going to bring up a bunch of other stuff you're committed to not dealing with. Maybe I should come."

"Stop. I'm fine with my stuff, it's all packed away, and you don't have the vacation days." I am trying to be light about it, but she really does look worried. It's not helping to see the people who know me best terrified that I'm going to implode.

Clem folds my jean shorts in half and tucks them into the suitcase.

"Clem, I've got my revenge dress locked and loaded and folded into fours. I'm bulletproof." I try to catch her eye so I can convince her that this is okay.

"Don't do that."

"Don't do what?"

"Don't do the thing where you hide inside the perfect outfit. You don't need a costume. Or a script. I just . . ." She pauses, and she looks legitimately upset, like she's wanted to say this for a while. "I just hate how you hide your good bits, you know? Use your actual voice. Be funny and raw, and I swear this will work out. Go to New York, see Jack Quinlan, and bust on his stupid Elvis sideburns. Tell him how lucky he'd be to work with you again. You're the goddamn bomb, okay. Make sure he knows."

~~~~~~~

CHAPTER 9

I DON'T GET US SEATS TOGETHER BECAUSE (1) WE BOTH prefer aisle seats, and (2) I don't want to talk to Dan for six hours. I cross my arms and legs in a sort of self-hug. I do not know where I got the idea that this was going to be easy. Just like that, I'd find a script on my desk and live happily ever after.

I look two rows up to where Dan is watching something in black and white with subtitles on his laptop. So on brand. He is also, and I hate to admit that I remember this, wearing the same flannel shirt that he was wearing the first time we met. It's celery green and light blue checked, softer colors than the flannel the paper towel guy wears.

I met Dan for the first time four months ago. I saw him before he saw me. Mandy and I had just finished lunch at Mystique, and we walked outside as he was crossing Sunset Boulevard, barely dodging traffic. I'd like to say I noticed him because of the Tesla that came to a screeching halt, just missing his leg, but the truth is he's a person you'd notice anyway. Maybe for the way his black jeans gripped his legs or the way his camera bag made him look slightly threatening, like he was armed. He's a few inches over six feet, with that uncombed hair and those rectangular eyes. His face is sharp lines—high cheekbones and a square jaw. He's striking, but take all of that away and you'd still notice him for the way his eyes were trained on a spot behind me. There was a certainty and purpose in the way he carried his body through traffic.

The Tesla must have made some kind of contact, because when he got to our side of the street he stopped, looked around, and rubbed his leg, like he'd just come to.

"Are you okay?" Mandy asked.

He looked at her and then at me, as if he was surprised he wasn't the only person in Los Angeles that day. There's a certain arrogance to not taking in your surroundings, and based on what I now know about Dan and his single-mindedness, I'd call his arrogance dangerous. He rubbed his leg again. "I guess I deserved that, crossing the street like an asshole."

"Well, yes," I said. I remember immediately thinking, *Very attractive, but absolutely not.* I was eight months into my Manifest a Solid Partner project, and one of my rules is that no one gets completely overlooked. So I gave him a once-over and ran him through my basic checklist. It was a quick decision, even for me, but it was a hard no. It wasn't the way his hair seemed to have never been combed. Or the way his navy blue eyes seemed dark where they should be light. It was because I could never tell our kids that the first sentence their father ever said to me contained the word "asshole."

I was about to walk away, but his eyes locked on mine and I couldn't help but think of Batman. Batman, but not at all Bruce Wayne. He'd still be in that leather suit, stepping out of the Batmobile, and I'd be the only one who was able to see his face when he pulled off his cowl, his hair sticking up in literally every direction, his eyes telling me he'd rid the city of danger. And yet, still, not partner material, which was great because I'd just had a really big lunch and didn't feel like acting datable.

He looked back over my head and said, "I'm trying to get that." I turned around to see a hawk perched on the corner of a billboard above the restaurant. It was turned in profile like an eagle on the back of a quarter. There was a eucalyptus tree behind it, and the billboard said DON'T GIVE UP, like that was advice we needed.

"Los Angeles is so crazy," he said, almost to himself. He took his camera out of the case, and we made no move to leave. I wanted to see if he could get the shot, and I also just wanted to stay. "Do you mind holding this for a sec?" he asked, handing me the camera case.

I took it and slung it over my shoulder, and he held my gaze for a second. It was unnerving the way he looked at me like he recognized me and also the way he asked me to hold his stuff like we'd known each other forever. I had the sense that I was not in my normal reality, as people maneuvered around us on the sidewalk. So when Mandy motioned for us to leave, I did the not-normal thing: I told her to go, and

I stayed. Dan took a dozen shots before I saw it: the hawk turned its head and looked directly at him.

Dan looked down at his camera, "Got it. Don't give up." He showed it to me, and it was perfect. It was like he hired that hawk as a model. We both looked back up at the bill-board as the hawk flew away, disappearing into the hills.

"Do you sell greeting cards?" I asked. I was sort of kidding.

He laughed and I saw his smile for the first time. Not Batman at all. His smile chased away all the darkness. "No, I just saw him from my apartment. I live right over there." He motioned to a pink building across the street. "I liked how he was sitting there for emphasis, worried we might miss the message."

"I like the way he was sort of stern there, staring at us," I said.

"You like someone giving you a stern look?" he asked. He turned to me as he said it and locked on my eyes.

I made my sternest possible face—eyes pinched, fore-head scrunched. "Yes, it's my favorite." I don't know why I did this. But there was something about this stranger who'd just risked his life to take a photo of a bird for no reason in the middle of the day in West Hollywood. Something about the whole situation had me a little out of my body, out of my put-together Jane costume.

Dan matched my stern eyes and we both laughed. Later, when I recounted this meeting in more detail than neces-sary, Clem accused me of bringing Actual Jane into a flirt-ing situation. And I know what she meant—there was an unprecedented amount of unplanned speaking and joking, particularly given how objectively attractive Dan was.

"Who do you think pays for that billboard?" I asked Dan.

"Who knows. Some kind of nut. A lot of nuts out here."

"Out where?"

"California."

"Where are you from?"

"New York. Long Island," he said.

"No nuts there?"

He laughed again. "Just my family. Everyone else seems pretty normal. I'm Dan," he said and extended his hand.

I looked at it for a split second before taking it. It was in that second that I realized we were in the middle of an actual meet-cute. A wonky, distracted meet-cute with a near hit-and-run. I'd just made him laugh twice, which is two more than the recommended number of times you should make a guy laugh if you want him to ask you out. But Dan was (and is) absolutely not my type, not partner material. He's rough instead of smooth; his hair does not rest in a crescent over his ears. And yet, as previously established, he's objectively handsome and I'm an idiot. "I'm Jane," I said and took his hand.

"It's nice to meet you. Want me to send you the photo?"

Okay, believe me when I say that Dan is the worst, but this was an impressive way to low-key ask for my number. I stand by my respect for it. I had never once given my number to an unvetted guy, but inexplicably, I said, "Sure," and put my number into his phone.

He looked at his phone and then up at me. "Okay, Jane Jackson. See you later." He turned and crossed the street toward his pink building, and I watched him go.

He texted the next day, which was a Wednesday. Not that this matters or is burned into my memory, but I still have the conversation on my phone. It seems impossible now how light we were being. He texted the photo and the words: Worth risking my life for, right?

Me: For sure. I'm glad to have it

And I remember thinking that I hope he knows I mean I'm glad to have the photo, not his life. I mean, obviously.

There was a long pause that made me think he was done with the conversation, then he texted: What should we call him? Our hawk?

The "our" changed the tenor of the conversation. I replied: Tails

Dan: Tails? Like he has more than one tail? I don't see it

Me: No, look at the back of a quarter

Unnecessarily long pause. Then: Oh I get it. I like that. Tails

Now it was back in my court. I have never been good at small talk and keeping things going. Of course the second I started typing I would have committed to a comment because he'd see the three little dots of anticipation there. I remember I started to sweat, and then he called.

"Hi," I answered.

"Hey. Hi. It's me."

"I know."

"I was going to try to keep the conversation going by texting another thing about the hawk. But to be honest I'm sort of out of hawk talk."

"Hawk talk." I actually repeated it.

"Yeah, so I was wondering if I could take you to dinner on Friday. Do you eat seafood?"

"I do. Sure." I said something like this. I remember being flustered, both by the fact that I'd been asked out by this stranger and that I'd let him slide in under the radar. He said he'd text me Friday, and we got off the phone. And maybe I was excited. Well, I probably was. I mean, I didn't know any better.

THE NEXT WORDS I heard him say were "It's trash."

It was two days later, Friday, and he was sitting next to Nathan in the conference room where I was supposed to be meeting the team for my new film, *Star Crossed*. He had his back to the view of the partial Hollywood sign, with the letters *HO* crowding the edge of the frame. He looked up when I walked in and smiled that smile like he was glad to see me. It started in his eyes and then spread throughout his face. Batman on Christmas morning. I probably smiled back.

We both had yet to realize that he'd just insulted me and, more importantly, the first script that I was solely responsible for bringing to Clearwater.

"What are you doing here?" I asked him, tucking my hair behind my ear and wishing I'd worn heels.

"You know each other?" asked Nathan. "Perfect."

Dan said, "No. We just met. About a hawk." He seemed totally thrown. "I might be working on this thing. Why are you here?" He was seated next to a woman who I would learn was Amy Halstead, an up-and-coming director.

"It's my project," I said.

"This?" He slid it away from himself toward Amy, like it was a bowl of cereal and the milk had gone bad.

I shook Amy's hand and sat opposite Nathan. I needed a minute that I didn't seem to have. I scanned the big bowl of peanut M&M's and the sandwich platter. "Nathan said he was hiring a director. What is it that you do?" I was trying to sound even, businesslike.

"I'd be director of photography." He looked at Nathan and then back at me. "I was just saying I have some thoughts about the script. It's so crazy that this is you." Dan Finnegan. Nathan had told me about a cinematographer he'd wanted to get on a project. He'd won an award for an indie film he made with the great Vinny Banks that I'd never seen and Nathan had loved.

"Jane optioned this script cheap, so I'm open to talking about it. We don't have to green-light it," said Nathan.

I opened my mouth to speak, but the words *Yes, we do* didn't come out.

"I read it very quickly," Amy said, and I didn't quite know what that meant.

"It's just a little light," said Dan.

"Light?" I asked. He'd said "trash."

"Maybe trite?" he went on.

Nathan laughed and poured himself a green juice from

a pitcher in the middle of the table. It's a wonder he ever leaves the bathroom. "It's a love story, Dan," he said. "Trite is the name of the game."

"No," I said. "Sweet and emotional is what we're going for."

"Please," said Dan.

"Please what?"

He smiled at me softly, like he was sorry. Like he didn't want to say what came next, which happened to be: "This isn't exactly *The Notebook*. It's insta-love followed by activities with opportunities for hands to touch, followed by— shoot me—a misunderstanding. I'm sorry, Jane, it's got no heart."

If there's one thing you don't want to get me started on, it's *The Notebook*. He waits all that time and builds her a house? Come on. "*The Notebook* is insta-love followed by activities."

"*The Notebook* is not insta-love. It's attraction leading to love based on mutual appreciation of particular qualities," he said.

I looked at Nathan for a reaction. I don't know when I'd ever debated *The Notebook*, but Dan had gotten something boiling inside of me and I was all in.

I leaned forward a bit. "He sees her and immediately climbs the Ferris wheel," I said. *Like a maniac*, I don't add.

"Because Noah likes Allie's exuberance and sense of fun, that's not insta-love."

"You really know your *Notebook*," I muttered under my breath.

"I do. I'm sorry, Jane, I don't hate love stories, but they need to dive a little deeper emotionally to grab me. This isn't that." He slid the script toward me.

"It isn't what?" I asked.

"I think he's telling you it isn't *The Notebook*," Amy said.

"Well, of course it's not *The Notebook*. No one ever said it was." *Dan*—I suddenly hated that stupid name. Rhymes with "can" and "fan." Hit a man with a pan. "Only *The Notebook*'s *The Notebook*." My voice cracked—I remember this. And I was annoyed because we could be disagreeing about any movie, it's only this one that feels so charged. The end of my total lie of a childhood bedtime story. "And the whole twist in that movie, by the way, is a misunderstanding."

Dan let out a breath like I'd totally just worn him out. "It's not a misunderstanding, Jane. That was sabotage. By her mother."

I leaned back in my chair. I was clenching my peanut M&M's so hard that I could feel them melt against my palms.

"Is this the one where they're old and then not old?" Nathan asked. "I found it confusing."

"It's the worst," I said.

"How could you say that?" Dan replied. "It's romantic and true and perfect. But this, and I'm sorry, Jane, it makes me feel absolutely nothing. I mean, Harry and Sally—pretty sure the names have been done, by the way." And he rolled his eyes at Nathan. "They just meet and hook up because they're in the same place? It's not interesting."

"Well, people don't paddle around on a lake full of swans either. Did you know they had to raise those swans in that marsh or whatever just to get them to stay? That whole movie is just a big fake." I was sweating by then. I could feel heat moving from my chest to my face. "Can we maybe get off this topic? Though I do feel so much more enlightened having had you mansplain *The Notebook* to me this morning." I turned to Nathan, giving him his cue to ask Dan to leave so we could move on.

Nathan sat with his arms crossed, nodding. "Amy, what do you think of it?"

"I agree it's not *The Notebook*," she said, and I suspected she hadn't read it. She had that no-eye-contact energy of a kid who's been called on in class and didn't do the homework.

Nathan sighed. "Okay, I read this pretty quick, mainly because it was so cheap. Let me read it again and decide."

"Fine," I said, getting up from the table and looking at Dan. "So nice to see you again. Let's consider our later appointment canceled." I gave him a tight smile, my mean smile that I normally reserve for the third postal worker at the Brentwood post office. She vacillates between annoyance that I don't use enough tape on my packages and exasperation that I use too much tape on my packages, and I stand there with my murder smile until she has corrected the situation and handed me the receipt, pointing out that I should fill out a survey at the bottom. "Oh, I will," I tell her every time and never do.

I took the stairs down to my office because I didn't want to have to stand there and wait for the elevator. My heart was beating with rage and my hands were sweating, like I was about to turn into the Hulk. I got to my office and steadied myself on my desk. This was my big break. The studio gave me actual money to buy a script and run a project. I was finally going to step into my life, shoulders back, maybe in a pantsuit, maybe in a dress. I hadn't worked out the details.

"I'm sorry," I heard him say, standing at my office door, and I thought, not for the first time, that security around here is really for shit and where the heck was Mandy.

I turned around. "Sorry? Seriously?" He was leaning on the doorjamb, and he did look sorry.

"I need the work, for sure," he said, "but I cannot make that movie. And I might have, because I really do need the work."

"You've said."

"But I can't let you make it. I mean, you know it's crap."

"Where'd you learn to apologize? This is really moving."

"You've got this studio in your corner, you could make anything. You could put a real love story out into the world. Making that movie would be like building another strip mall. It's fake love."

"Oh, and you're an expert on love too. How many love stories have you filmed?"

"Same as you. None." He meant this as a barb.

"Ah, then I guess neither of us is an expert, so neither of us knows how that movie was going to turn out. Before you killed it." My hands were balled up by my sides, and I forced myself to open them and place them on my hips because I was afraid I looked like a little kid having a tantrum. "Arrogant," I said to my feet, all in one breath.

"What was that?" he asked. He took a step into my office,

not in a threatening way but like he wanted to hear me more clearly.

"Arrogant," I said again. "You're arrogant. I should have known, the way you crossed the street like everyone should come to a screeching halt for you. I bet you use organic shaving cream that squeezes out of some kind of weird bamboo packaging. I bet you understand Jackson Pollock and make sure everyone knows." He was looking at me like I was very close to going completely off the rails. It's possible that he smirked. Whatever it was, it made me feel like he was about to laugh at me, and let me tell you that was not something I was going to be able to deal with on that particular day, so I said it: "I bet you went to Brown."

He just looked at me. It was almost like he was seeing me for the first time. I stared back, waiting with my hands in fists again like a toddler. "Well," he said. "Again. I'm sorry." He put his hands up in mock surrender. "When I met you on the street, I didn't realize. You're completely insane."

"Am not," I said to solidify my role here as a toddler.

"Are too?" he said and actually laughed. "I'm thinking we call our date off? I'm just going to grab a quick organic shave and meet up with some of my Ivy League buddies instead, if that's cool."

"You're not even my type." I said it like it was a machine gun full of expletives. This spectacular disaster is why you don't give your number to some random guy on the street.

"Well, that's the nicest thing you've ever said to me, crazy lady." With hands up to shield himself from more of my violent words, he backed out of the room.

CHAPTER 10

~~~

I T'S HOT IN NEW YORK. I MEAN, IT'S HOT IN LOS ANGE-
les too, but here it's a thicker, wetter kind of hot. My hair
is drinking it up and preparing to explode. I am regretting
my jeans-and-sneakers travel look. Standing outside the
terminal at JFK with Dan, I wonder if he's regretting the
flannel. There's no small talk as we wait, and I really appreciate that. I pull my hair into a ponytail. He takes off his
flannel and shoves it in his bag. His jeans are Levi's—I can
tell by the denim—and his white T-shirt is from a pack of
three that you get at Target. My jeans are also Levi's, but
my white T-shirt was expensive. Something about this
makes me feel dumb.

A green Subaru pulls up, and a man who could be Dan's
twin gets out. He has the same black hair and the same rectangular blue eyes. They fall into a long hug, and I see that
they are the exact same height.

When the hug is spent, he turns to me with an outstretched hand. "Hey, I'm Aidan." He's movie-star handsome with an easy smile that lights up his face.

"Are you twins?" I ask. They are truly identical.

"We are, but Danny and I don't dress alike. You two are embarrassing."

"I'm Jane," I say. "And this was an accident."

"All the girls in LA try to dress like me," Dan says, putting our suitcases into the hatchback. "It's a whole thing."

"That's very sad," says Aidan.

I get in the back seat, and Aidan pulls into the traffic and onto the highway. He's wearing a wedding ring, but his hands are otherwise just like Dan's, tan and muscled.

I text Clem: Landed, headed to their house. Turns out there are two of them—Dan has an identical twin who is hot and nice but married

Clem: You just said Dan's hot

Me: No

Clem: Scroll up, you did

Me: Fine but his subscription to Beanie of the Month Club cancels it out

Clem: Send me a pic of the beanie he's wearing right now

Of course there's no beanie. I lean back in my seat and watch them as they talk. Dan and Aidan have the same longish black hair, with the same natural part. The rhythm of their conversation comes in short bursts, that back-and-forth of fragmented thoughts you have with someone whose approval you're not looking for. I watch the cars go by as the airport disappears in the distance, and I wonder what I've gotten myself into. I have been highly focused on getting to where Jack is, but in the process I have made myself a houseguest. A houseguest to complete strangers and the one person I really can't stand. Dan punches Aidan in the arm. Aidan laughs, inexplicably.

WE'RE OFF THE highway driving through Oak Shore. It's a classic small town, like you'd see on TV. Andy Griffith could live here. Library, gift shop, bakery, diner. Old-fashioned streetlights and leafy elm trees. Kids are riding bikes without helmets, steering with one hand while holding ice cream cones. We have pockets of this in Los Angeles, small neighborhoods tucked into corners of the city, but they look different, like they're too new.

I'm picturing Dan's family home again. They'll have a wine cellar with seating, in case you ever wanted to have a conversation about wine that lasted so long you'd have to sit, and framed photos of people in ruffled shirts. His mother will be named Catherine, with all the syllables drawn out.

I'm deciding if Catherine has a French twist or a sensible bob when Aidan turns right off of Main Street, past a berry stand, and down a country road. I scoot up between the two front seats. "Is this farmland?"

"Potatoes," Dan says.

Twins with Irish names driving me by a potato farm. This feels made up. "Is your family in farming?" I ask.

"Air-conditioning," says Aidan, and Dan laughs. "But

our grandfather worked on this potato farm for most of his life. Our grandmother was actually the Potato Queen in 1951."

"Okay, stop, now you're just bragging," Dan says.

Aidan has the easiest, most generous smile, and I remember seeing that smile twice on Dan, when we first met and right after he called my movie trash. Since then, it's been a lot of eye-rolling.

"It's all automated now, but we grew up here, running through the sprinklers in the fields and then rolling in the mud," says Aidan.

"Mom hated that," Dan says to the window.

"She did. It's noisy during the harvest in the fall, but the rest of the year it's just a vast expanse of peace and quiet."

Dan turns to me. "Which is why he lives in a house in the center of town."

"Well, yes. It's too much peace and quiet for me."

At the end of the road there's a small shingled house with a sprawling rose garden out front. The roses are red, which strikes me as overly romantic. I wonder if they were planted when the people living here were newlyweds.

We pull into the driveway, and Aidan says, "This is us," and gets out of the car. I run this pretty little house through my brain, trying to reconcile how a person as pretentious as Dan could come from a home as unpretentious as this. There's a low wooden table by the front door with a serrated knife and a bucket of recently cut roses. We are inland from the ocean, but when I get out of the car, I can still smell a bit of the salt air.

A woman who must be the mother of these twins comes out and throws her arms around Dan. Her hair is the same shade of black with a single white stripe along her face. This is not a perfunctory greeting hug. Dan's face is in her hair; her arms encircle him like he's the thing that will keep her from drowning. I don't know what it's like to have a child, and I don't know what it's like to live that far away from my mother. But I am self-conscious for all of us as this hug draws on.

Aidan seems unfazed and carries our suitcases around the hug into the house. She takes Dan's face in her hands. "You're thin, Danny. You look terrible."

He turns to me. "Mom, sorry, this is Jane Jackson. From work. Jane, this is my mom, Maureen."

"Call me Reenie," she says, taking both of my hands in hers. She is the source of the wide navy blue eyes. "You're so pretty. Danny didn't say. But of course you are. Danny always likes a pretty girl."

"Thank you," I say, trying not to make it sound like a question. "And thank you for having me. I know it's a big week with the anniversary."

"Well, of course. Danny hasn't brought a girl home in years. What was her name? Esme? Ethel?"

Dan is the tiniest bit flustered, and I like it. I like seeing him take a few steps off his high horse and squirm a little like the rest of us. "Elizabeth. Her name was Elizabeth. And Jane is not my girlfriend. Like I told you on the phone, she works at the studio and needs to be at the festival this weekend. That's all."

"Oh, all right, if that's how it's going to be," Reenie says with Dan's trademark eye-roll. It's more playful on her. "Come meet everyone."

Everyone. How many people could possibly be in this little house? She leads me inside into a neat entryway. There's a staircase carpeted in seagrass and children. There are four of them, between three and seven, I'd guess. Dan dives into the pile of them like they're a ball pit at Chuck E. Cheese. When he emerges, he has one on each knee, and one hanging from each arm. He seems to have bathed in them, and some of his hardness washes off. He catches me noticing and quickly lowers the two on his arms to the ground.

"I'm Sammy," says a little boy. "Who are you?"

"Rude," says Reenie, giving a fake swat. "This is Uncle Danny's girlfriend, Jane."

"I'm not . . ." I start.

"It's a bit of a madhouse around here this week," says Reenie. "Come." We pass a wooden table with a framed photo. Five nearly identical boys, in ascending height order with the twins in the middle.

"Who?" I say to no one.

"These are the boys," she says. "It was the Fourth of July. This is Brian, Finn, the twins, and baby Connor. Can you tell which one's Danny?"

The children rush past me toward the back of the house as I pick up the frame and look at the boys. I had no idea Dan had so many brothers. I study the twins. Hair brushed identically. Matching blue-and-white-striped shorts and red sweatshirts. One is grinning into the camera; the other is staring at something in the distance. I point at the starer. "This one."

"Ah, you know him well," she says and laughs. "Come."

"Five sons and four grandchildren," I say almost to myself. It's impossible to imagine it.

"Oh, I have seven grandchildren, plus one on the way," she says and leads me to a rustic but neat kitchen where pots are bubbling on the stove. She rushes to stir something, and Dan rests his hands on the back of a spindled kitchen chair and takes a breath.

"Are you ready for this?" he asks.

I look down at the farmhouse kitchen table. It's three long planks of wood with a lazy Susan in the middle—salt and pepper, hot sauce, sugar, Splenda, honey, and a tiny votive candle. Someone's thought of everything.

"Ready for what?"

"My family." He says it quietly, like it's a secret, like he doesn't want his mom to hear.

"So far, they're a lot nicer than you, but if you insist, I'll reserve judgment."

"All right," he says and opens the door to the patio. The sound that greets us is deafening. At first I think we've walked into a children's birthday party, balls and screams flying across the lawn. Then I think they've invited the town for a barbeque to welcome Dan home. But all the men in this small crowd look similar, and I realize they're all Finnegans. I feel like I've walked into a fashion shoot for a laid-back, high-end men's clothing line. All of them with their sharp jaw lines and sculpted muscles pressing against cotton in a way that suggests they've just gotten off a fishing boat or a rowing machine. "Here we go," Dan says.

A long table is set with white napkins and jelly jars full of yellow daisies. There's a picnic blanket on the grass for the kids. Beyond the grass is an expanse of potato fields. Perfectly straight lines of dark green bushes converge in the distance. Some kind of shed covered in ivy blocks a portion of the view, and I wonder if I am the only one who wants to tear it down. This field would be completely Zen without that eyesore.

A leaner version of Dan crosses the patio to greet him. "Ya ugly fuck! How are you?"

I turn to Reenie for an explanation, and she just beams. Dan is a lot of things. *Ya grumpy fuck*, sure. *Ya pretentious fuck*, okay. But ugly, for sure no.

"I'm good." Dan hugs him. "Good to see you, ya old bastard."

The old bastard laughs. "I'm Brian," he says to me and pulls me into a hug. "I'm the oldest, which is why I get so much respect."

"This is Jane," Reenie says to everyone. "Can we try to act civilized for just one night? Danny's brought a girl home." She makes big eyes at the crowd for emphasis.

"What? Did you lose a bet?" another one says to me. He's a bit fairer than the others, his hair more brown than black, but with the same navy blue eyes. "I'm Connor. You look familiar."

"He's the baby, but we call him the professor," Brian says.

"Because he's a professor?" I literally don't know how to jump onto the freight train that is this family.

"He's a dentist. Big shot." This is from a shorter man who has to be Dan's dad. He is the source of the cheekbones and sturdy jaws. "I'm Cormack Finnegan. Welcome." He shakes my hand and gives me a beer.

All of these brothers look like they were produced from a Xerox machine, differentiated by some slight smudges in the printing. Aidan introduces me to his wife, Paula, who gives me a hug and says, "Thank you for not being platinum blond. Brian dates so many platinum blondes, and I get confused as they come and go. For a while I was just calling them all Heather, and twice I was right." This appears to be a joke, not that it's one I get, but all of the brothers are laughing, including Dan. "Don't try to remember any of our names, it's impossible," she says. "And avoid the children, the worst of them are Finn's."

Connor's wife, Marla, is both pregnant and carrying a baby, and I don't know quite how to process this. "Hello," I say. "I don't see how . . . Is that your baby?"

"Baby?" she asks and then looks at the baby like she's surprised to see it there. "God, no. Whose baby is this?" she shouts into the crowd. Everyone laughs, and Aidan claims the baby.

Dan doesn't speak directly to me, but he stays close like he's responsible for me, worried I might get trampled in the crowd. I think of how much time I used to spend as a kid searching for my dad's face in a crowd, and I wonder what it would be like to be surrounded by so many people who look just like you. Reenie calls to Aidan from the kitchen, and he hands me the baby. "Katie, this is Auntie Jane, be right back."

"I'm not . . ." I start again. But Katie is in my arms and has one fist wrapped around my hair and another in her mouth. She's staring up at me with those deep blue eyes like she's a hundred percent sure I can handle this. We have a quiet moment where the din of the crowd softens and she and I lock eyes. I don't know what to say to a baby, so I make my *oof* face and she laughs. Just a tiny *I love you too*.

"She likes you already," says Reenie, leading me to a seat at the table. I don't know if I'm responsible for this baby now or if she's just the general responsibility of this giant, pulsing Finnegan organism. We all sit, and no one makes any move to take the person in my arms.

Cormack pulls chicken kebabs off the grill, and Reenie brings roasted potatoes from the kitchen. The sun lowers over the potato fields and the humidity starts to lift. Aidan's wife, Paula, takes Katie from me and is feeding her something from a jar. I meet Finn and his wife, Eileen, and their small brood just as we're sitting down, and I'm counting on my fingers: this is five; it has to be all of them. And only Dan and Brian are single. In a shocking turn of events, a sum total of zero Finnegans are pretentious or hairsplitting, even Dan, actually, now that he's home.

Dinner is served, and I am starving. I find kebabs hard to deal with, and I forever hope that someone else will un-kebab them for me. There's always the possibility of the awkward moment where your fork catches on the spear and you pull too hard and send a chicken cube flying across the table. So I start with the potatoes and the salad.

"How are things looking for the festival?" Dan asks Finn. Mention of the festival refocuses me. I'm on a business trip, a mission to confront my past and win my future. I don't need to be worried about what I'm supposed to be talking about with these absurdly attractive strangers.

"Good, I think. I only see the parts I'm involved in, mostly wires."

"I can't wait till it's over," Cormack says to me. "This thing causes such a frenzy. Brings in money, but it definitely disrupts the peace and quiet. As you can see." He gestures to the full table.

Aidan rolls his eyes, and it's appealing on him. "He's just annoyed that Paula, the girls, and I are freeloading. We rented our house for ridiculous money for the week, so we're crashing here."

Dan drops his fork. "How's that going to work?"

"Oh, it's fine, honey," Reenie says. "You two are grown-ups."

"Mom. We're grown-ups who *work* together. And honestly, we barely even do that. I thought we'd have two rooms."

And boom, just like that, there's just one bed. My face goes hot, and I concentrate on the brain-surgery-level work that is getting this kebab off the spear. I have an elbow in the air for leverage and tug with increasing pressure until it gives and, you guessed it, flies across the table.

"Janey Jakes!" Connor says and starts to laugh. I can feel it: I've just made my *oof* face. Braces sparkling, glasses in disarray. He has seen my essential awkwardness, and he knows who I am. I sit up straighter and try to *Mona Lisa* my features. "I knew you looked familiar, but you're so hot now." He looks at Dan, then his wife, Marla. "If that's okay to say."

"What's Janey Jakes?" Paula asks.

"Holy shit," says Aidan. "You are her. Danny, are you joking? How did you not tell us this?"

Dan turns to me and stares. He scans my face and my hair, like the PIN for his debit card is hidden there. Then he turns back to Aidan. "Are you talking about the geek from *Pop Rocks*? There is no way."

"Was that the show Connor loved that you guys were always watching? With the catchy song?" Reenie asks.

"'Jump-Start Love Song,'" Connor says, then starts singing and strumming his hands on the table. *"I want to write a jump-start love song, figure out how we went so wrong."* My face goes hot. This is a nightmare. I came to New York to pose as a Hollywood dealmaker, not a chronic punch line.

Aidan joins in. *"I don't know how you've stayed gone so long, calling you back with my jump-start love song."* They all start to laugh.

"I don't know what you nitwits are talking about," Cormack says, effortlessly forking a piece of chicken.

"I never watched it," Brian says. "It was after Finn's and my time. But God, these guys were so into it."

I must not be here. It's like they're all talking around me, so I sit and wait to be addressed directly.

Aidan says, "Dad, she's Janey Jakes, from *Pop Rocks*."

And then, finally, to me, "You are, right? There's no way you're not."

"I am," I say and wince a little. I wait for one of them to say, *Poor Janey, do do do do do do.*

Dan turns all the way toward me, as if I've just appeared. He scans my face again in that unnerving way he has of taking in every single detail. "Seriously?" He almost whispers it.

"How could you not have noticed this?" Paula asks.

"Or talked about it?" Reenie asks. "How long have you two been together?"

"Mom. Since this morning. We're not together. Wow," he says, looking at me. "Now that I've seen it, I can't unsee it."

I lean back in my chair. It's been a long seventeen years trying to be taken seriously. Braces off, better haircut, moderate success. One piece of flying chicken has shattered my hard-earned smoke screen. But on the other hand, the only way I'm going to get anywhere with Jack this week is by playing the Janey Jakes card. And the stakes are very low here. I'm not trying to date any of these guys. I'm never going to see any of these people again.

"That was me," I say. "Until I was sixteen."

"Connor was so into Hailey Soul," Aidan says.

"We all were," says Dan. "I mean every guy in the country."

"Well, you're hot now," says Connor.

Marla says, "Honey, the more you say it, the weirder it gets."

Connor makes a face like he's pretending to be embarrassed and turns back to me. "You were funny as hell on that show. Your timing, everything." He's laughing as if he's rewatching the episode where I accidentally booked us a mobile pet-grooming truck as a tour bus.

"Thank you," I say. I am surprised at how calm I sound. I take a sip of wine and decide to just go with it.

Dan leans back in his chair and looks around like he's reconsidering everything he's ever known. His eyes settle on me in a way that reminds me of the day we met. "You know, the first time I saw you, I thought I knew you. Remember? On the street with the hawk? I was a little distracted, but then I swear I recognized you."

"Is that when you started dating?" Reenie asks.

"No, it was when I was considering dating her."

This is the first either of us has ever acknowledged the brief moment that our relationship was going in a totally different direction. I'm uncomfortable opening that door, so I slam it shut. "Days before he ruined my career," I say.

"You didn't need me for that," he says and raises his eyes to me in challenge.

I let out a breath and lean back in my chair, feeling myself relax again. Arguing with Dan is a safe space.

"She picks terrible scripts," Dan goes on.

"Of course," I say. "And I'm sure you all know Dan has a PhD in *The Notebook*."

Everyone at the table laughs. They laugh hard, and I like it. There's no satisfaction like saying the right thing at the exact right time and getting that happy energy in return. It takes me back to the early days of *Pop Rocks*, before Pantheon Television learned that it was a lot cheaper to work with a laugh track. (I'd later think that the laugh track is to a live audience what porn is to sex. It can sound the same from the next room, but really, it's not the same at all.) The laughter around the table now is raucous and alive, like they've been waiting all day to let it out.

Finn is wiping his eyes. "Jane, literally, he would watch *The Notebook* and sob. It was part of his whole quiet-time weird thing, so we'd leave him alone . . ."

Aidan says, "But we knew when to come in . . ."

"Minute fifty-four," says Brian. "Tears, like clockwork." Everyone laughs again, including Dan.

"It's true," Dan says. "Watching *The Notebook* was the only way I could get them to leave me alone."

"Until minute fifty-four and the tears," Connor says. "Then we pounced."

"He's an introvert," Finn says with air quotes, as if the whole idea of introversion is a made-up excuse for people who don't want to deal. They all laugh again, but Dan doesn't.

"What happens at minute fifty-four?" I ask. "That can't be the end when they die in each other's arms. Which, incidentally, is ridiculous." It's freeing to be so far from home, so far from my mom that I can speak this essential truth to strangers.

"Of course you hate it," Dan says. "The most romantic part."

"Yeah," says Marla, pulling a child onto her lap. "What's annoying about them dying like that?"

"It's absurd. It's more likely it was a murder-suicide than they both just spontaneously died," I say.

Dan turns to me in mock seriousness, but there's a smile behind his eyes. He likes this debate as much as I do. "She died, and then he died of a broken heart immediately after. It's true love, Jane. Look it up." They're all looking at us, and I wonder if they have any idea how long the two of us can argue about this movie.

"Doesn't happen. Not a thing." I take a bite of my salad. "So what happens at minute fifty-four?"

"Noah comes back from the war and sees his dad," Dan says to his plate.

"Dude, you're such a wuss," says Connor. "I don't know how your fake girlfriend can stand it." Dan shakes his head while his brothers laugh. He's on the outside but is somehow fine with it. I look around the table at all of these happy people and know there's something here that I want.

CHAPTER 11

AS IT TURNS OUT, WE HAVE THREE BEDS. THERE'S one set of bunk beds and a twin bed next to it, with enough room for one person to stand between them. At the very end of the room is a large dresser with three drawers, and on top of it is a television from back when they invented televisions. Dan and I are standing at the threshold.

"Home sweet home," he says. "I was totally going to take the other room with the queen-size bed and make you stay in this used-bed warehouse. I guess this serves me right."

I take two steps forward and sit on the twin bed. "I claim this one."

He's looking at me with the shadow of a smile on his face. "It is so weird that you're here, and even weirder that you're Janey Jakes." He looks at the little TV and back at me. "I'm having a sleepover with Janey Jakes."

"I'm the poor man's Hailey Soul," I say and shrug. I want him to think I'm kidding.

Dan looks at me for a beat before saying, "I don't think so." It's a kind thing to say.

He throws his stuff on the bottom bunk and looks around. "The bathroom's next door, definitely lock the door. No one has any boundaries around here." He unzips his duffel bag and pulls out a sweatshirt. "I'm going to go hang out for a while."

"Didn't they go to bed?"

"Yes, they're in bed or gone, which is exactly why I'm going to go hang out."

"You have a lot of brothers," I say.

"I do. It's hard to get any peace and quiet. So I'm going to . . ." He motions to the door.

"Okay," I say. This may be part of his arrogance, but I respect how Dan takes the quiet time he needs.

He doesn't make any move to leave though. He's just looking at me.

"I don't hate the part where Noah comes back from the war and sees his dad—everyone cries at that point," I say.

His smile is wide and bright, like I've just shown him a photo of his favorite thing. "I mean, he sells the house so Noah can buy the old Windsor plantation. How cool was that guy?"

I feel a tiny tug on my heart for that dad. I don't like this tug, so I deepen my voice and deliver my best Sam Shepard imitation: "I'm gonna live with you, dummy. Gonna help you fix it up."

Dan doesn't ask why I can recite a line from a movie I

hate. Instead he laughs a real laugh and locks his eyes on mine like he did the first day. I like the sound of his laugh and the way his eyes dance around my face before settling on my eyes. This is an odd thing for me to notice about a person I wanted to punch in the neck as recently as this morning, but something's different. It could be that we're on the same inane quest. It could be that I've seen his people and none of them seem like they purchase bespoke anything. It's fine, and even fun, to carelessly make Dan laugh, breaking all dating rules, because that ship has sailed.

"Well, thank you. That almost feels like a peace offering," he says and turns to go. "You probably know how to get a glass of water and stuff?"

"I can figure that out."

"Okay," he says and stands there for a beat. He's going to say something else, but then he shakes his head and closes the door.

It's hard for an only child to imagine growing up with all of those people vying for attention and space. And food. Tonight wasn't a party; it was just his family sitting around the table exchanging good-hearted insults. I try to picture doing that every day for eighteen years. I try to imagine coming home to my very own people. I feel the ghost of a million laughs in this room.

I lock the door and change into my pajamas. If I'd known I'd be sharing a room, I'd have brought a full-length pajama set, maybe the crisp blue ones that feel like a man's shirt. They're practically business pajamas and would have been perfect for this trip. Instead I grabbed the short pink set that my mom gave me for Valentine's Day. The top has little conversation hearts for buttons, and "Hug Me" in this setting feels all wrong.

When my teeth are brushed and I'm under the covers, I text my mom: Arrived safely, sorry I forgot to text. Love you!

She does not reply, which is fine but odd. She's in Santa Barbara, not on the moon.

I close my eyes and try to picture Dan, Aidan, and Connor watching *Pop Rocks* on that little TV. I imagine them all lusting after Hailey and laughing at our carefully scripted predicaments. It's no wonder Hailey's still on top; she grew up believing that's where she belonged. I used to spend a lot of time imagining what that would feel like, walking around in her skin and feeling the power of that adoration. I used to read her lines into the mirror at home, trying to channel my inner Hailey. "Oh, as if I'd ever be caught dead at that party," I'd say with a hair toss.

I am a witch and I've conjured her, because my phone dings with a text. Hailey: Any luck tracking Jack down? The idea of us seeing him again is hilarious

Above this text is our conversation where she told me to contact Angelica. Above that is Happy birthday!, followed by Thank you! over and over again. Years of it. It's crazy that Jack's rise from the ashes has us talking twice in a week.

Me: Not yet.

Hailey: I hope you find him. I hope this album hasn't turned him into a dick, he was such a sweet guy

Barf, no. Me: Yeah, the sweetest

I call Clem and get her at her shift at the bar. "Sorry," I say. "This was a crazy time to call."

"Cover for me for five minutes?" she says to someone. I hear a door open and close, and it's the kindest silence. "What's going on?"

"Nothing really. I mean, I'm in Dan's childhood bedroom and his brothers immediately recognized me as Janey Jakes and Hailey texted and I feel like I'm being dragged back in time."

"That's got to be weird. Are they all hot?"

"All of them."

"Married?"

"All but the oldest, Brian. And Dan."

"Interesting."

"Not interesting. I don't know why I'm calling. I just needed a little courage."

"You're going to see Jack, and you're just going to be easy, jokey Actual Jane. Repeat after me: 'Nice sideburns, Elvis.'"

"Come on." Jack does sport a ridiculous set of pork-chop sideburns these days.

"You can't seem nervous if you're busting on him. Say it."

"Nice sideburns, Elvis." I'm not as convincing as she was, but I do feel a little more confident.

When we've hung up, I pull the quilt over my head and open Instagram before I can really think it through. I find Jack and send him a message: Hey it's Jane Jackson from Jump-Start Love Song. Remember that? Ha! I'm in Long Island for the music festival and wanted to talk with you quickly about a movie I'm making with Clearwater Studios. Let me know if you have time to talk.

I delete "if" and replace it with "when." That's what decision-makers do.

Send.

I pull down the covers and look around the room, half expecting someone to say, *What have you done?*

CHAPTER 12

~~~

I WAKE UP AT SIX, WHICH IS THREE A.M. IN LA. I SHOULD be tired, but that first adrenal rush of waking up and not knowing where I am has me overly alert. The sun is up but barely, which is the best part of the day. My mom texted in the middle of the night: Great, have fun!

I check my Instagram, and there is a reply from Jack: Thanks for reaching out. If you are interested in upcoming tour information, please visit my website.

There is nothing less satisfying than a reply from a bot. It took all of my courage to send a message he'll never see. In the story of Jack and me, this tracks.

Dan is just across from me, an arm's length away in the bottom bunk. He's on his back, still in the white T-shirt he traveled in. He looks younger when he sleeps, and his face is monochrome without the flash of his blue eyes. His black eyebrows look penciled in, like he's an ink drawing. The straight line of his nose makes me think of the statue of David. His lips are at rest; they're not preparing to debate me.

They're just resting there, soft. He turns toward me, and the thing I want more than anything is to not be caught staring at him while he sleeps. I slam my eyes shut and count to thirty. Then I stretch a little in my sleep and make a big show of just having awakened. It's a waste of perfectly good acting because he's still sound asleep.

I will the bed not to creak and beg my body to be light as I peel off my covers, stand, and grab my suitcase. I cannot risk the sound of a zipper unzipping in this tiny space, so I take my whole suitcase into the bathroom with me. When my teeth are brushed, I rinse with a tiny, silent stream of water and get dressed. Unfortunately, the toilet has to be flushed, and the sound roars throughout the house. *She's up! She's peed!* the toilet screams.

I carry my running shoes as I tiptoe by the kitchen to the front door.

"Coffee?" Cormack is at the kitchen table with the *New York Post* and a big mug.

"Good morning. No, thank you. I'm going to go for a quick run first."

"Where?"

It's a great question. I'm not really sure where I am. "Maybe I'll run twenty minutes in one direction and then turn around."

Cormack tears off a corner of the newspaper and scribbles something on it. "That sounds like a terrible plan. Call me if you get lost." He holds out the paper to me without getting up. He's written "Dad" and his phone number.

Maybe it's because I've just woken up and I'm still tangentially close to that dreamlike state where anything is possible, maybe it's because I am on the hell path of memory lane and I've been transformed back into Janey Jakes, but looking at that word makes my throat burn with prickly tears. It's a noun that's magically transformed into a name just by capitalizing the first letter, like "dawn" or "rose." It's a name that could have been on the bottom of so many birthday cards but wasn't. I tuck it into the back of my phone case, and leave without saying anything.

It's a cool morning and perfectly quiet. I normally run to the melody of the cars on San Vicente Boulevard, but here I don't hear anything. Potatoes grow in complete silence. I run alongside a mile of fields until I get to the left turn that takes me to town. On Main Street I start to smell the salt in the air. There's a faint crunch of sand on the sidewalk as I run, left by yesterday's kids coming straight from the beach for ice cream. It's hard to imagine this town overrun for a week with concertgoers and rock stars. I pass a gift shop called Sundries with a rainbow of Oak Shore T-shirts in the window.

When I've reached the edge of town, houses line the road, and beyond them is the ocean. The sun is low still, dappling pink light on the water. I turn around at the end of a big park and head back to town. Chippy's Diner is the only place open. I order a black coffee to go, and the man behind the counter asks me if that will be all. Without thinking, I take the little scrap of paper out of my phone

case and text Cormack: It's Jane. I'm at Chippy's, want anything?

Cormack: Yes! Can you get me a blueberry muffin? The
kind without the flaxseeds and stuff

I ask for six of them, and while I wait, I add Cormack to
my contacts. Where it says name, I type: Dad. I don't know
why I do this, though I do know why.

CORMACK'S SITTING OUT on the patio with a little black-
haired girl, maybe six, at his feet. She's Aidan's, I think. I
stop before I get to them because the view has changed.
Instead of the old shed blocking the rows of bushes, there's
an arbor covered in ivy that perfectly frames a bit of the
potato field. It's the thing you'd stand under to recite
your wedding vows. The lines of crops converge in the distance, brown stripes of dirt alternating with green rows of
bushes.

"What is this?" I ask, handing him the bag of muffins.

"It's art or some nonsense," he says and hands one to the
little girl. "Top secret," he tells her. There's steam coming
out of the bag, and he lets it touch every part of his face. He
smiles at me. "Thank you."

I take a muffin and settle in next to him. "Hi," I say to
the little girl. She's arranging pebbles on the deck.

"I'm Ruby," she says and looks up at me with Dan's
eyes. It's astounding, the resemblance, and also her mass of
loose black curls.

"I'm Jane," I say.

"I know," she says and goes back to work.

"Aidan's," Cormack says. "The rest of them will swarm this place soon. They've all taken some time off this week. I don't know why. It's August, not Christmas."

"Where did this arbor come from?" I ask him. "Wasn't there an old shed there?"

"It's Danny. An old project of his. You know he's a little . . ." He moves his hand like he means Dan's so-so. "It wasn't a shed. It's the frame of their old swing set. When he was about thirteen, he moved it to that spot, removed the swings, and then trained all that ivy crap to grow up the sides."

"It's beautiful," I say.

"I suppose," he says. "He comes home and trims it, and then he takes pictures and stares at them like the potatoes are Greta Garbo."

I laugh.

"It is nice to have Dan back," Cormack says. I feel that old ache for that simple thing—a dad who would be happy to see me.

"It must be hard having a child live so far away."

"Well, yes, I guess. We always thought he'd come home, get a real job."

"In LA, working in movies is a pretty real job."

"Artsy jobs end in homelessness. No offense. It's just a fact." He looks at me sideways. "I work in heating and cooling. Done it my whole life. And let me tell you, it always gets hot and then cold. People always need their systems serviced and fixed. I always have work."

Regular work does sound oddly relaxing at this point in my life. "And Connor's a dentist," I say.

"People are always going to have teeth."

"Finn's an electrician."

"Someone's gotta keep the lights on."

"What does Aidan do?"

"Plumber," he says.

"Everybody poops," I say. Cormack laughs, and I feel a disproportionate amount of joy at having caused it. His laugh has fingers that wrap around my heart.

I polish off the rest of my muffin, still warm. The sun is all the way up over the potato fields and the straight brown lines between the green bushes seem brighter. There's noise in the kitchen, and Paula comes out with baby Katie and pulls a chair from the table so that we are all in a row.

"Who got muffins?" Paula asks.

"Jane," says Cormack. He hands her the bag. "You're sworn to silence."

"The calm before the storm," she says.

"Is there going to be a storm?" I sort of like the idea of it. We don't really get weather in Los Angeles, and it would be exciting to see dark clouds roll in over the Atlantic, like in the movies.

Cormack laughs. "No, she just means breakfast. Reenie's going all out this week because everyone's around for the anniversary party. It's like a diner for a couple of hours and then she throws everyone out."

"Did I sleep late?" It's Dan, behind us. He walks out with coffee. His hair is wild and his sweatpants are low on

his hips. I have a quick thought that he looks like a bed
you'd want to climb back into on a Sunday. Because it's
raining outside, and your body just wants to sink back into
the warmth. I look away from him and shake off the thought
before he sees it on my face.

"No, but we ate all the muffins," Cormack says.

"Muffins? Who smuggled those in?"

Ruby gets to her feet, arms up to be lifted and swung
onto his shoulders. No one seems to blush about the way his
shirt rides up when he does this, revealing the low ridges of
his stomach. I raise my gaze to the safety of their matching
sets of eyes.

"I got some on my way back from my run," I say. Cormack gives me a sideways glance and then looks away, in-
nocent.

"Where's the bag?" Dan's voice seems kind of intense
for a man with a six-year-old balancing on his head.

I pick up the bag from where it's sitting by my feet and
hand it to him. He shoves it under his shirt as his mom
comes through the door. "Good morning! Who's hungry?"

"Starving," says Cormack, who's eaten two muffins already. He gets up and gives her a quick squeeze.

Paula shakes her head. "You'll get used to it."

BREAKFAST IS A circus. We spin the lazy Susan and pass
plates of bacon and sliced grapefruit. The pancakes are thin
and crispy on the outside; Dan rolls his up and eats it like a
crepe. When everyone leaves, I can still feel the hum of

their conversation. Who's going where, who's grabbing whose kids. Who needs to chew with their mouth closed.

"So you've already been to town and won over my dad?" Dan asks when we're loading the dishwasher.

"Yes, but it was early, everything but the diner was closed. What's our plan today? Stake out the town? Hang around the Owl Barn?"

"Jack's definitely here, and he stopped by the Owl Barn yesterday afternoon. I told Finn we'd go around four, but he'll text us if Jack shows up earlier. So we sort of have the whole day till then."

"I should work," I say. I cannot imagine how Dan and I would spend a whole day together.

He's drying his mother's cast-iron skillet and is a million miles away.

"The library," I say. "Maybe I'll go there today to work." He doesn't reply until he's placed the skillet back on the stove.

"I love pancakes," he says. "Did you like them?"

"I did. But tomorrow I'll remember not to have a muffin before . . ."

He reaches out and covers my mouth with his hand. He seems as surprised as I am that he's done this, but he leaves it there for a second. I take in the smooth feel of his palm on my lips, and he watches me. His hand smells faintly of lemony dish soap, and for a quick second I think that lemony dish soap on smooth warm skin might be sexy. When he finally removes his hand, I force my lips into a hard line to squeeze away the tingle he's left there.

"Sorry," he says and hides the offending hand in his pocket.

"Yes," I say, though he didn't ask me a question. I'm nonsensical now that his palm has been on my lips. I don't know what that was, but it is unsettling. Dan has plenty of ways to get under my skin; we don't need another one.

"She cannot know about the muffins," he says. "She'd kill a man for less."

I smile at that, the fierceness with which his mother runs her kitchen. He smiles back.

"So the library today?" I ask, folding a dish towel and hanging it on the oven.

"Jane. Janey—I still can't believe that. We're on Long Island. In August. You have no projects going and are probably going to get fired. Let's go to the beach."

CHAPTER 13

~~~~

THERE ARE A HUNDRED GOOD PLACES TO BUY A BATH-
ing suit in Los Angeles. Four of them are within a mile
of my house. I have several in my middle dresser drawer
that I like and that would be better than anything currently
on offer at Sundries in Oak Shore. This is a business trip, to
New York. Nothing in those words indicated that I'd need a
bathing suit.

Dan knows the girl who works there. Her name is Tay-
lor, and she's in her twenties. Early twenties, I'd guess. She
brightens when she sees him and touches his forearm unnecessarily. "It's sort of late in the season," she tells us. "And
we don't really restock. Let me pull what we have in your
size."

She busies herself at the racks, and I swear to God she
just pulled a yellow one-piece with strawberries on it. It
looks like a bathing suit for a very tall five-year-old. "Has
anyone seen Jack Quinlan in town this week?" I ask.

"Karen from the pharmacy said he was in buying Tylenol yesterday, but he left immediately in a Mercedes G-wagon. He hasn't been hanging around."

I practice again in my head: *Hi, Jack, I'm Jane Jackson.* *"Jump-Start Love Song"? Yeah, right. Good times. Listen, I need you to write a song for me.*

I am trying not to feel hopeless as I head to the tiny dressing room with an armful of bathing suits, even though my pitch is lame and Dan and his lemony hands think I'm going to get fired. The strawberries become more appealing as I sort through the ruffles and eyelets. One even has a little skirt. I settle on the quietest one, a royal blue one-piece with pale blue polka dots. I am a hundred percent sure Eleanor Roosevelt had this exact same suit.

I rip off the tag and put my shorts and T-shirt back on. I buy a straw hat and a bag of peanut M&M's out of habit. "Don't tell your mom," I say.

"It's fine, she doesn't make lunch," Dan says.

BACK ON OUR bikes, we head through town to the beach. We drop our bikes by the dunes without locking them or even discussing it. I don't bring up the fact that we'll be walking home after someone steals those bikes because I am trying to fit in. We kick off our sneakers and carry them as we walk along a narrow path of sand through the grassy dunes. The sand is silky white and peppered with shells and hot rocks that press hard against my feet. It reminds me of Clem's birthday when I took us to a spa for hot stone massages, except this is free. When the path ends, we are on a wide stretch of beach and the ocean roars in front of us. Groups of kids are busy digging and building things, and behind them, gulls break the straight line of the horizon. As we get closer to the water, the cool mist of the waves hits my face. I try to remember the last time I went to the beach at home. Most days I run to the water, have a look, and then head back.

Dan pulls two towels out of his backpack and hands me one. We spread them out on the sand and plop down. He's brought a book, a not-so-subtle clue that he doesn't intend to talk to me.

"*Moby-Dick*?" I ask. I can't wait to lie here and have him explain existential angst and the quiet merits of the seafaring lifestyle.

"*Sula*," he says. He's flat on his back and holds the book up for me to see. I read it in college and highlighted the part where she wants to dig into his skin to get inside of him. Something about fertile loam underneath his hard gold exterior. I'd wondered about Toni Morrison, such a genius, letting herself get so romantic. I'd wondered if she'd ever fallen in love like that and then had to claw her way out.

I'm about to say something to this effect, but he closes his eyes, so I do the same. It's strange that we're not talking. Who ever heard of two people going to the beach together in complete silence? I try to think of something for us to argue about. I wonder if there's something I could say about *Sula* that would make him put his hand on my mouth again. I wonder if I'm starved for touch; I think this is a thing that happens to primates.

I fidget with the bottom of my shorts and try to mold my back into the sand beneath me. I am not stripping down to my polka-dotted bathing suit. The other thing I'm not doing is relaxing. I know about relaxing because I live in the world, but it is not a thing I seem capable of. On the days I don't run, worrying is my cardio.

I steal a look at Dan, and he is dead to the world, barely a breath rising in his chest. I don't know how he does it. I take a deep breath. The waves crash in a regular rhythm and a breeze blows off the water. I concentrate on the soft touch of the air as it moves up my shins and along my body. I pull my phone out of my bag and check my work email. Nothing.

"Do you hear it?" The sound of his voice startles me.

"The ocean?"

"No, the quiet," he says. "Nothing makes me appreciate the quiet like coming home." He turns his head to me and squints against the sun, one eye open. "They're really loud."

I laugh. "I like them. They're all so good-natured."

"Mostly," he says. "For entertainment in my family, we just bust on each other and argue. About sports, about music. We once argued about asparagus for an entire meal."

"Asparagus." I turn my head toward him, and our faces are no more than six inches apart. I don't know when I've seen him this close, the way his eyelashes seem even darker than his hair. The way his upper lip bows at the top.

"It was very heated," he says. "Good source of vitamin E versus makes your pee smell. It was a whole thing."

"So this is where you learned to be a pain in the ass?"

He smiles at me. "Yes." The back of his hand shades his eyes, but I can see the playfulness there.

I look back to the sky.

"I'm an only child," I say after a while. "And my dad died when I was five. It was very quiet." I don't know if it's my discomfort with the quiet that's made me say this. I don't know if it's the whole Jack Quinlan thing or all this *Pop Rocks* talk, but I am feeling unusually unmasked, digging up the old ghosts and tossing them out there. My eyes are closed against the sun, but I can feel him looking at me.

"I'm sorry," he says. "About your dad."

"It's fine," I say.

"It's not fine," Dan says. "I mean, your dad being dead can't be fine." He turns onto his stomach and rests his chin on his hands.

I turn my head and find his eyes right there. "It's a long story," I say. It's not really even that long. It's a sentence. But it's something I've never said to anyone besides Clem. Not even to my mom. Sometimes the simplest facts are the most painful ones. They're the ones that cut to the essence of who we are.

His eyes are intensely focused, and this is the difference between Dan and his brothers. They let things roll right over them, and Dan doesn't miss a thing. It's almost like he could pull that sentence right out of me.

I hold his gaze for a few beats before I actually feel myself weakening. There's power in his quiet; it makes room for something. But I've said way too much on this topic already, so I say, right into his eyes, "You totally listen to folk music on a gramophone."

He laughs, and I feel better. "Yes, obviously."

"It must be so weird to have all those brothers who look so much like you."

"I even have an identical twin," he says. He smooths the sand between us with his hand.

"Well, yes. Even weirder."

He doesn't say anything more and I want him to. So I go on. "Do you like that, coming home to people so much like you?"

He looks at me, and there's something in his eyes; it's a vulnerable something. "Sometimes when I'm here with all of them, I worry I'll get swallowed up. Like I'll forget who I am."

The white noise of the ocean surrounds us, and it's an active sort of quiet. It reminds me of the quiet in an airplane, that loud hum that shifts your brain waves.

"I have no idea who I am," I say. It comes out more solemn than I intended, as if it was something that should be said in a church. I don't know where this thought came from, but I do know this is something I've never said out loud. I grew up pretending—for the camera and even for my mom. I've never stopped.

"What does that mean?"

I turn onto my side to face him, propping my head up on a hand. "I grew up in a costume and reading from a script. That's not a metaphor, as you know. And every once in a while I sort of saw something underneath all of that, and I thought that might be who I was." I scrunch up my face. I don't know why I'm telling him this.

"And you liked it?"

"I did, I think." For a second, I thought I was beautiful and important. "But then a bunch of stuff happened and I decided maybe chasing that girl down wasn't worth it. It seemed easier to just come up with a better costume and show up as the kind of person the world liked."

He doesn't even blink. "I hope we read the same script, Jane. It's all about being brave enough to be your full broken self. You need *True Story* more than anyone." He turns back to the sun. I feel the truth of those words in my heart, though I don't have an adequate reply.

We listen to the waves for a while, and I try to get comfortable with the silence. I just overshared and there's something seeping out of me now that I've said that thing to Dan. I know it's the script that has these old feelings brushing up against the surface. I look at him with his eyes closed and the hint of a smile still on his lips, and I'm glad I'm not currently working on *Star Crossed*. I'm glad there's a chance that *True Story* might be my first movie. The quiet complexity of it is like Dan himself, authentic and weirdly under my skin.

"Aidan, can you come help us?" There's a twelve-year-old boy casting a shadow over Dan.

"I'm his brother Danny," Dan says.

"Wow, weird," the kid says. "I'm Tucker. My parents know him."

"What do you want help with?" I ask.

"We're digging a pit for a big tug-of-war, losers get wet. But my friends aren't here yet and I just have a bunch of little kids helping and it's taking forever." He holds up his shovel.

"Sure," Dan says and gets up. From where I'm still lying, I am now looking up the length of his legs; they're legs you'd see at the Olympics or on a drawing of the human muscular system at the doctor's office. I need to stop looking at his legs, so I get up too.

I follow Dan and Tucker over to the hole in progress. Dan jumps in and holds out a hand for me. I was going to jump in too, but I take his hand anyway. And there's that feeling again; I am definitely a monkey starved for touch. The hole is filled with eight-year-old kids and too-big shovels, and I love the squishy feel of the wet sand under my feet. I pick up a shovel and start digging. This hole feels like another world with no wind and a distant threat of waves crashing. Each time I toss a shovel full of heavy, wet sand out of the hole, I see the waves coming closer. The first one to hit trickles cool water up to our shins, and everyone screams. It's exciting, digging deeper and deeper and knowing what's coming.

"We're going to get soaked," Dan says, looking at my legs.

"We'll be fine, get back to work," I say just as the big wave comes and crashes over our heads. The hole is deep enough now that the water settles at Dan's shoulders. The surprise of the ice-cold water has me disoriented, but not as much as the feel of his arm around my waist.

"Okay?" he asks. He wipes water from his eyes with his free hand, and his hair is briefly neat, slicked back against his head. The rectangular shape of his eyes seems exaggerated, and I have the thought that I would cast him as a vampire. The kind that wouldn't kill you but might break the bed.

"I'm soaked," I say, still close. He picks a strand of seaweed out of my hair and lets go of me.

The kids scramble out of the hole, and Tucker says, "You two against us." Which is how it came to be that I am soaking wet on one side of a giant hole with the Atlantic Ocean to my left, pressed in close to Dan Finnegan behind me, pulling at a thick rope with all my might against a bunch of little kids. The newness of this fills every part of me—as the screams and laughter fill my ears, I realize I did not play like this as a kid. And as the back of my thighs rub up against the front of Dan's, I realize the lemony hand on my tingly lips was just a warm-up. Dan's head is right over my shoulder, and his arms are around mine as we pull. I can feel the strain in my shoulders, but not as intensely as I feel the brush of his stubble on my cheek. "Ready?" he says.

"Yes," I say because that's the only word my body knows right now.

He gives a giant tug, and we fall backward into the sand. All the little kids land in the hole. We're side by side on our backs, recently wet and now covered in sand.

"We won," he says, breathless.

"Feels good," I say. We look at the sky for a bit, catching

our breath, the hot sand warming our backs. "I don't know how I'll ever get all this sand off."

Dan gets up and leads me into the ocean. "This is the only way," he says.

He dives under a wave and then peels off his T-shirt. He does it in a functional way and dunks it again and again in the ocean to get the sand off. But I see it in slow motion, like he's a vampire who's also a firefighter, and he's just left the burning building.

He mistakes my stunned expression for confusion about the de-sanding process. "Come on," he says. "It's like laundry."

I pull off my T-shirt and shorts and dunk them in the water. I empty my pockets of sand. I honestly cannot believe I'm wearing this bathing suit.

Dan dives under another wave, shakes out his hair, and comes toward me with that muscled chest and ridiculous stomach. My hands want to poke him to see if he's real. "I'll lay this all out to dry," he says and takes my clothes. "Are you staying in?"

I need to gather my thoughts and monkey hormones, so I say, "For a minute."

I dive under a wave. I imagine there's a sound that goes along with it, a whoosh as I'm washed clean by the salt water. I dive under the next wave and the next, feeling the water cool my shoulders. I look out at the horizon, and I realize I have my back to Hollywood. If I had a giant's legs, I could take big steps over to England and start new there.

Maybe I'd sing in a pub and pour pints during the day, greeting the regulars and not caring what my future looked like. *If I can't get this movie made, pints are always going to need to be poured*—I think this in Cormack's voice.

The air is starting to feel cold, so I head back to our towels. Dan has placed two of Tucker's big shovels upright in the sand to hold our drying clothes. He's leaning back on his elbows and he's watching me. I train my eyes on the sand and try not to envision what I look like in this bathing suit.

"I wasn't checking you out," he says when I'm lying face down on my towel.

"Oh yeah? Was there a very important hawk behind me?"

He laughs. "Are you funny? I'm starting to think you are."

"Try not to be," I say. My head is resting on my hands and I'm turned away from him.

"You don't try that hard," he says.

I turn my head toward him, and he's rolled onto his stomach, chin on folded hands, a clump of hair resting like a single parenthesis over his forehead. We are very close, and I can see each of his black eyelashes, a dusting of white sand on the ridge of his left cheekbone. I want to wipe it away with my thumb. I have the sense that we are in a small space now, that the sound of the waves and the kids has been muted. He's looking at me like I'm something he's unsure of. His eyes run along my hairline, my jaw. They land on my eyes. My body feels hot and loose like lava. Anyone lying this close to shirtless Dan would feel this way, but it's neither convenient nor appropriate for me at this particular time. One thing that's abundantly clear as I scan the slope of his shoulder and the way it flows into the ridges of his back: Dan needs to put his shirt back on.

"Men don't really like funny women, like to date," I say.

"Not true."

"It's absolutely true. Name a comedian you want to sleep with."

"I'd have to think about it."

I have successfully broken the tension. You're welcome.

"Don't bother," I say. "It's a thing. If you want to be the leading lady, you need to be capable, thoughtful, a little vulnerable. The funny one is the sidekick. She goes stag to the dance."

"You've given this a lot of thought."

"Well, I'm Janey Jakes. So I'm kind of an expert." I turn onto my back and let the sun warm my face.

"Janey Jakes," he says after a while. "You were funny. I watched a few episodes on YouTube last night."

"No, you didn't. Please don't do that." My stomach drops at the thought of him watching that version of me. Of course I'd grow up to wear this bathing suit.

"It's not every day you meet a girl and then get to stalk her all the way back to twelve."

I turn my head toward him. "How do I erase the internet?"

He moves so that we are a bit closer. "Make the face, like *oof*," he says, so I do and he laughs. The light hits his eyes and the blue deepens. "Do you really play the keyboards? I zoomed in and it looked like you did."

"I do."

"Sing?"

"Yes."

I have his absolute full attention. His eyes hold me in place. "And what about Will Powers? Were he and Hailey really a couple? I mean, it felt like they were."

"You know the show ended seventeen years ago, right?" I say. "I mean, this is gossip about kids from a lifetime ago."

"You are so mean if you don't tell me. Connor was Aidan's and my excuse to watch it. We loved it. Connor was sworn to secrecy because we were in high school and that was clearly embarrassing." The sky lowers again and the sound of the waves goes fuzzy. I don't know why this feels intimate, lying here talking about an old TV show, but his eyes have me trapped.

"You're not that pretentious," I say, and I don't blink.

"But I love my gramophone."

I smile at his mouth, turned up just at the corner. I smooth the white sand between us. "You're just kind of honest." It must be Dan's honesty that's making me put so much of myself out there. He's like a human invitation. I don't know why I've said this, so I look away and answer his question. "Hailey and Will were never really a couple, but Will and Dougie were both madly in love with her. I was the sidekick." He's watching my hand as it runs over the sand, and I watch him watch.

"And you never had a boyfriend of your own?"

The truth is no, of course I didn't have a boyfriend. Except for the twenty-four hours I convinced myself Jack

Quinlan was my soulmate. "With a mouthful of braces and nachos all over my pants? No."

"Well, you're all grown up now, Janey Jakes, and you're killing it."

"How so?"

"Connor thinks you're hot, and you came this close to going on a date with me." I kick a little sand onto his towel as he smiles, rolls onto his back, and closes his eyes.

CHAPTER 14

~~~~~

THE OWL BARN IS NOT IRONICALLY NAMED, AS I'D EX-
pected. I was picturing a big music venue that had been
decorated in a modern farmhouse style to give it some folksy
charm. In reality, it's basically a barn where you might find
an owl creeping in the corner, cleaned up and wired for
sound. I love the feel of it. It's open and authentic without
an ounce of Hollywood glitz. No one would ever consider
lip-syncing here. Any crack in your voice would mirror the
uneven slats that are holding this place up so perfectly.

It's also surprisingly cool, which is a relief after riding a
bike around in the hot August sun all day. My hair has
dried in hard curls after two swims in the ocean and a trip
back to town for Dan's favorite sandwich. We got two because he didn't want to share—turkey, Swiss, coleslaw, and
Thousand Island dressing on rye bread. I am now ruined
for all other sandwiches and have a big pink glob of dressing
on my shorts.

I eyed that pink glob on the ride here, chastising myself

for getting so swept up in the glory of that sandwich that I lost track of the main goal, which is to not look like a hot mess when I run into Jack. I stand here now, sunburned shoulders coated in a little sweat, and let the relief of the air-conditioning roll over me. Jack's big enough in every way that I would know if he were here. The air would be electrified.

"Like it?" Dan asks as I look around.

"Love it," I say. My eyes rest on the stage, which is just a raised platform with a few spotlights overhead. "How many people does it hold?"

"Four hundred."

"It's perfect." They're going to lose their minds when Jack shows up.

Finn walks onto the stage and sees us. He says into the microphone, "Can you hear this?"

Dan gives a thumbs-up.

"How does this sound?" He starts to sing "Twinkle, Twinkle."

Dan gives a thumbs-down as we approach the stage.

A man in all black walks out behind Finn. "Awful, but it might just be you."

Finn shrugs. "This is Leonard. My brother Dan and his friend Jane."

"I think it sounds fine," Dan says. "And it'll sound better with a room full of people."

Leonard shakes our hands. "I hope so. Last year we had a bunch of divas complaining while I was adjusting amps and things. Let me go to the back of the room and listen." He shakes his head at Finn. "Try not to suck so bad."

Dan asks, "Any Jack Quinlan sightings today?"

Leonard shakes his head. "Someone saw him at the berry stand on Main Street. He hasn't shown up here."

Dan turns to me. "It's just the first day."

"Too soon to panic," I say, though it's never too soon to panic.

Finn turns to me. "Can you sing, Janey Jakes? Were you on backup, or was it just the keyboard?"

"No," I say. It comes out so fast and hard that it's clearly a lie.

"You literally just told me you could sing," says Dan. "You've got to be better than him."

Finn walks over to a small keyboard and bangs on a few keys. "Come on, Janey, give us a little 'Jump-Start Love Song,' you know you know it."

I don't dislike singing. In fact, sometimes it feels like magic. A breath in and then a breath out brings music. It's amazing to be able to access something like that, a lifetime of songs that are stashed away somewhere waiting to come out after your next inhale. But it's not a thing I do in front of people anymore. Not even my mom. It was a joyful thing that turned sour and false. What's inside of me can stay right where it is.

"No," I say again, but I'm lighter about it. "But I'll play it, and you two jokers can sing."

Dan says "No" at the same second Finn says "Danny doesn't," and they sort of laugh.

Dan explains, "I'm not that kind of Finnegan."

"Well, Friday night you will be," Finn says. "We're giving a group toast. I picked the song."

"No," says Dan. It might just be the hardest no I've ever heard.

"It's their fortieth anniversary. Get over yourself. It's five minutes."

"Finn, come on." Dan says it like it's definitely not the first time. It seems impossible now that I've met this family that Dan wasn't sure if he was coming here this week. Until I needed help, he hadn't told them one way or another. This reads rude, where Dan does not.

"You can lip-sync, Danny. And Aidan wrote you the shortest part of the toast. It's so easy." Finn turns and walks back onstage and announces into the microphone, "Janey Jakes on the keyboards." I follow him up the steps to the stage and play the first few notes. They come from my subconscious. It's been almost two decades, but I've played this song so many times that it's just muscle memory, like braiding a piece of your own hair. My body also remembers how to withdraw into the background, how to subvert my own confidence. I am so, so small playing this song that I made a hit.

I leave my body and focus on Finn as he sings. He throws himself into the song, terribly singing both Hailey and Will's parts, only getting half the words. Dan stands back and watches, as if this is a show he's been watching his entire life.

Leonard's waving his hands from the back, and Finn stops. "It's fine, the sound works. I heard every awful note."

Finn grabs the mic. "Are you sure you don't want one more?"

"Yes!" Leonard shouts.

Dan is leaning against the bar, arms folded across his chest, and clearly happy to be out of the fray. Finn waves him over, and the two of them lift some equipment onto the stage. Whatever disagreement they had about the toast is forgotten. It's such a basic thing, siblings. I look at Dan with his quiet but twelve-dimensional perspective on everything and Finn with his big energy. I wonder what it would be like to live with so many distinct versions of yourself. And I wonder if things would have been different if I'd had a sister or two and we could take turns worrying about my mom. Maybe we'd fight and make up; maybe I'd know how to fight and make up. I'd have a favorite who I would text right now so that I could tell her that Dan is softer at home. I'd tell her that when he's not saying something annoying, I want to touch the back of his arm and I have no idea why.

I text Clem: It's so humid here, I can't think straight

Clem: What does that actually mean?

Me: Okay, he's hot. And not the worst

CHAPTER 15

THE KITCHEN IS SURPRISINGLY QUIET WHEN WE GET back to the house. Reenie and Cormack are sitting outside, and I race to the shower. I showered after my run, but then biked and sweated and rinsed with salt water and rolled in sand and rinsed and sweated again. I am sodden and dried and sodden again on repeat, and there is sand in the creases of my ears. When I am out of the shower, I am cleaner than I have ever been before. I look at my reflection, naked, and I have the sense that a layer has been removed. I've had a spa day by accident.

I dress in luxuriously clean jeans and a white top that makes the tiny new freckles on my cheeks pop, and I return to the bedroom, where Dan is dangerously shirtless again. I grip the doorknob and look for a spot over his shoulder to rest my gaze. He grabs clothes from his bag and I just stand there.

"I'm going to shower too," he says.

"Yes." It's a word I cannot stop saying.

"So tonight, I sort of forgot, my brothers are all going out for dinner. It's a thing we do when I come home, and Aidan planned it for tonight." He's cradling a pair of khaki shorts and a faded blue button-down in his arms, and the cotton of the shirt is resting against his chest.

"Could you put your shirt on?" I ask.

"I'm about to take a shower."

"I know, but I just . . ." I look down at his feet, also bare. "You're so naked, I'm not following what you're saying. You're going somewhere?"

He smiles and pulls his shirt on, buttoning just one button. "Better?" The blue of the shirt and the smile both do something to his eyes. No, not really better.

"Thank you."

He's still smiling. "So we do this brothers' dinner."

"Oh, got it. Yes. That's totally fine. I was thinking about biking back to town, maybe grabbing something at the diner. Maybe I'll catch Jack getting ice cream." Not being with Dan tonight is probably for the best. I need to get back on task, and that's going to be a lot easier when I'm not standing here watching him bite his bottom lip the way he is right now.

He takes a step toward me, and now we're both in the doorway. "Will you come? The wives don't come, so it would just be you. But the food is good, and I could use a little backup."

"You want me as backup?"

"Yeah, I couldn't have taken those kids today without you." He smiles again. "Aren't we trying to be a team?"

"Yes," I say again.

NELLIE'S CRAB SHACK is on the beach just outside of Oak Shore. From the road it looks like it could be a small bait shop, a door with two windows on either side and a shingled roof. But the back opens up to tables on the sand under thatched umbrellas. I kick off my sandals before I even realize I've done it.

We sit at a round table that would have been fine for six smaller people, or even the five of them without me. As it is, we are wedged in tight. They insist on giving me the seat with the best ocean view. I take it and wiggle my toes in the still warm sand. Dan sits next to me and kicks off his flip-flops too. He has rolled up his sleeves since we left the house, and his forearms rest on the table, dwarfing mine. The waitress greets us with "Danny's home!" and brings two pitchers of beer we didn't order.

"Against all odds," Connor says and shoots Dan a look.

She starts to hand us wooden menus, and Brian raises a hand to stop her. "Do we need menus?" he asks us. "Soft-shell crab and fries? Chopped salad and cornbread?"

Everyone agrees on the order, and Aidan pours us each a beer. "Before you all get drunk and disorderly, can we talk about the party?"

Dan leans back in his seat and takes a long sip of his beer.

Aidan says, "Paula wants us all there by five to help set up. People are coming at six. And it's like a hundred people—I don't think anyone said no."

Brian says, "Marla picked all the food, I think. Connor did the toast and Finn picked a song."

Dan lets out a breath and shakes his head.

"You have to," Brian says.

"I know," Dan says. And then, to me, "I don't actually love acting like a jackass in the same way my brothers do."

"He gets stage fright," Finn says and makes a sarcastic sad face. *Boo-hoo.* Connor laughs, though I'm not sure at what.

Dan rolls his eyes. "It's not stage fright. It's idiot fright. I know I'm going to hate whatever stupid thing you have planned."

Aidan places his hand on the back of Dan's chair. "He'll be fine. And Janey will make sure he shows up."

"Of course I'm going to show up," Dan says.

"Seemed a little touch-and-go that you were even coming to town," Connor says with an edge. "We weren't exactly counting on you."

"Can we not do this?" Dan says. His hands are clutching the table like he's about to push himself away and leave. I feel like I'm witnessing something I shouldn't.

"Well, it was nice of you to give us a little time during your hunt for a pop star," Connor says. There's a smirk on his face that I'd like to punch.

"You're welcome," Dan says without missing a beat.

"I mean, it's their fortieth anniversary. We've been planning this thing since Christmas . . ." Connor trails off. For a second, I see his baby-of-the-family energy.

Brian says to me, "He's MIA for a lot of stuff." I don't know how to respond. Dan is under attack and seems completely used to it. I want to defend him, or at least let him know I'm on his side. It's not that easy to show up for dinner on Long Island when you live in Los Angeles.

"I'm not MIA," Dan says evenly. He leans back in his chair. "I don't know if you guys know, but they recently opened the borders around Long Island. You could stick a toe over the line and see how it feels, if you wanted."

Aidan laughs. "Not a chance, we'd never survive." He lifts up his beer and says, "To crossing county lines."

Everyone drinks to that, and the tension softens, but I don't like this. I don't like the four-against-one. I don't like the way Dan seems like he's on defense against the people he loves most.

"I'll run lines with him," I say. "I'm a pro."

"And then you've got to get him on the stage," Aidan says. "That was going to be my job, but you're prettier than I am."

"I think you're exceptionally pretty," Dan says to Aidan. His brothers laugh and I am confused. It's a joke because they're identical, but I didn't expect something light to come out of Dan's mouth. I think I expected him to sulk or storm out of the restaurant. I'm realizing what it is about this family that has me so rapt—it's the way they say what they mean and just move on.

Brian says, "Okay, Jane's in charge of Danny. I guess

that's all we need to deal with. Connor's texting everyone his corny-ass toast." He raises his beer. "Cheers to Mom and Dad." We all clink glasses again, and I feel a pressure in my heart. An old longing to be a person who could say *Mom and Dad* like it was nothing, but also the feeling that I'm part of this night, the sixth glass clinking. Reenie and Cormack feel like people I'd like to toast again and again.

When a mountain of food is placed on the table, Aidan asks, "Any Quinlan sightings today? Like, are you staking out his house?"

"If we knew where he was staying, I probably would have. We actually just rode bikes to the beach," I say.

"And we kicked ass in a tug-of-war," Dan says.

"They made a brief appearance at the Owl Barn," Finn says. "And Janey and I made music history."

"Yep, that was our workday," I say. I smile at Dan over my beer. It was a good day. I can't remember the last time I spent an entire day playing. I wore the world's dumpiest bathing suit and got covered in sand; I ate a sandwich the size of my head and biked and made music. I'm no closer to not getting fired, and yet it was an oddly good day.

Connor grabs a crab and shakes his head. "I don't know how you guys do it. I hope this movie thing works out, really I do. But the stress of not knowing if you're getting a paycheck, I can't imagine it."

Aidan says, "And Danny, can you imagine spending the day flossing crap out of other people's teeth?"

"I cannot," Dan says.

It occurs to me then why Dan loves *True Story*. It's the

kind of love he grew up with, where the real and maybe not-so-nice thing is said, and then you come back together. The love creeps in in small ways, a hand placed on the back of your brother's chair.

"I wouldn't worry about Dan," I say. "He took me through his retirement plan, it's ironclad."

Dan laughs and gives me a sideways smile. I guess it's okay to use his joke now.

The sun gets lower, and they tell so many stories. The time Aidan snuck a girl into their room and made Dan and Connor sleep in the garage. The time Finn got arrested for trying to buy beer using his dad's expired driver's license. The mildly erotic love letter Dan wrote to his kindergarten teacher. Brian's first mullet. Laughter rises up from the table, and just as it's about to settle down, someone starts another story. I have laughed so hard that my body idles with anticipatory laughter for whatever's coming next. I tell them about pranks we played on each other on set, harmless, uncreative pranks that invariably went all wrong.

Through all of it, I clock the nearness of Dan. When I laugh, he leans in, not away. When he leans back in his chair, he places a hand on the back of mine. I try on the feeling, just for a second, of what it would be like to belong to him.

I AM STUFFED with softshell crabs and ice-cold beer when I wander inside to find the bathroom. There's a line, so I check my phone and see that I have just missed a call from

Clem. I would rather wet my pants than miss this chance to talk to her between shifts, so I walk out onto the street.

"Hot?" she asks before I've even said hello. "Dan, who you hate, is hot at home?"

"I have a feeling he's hot everywhere," I whisper into the phone. "But maybe I just notice it more when he's not also dashing my dreams."

"What's the family like? Are you in a big mansion on the water? Like in *Revenge*?"

"Small house on a potato field," I whisper. "I love it. And we're sharing a room and he takes his shirt off and it's just like nothing I've seen before. I want to lick him? Is that a thing people do?"

Clem is laughing so hard that I need to pull the phone away from my ear. "People, yes. You, no."

"That's what I thought. Maybe deep down I'm people."

"Yeah, Jane, I think you are." We're quiet for a beat.

"His parents are married," I say. "Forty years, and they all fight, but it's fine. I honestly feel like I've stepped into an alternate reality."

"You have my permission to lick him all you want," she says.

~~~

CHAPTER 16

D O YOU NEED TO GO BE ALONE AND DO SOME ED-
ward Scissorhands stuff?" I ask when we're lying in
our twin beds. The lights are off, but there's a little bit of
moonlight coming from the window between us. We're both
lying on our backs, covers pulled to our shoulders.

"No, this is fine."

"I'm not used to sleeping with another person in the
room," I say after a while.

"Am I breathing too loud?" he asks.

"Definitely."

"I'll try to hold my breath," he says.

"Ha," I say. It's the world's dumbest syllable.

He's quiet for a while and then, "We missed *Dateline*.
It's on at eight and ten, but it's eleven thirty."

I turn toward him. "I love *Dateline*."

He laughs. "So that's going to be what we agree on.
Dateline and *True Story*."

"I find it totally relaxing."

"Same," he says. "Why is that?"

"It's because the bad thing has already happened, sometimes like ten years ago. So you can just relax and watch the pursuit of justice." *Dateline* is basically the opposite of dating, where I walk through it waiting for the blowup.

"True," he says. "And I like how they try to trick us into thinking the murderer didn't do it by dressing him in a nice polo shirt for his interview."

"Well, the orange jumpsuit is a dead giveaway."

He turns on his side and the moonlight illuminates his cheekbone. Part of me feels like I've been caught staring, but I don't blink. We're lying here little more than a foot apart, but the darkness provides some protection, as if we are half hidden in it.

"Tell me about the frame," I say.

"What frame?"

"The arbor out back."

He turns onto his back, so I do too. "It's just something I've been doing since I was a kid. I made Aidan help me move our old swing set one night. And then I bought potted ivy and figured out how to train it. Sort of a hobby."

"I like it," I say.

"I do too. I always wanted to paint something important there, or take exactly the right photo with that ivy edge. My dad thinks I'm a little . . ."

I laugh. "Yes, he told me. Does that bother you?"

"It used to, but I'm fine with it now. He loves me.

There's a difference between someone loving you and agreeing with every single thing you do."

This is an unexpectedly deep thought, though nothing about Dan is what I expected. We're quiet for a bit, and I stare at the shadow that the ceiling light casts in the moonlight. "I like your family."

"They're a trip."

"A happy trip."

"But you see that I'm different, right?" He turns his head toward me and I meet his gaze.

"Oh, you're different all right." I mean it as a barb.

"I am."

He doesn't say anything more, so I go on. "I was kidding, but I can tell that you're different, quiet where they're loud. Intense where they're loose."

"Yeah. My dad, poor guy, is still trying to get his head around it. Me being in my head a lot. When I was a kid, he thought I was just really distracted, because I wouldn't focus in school or soak up the thing he was showing me how to fix. I mean, my interest in fixing a toilet is nothing. Use it, flush it. I'm out."

"Same."

He smiles, just a little. "The thing my dad still doesn't totally get is that I'm not at all distracted, that when I find something that I think is interesting or true or beautiful, I'm hyper-focused."

"I can see that." To prove me right, he locks his eyes on mine, and I have this flash of what it might feel like to be interesting or true or beautiful to Dan. I'm grateful for the dark, where words can bounce around without consequence.

"Aidan helped me with the arbor, but he also marketed it to my dad as construction rather than art, which is why we got to keep it." I can only see his eyes now, the way the light's coming in. They move around my face, like they're looking for something. Dan says, "I have the feeling being Janey Jakes wasn't your favorite thing."

"It was and then it wasn't."

"Today, when you were playing the keyboards, I was watching you. It was like playing that song kind of hurt. I was waiting for you to smile, but you never did. Not once." He's looking right at me, his eyes in shadow.

"It's just a dumb love song. I don't really believe in romantic love like that."

His eyes go soft. "So do you not date? You were going to go out with me," he says, and the corner of his mouth, which I happen to be staring at, curves up the tiniest bit. I smile back at his mouth because I don't want to look in his eyes.

"I was, before I found out you're the worst."

He smiles like he loves being the worst. "So you date but don't believe in love?"

"I'd like to have a partner, I'm not a robot. But I'm just not all starry-eyed about it. I'd like to meet a solid guy, like a guy with dental insurance who shows up when he says he will and picks up milk when you need it. A guy who will stick around."

He laughs. "That's so hot."

"Right?" I don't know why it feels okay telling him this.

I should be embarrassed. "So I go on dates, I wear the right thing. I blow my hair straight and try to act datable."

Dan laughs, and it fills the room. He turns all the way on his side, his arm outside the covers and his bicep catching the light. "What does 'datable' mean? Of course you're datable."

"Well, when I focus on it, I am. It's a whole thing. My dating protocol. I act the right amount interested and the right amount bored. I mentally track his word count so I'm not blabbering on more than he is." Dan's smile fades a bit, like he's more concerned than amused. "You have to remember I was an actress. So when I'm dating, I use that. I act like a woman you'd want to date."

Dan shakes his head.

"No, I don't mean *you*. I mean anyone. A woman anyone would want to date."

We're quiet for a second. I've totally overshared and I don't know how to claw it back.

"And how do those dates play out?" he asks.

"Fine, mostly. I usually nail the first three dates, but it fizzles by the fourth. I don't really know why."

"Maybe you need to work your old-school bathing suit into the mix."

"Great idea."

"I'm kidding, it's terrible. But you should leave your hair curly. It's soft around your face. I like it."

"Oh," I say and press my lips together.

There's something happening here, and it's unfamiliar and frightening. It's a thing I'm opening up to because of this script and the humidity and all the reckless laughing I've done tonight. I need to change the subject.

"I came up with a backup plan," I say. "About the movie."

"Don't know why we'd need one of those. This whole plan to ambush a pop star so he'll write you a song seems foolproof."

I smile and look back to the ceiling. I need to not be staring at his mouth if we're talking business. "If he won't write us a song—I know it's a big ask—maybe he'll just license us one of his early songs. Like 'Fresh Eyes.'"

"I don't know that one."

"No one does probably, it was on the album before his breakout. It goes with the vibe of the story, the small-town feel of it and the innocence every time they try again." I hum the beginning. "Know it?"

"Not from that."

"Come on, it goes, *Look my way so I can see you, fresh eyes on us.*"

"Nope."

I hum the beginning again, and he still doesn't know it. So I start singing, just quietly. It feels perfectly natural because we're in the dark, sort of out of space and time. I sing half of the first verse before I remember to be embarrassed about it.

I turn to the outline of him lying on his side in the dark. "What?" I say. "Do you know it? It's a good song."

"I'm confused," he says.

"About what?"

"You sound just like Hailey Soul."

"No."

"You do. You've got me all worked up over here."

I cannot overstate how much I like the fact that he's all worked up. Even if it's over his teenage crush on someone else. I want to claim that crush for myself, reach right into his head and make it me he was thinking about all those years ago. So I do.

"Yeah. That was actually me. I recorded the songs and Hailey lip-synced." Once I've said it, the secret is out. You cannot unring a bell, as they say.

"What?" He swings his legs off the bed and sits up, expertly avoiding hitting his head on the top bunk. "And she got famous, and you got to sit in the background? This is outrageous."

"This is my life."

"Why don't people know this?"

"It was a secret. I signed an NDA. No one would care now, but keep it to yourself. At the time it was a big deal. The studio was worried we'd have a whole scandal on our hands." This is the time for me to tell him about Jack. And I almost do. It's a natural segue: *Jack sang Will's part, actually.* But I like the way I'm feeling right now. I like the way Dan listens and responds like I'm the main character in this story. I don't want to let him see whatever my face would do if I told the Jack story. I don't want him to see all my embarrassing parts.

"Why didn't they just put you up-front and let it be your song?"

"Because I was Janey Jakes." I think of the moment I

looked in the mirror and thought Jane Jackson might be different from Janey Jakes, a person worth looking at. I remember catching Angelica's eye and knowing I was right. That feeling flutters inside me as Dan holds my gaze. I want to grab onto it and make it true. "They'd gone to a lot of trouble to geek me up."

"This is insane." He runs his hands through his hair and shakes his head.

"Hailey couldn't really sing the song. She could sing, but she couldn't hit the high notes. But she was the one you guys were lusting after, so they wanted it to come from her."

"I feel totally duped."

"Well, it worked, two top forty hits."

"Two?"

"I sang 'Can't Find My You' too."

"Okay, this is madness! Were you paid extra at least?"

"Yes. And I got royalties from both songs until people stopped listening. I put myself through college and own a house in LA."

He leans forward with his forearms on his knees, and the space between us is impossibly small. There's a fizzy little energy between us that is not familiar to me. I've never felt this sort of thing before, and I want to keep him leaning in close like this so I can swim around in it for a while. He starts to lean away and I want to bring him back, so I tell him.

"Jack Quinlan sang Will's part."

"Oh my God. What?" Dan grips his knees. "This is just unreal." He stands up and walks over to the TV, completely foiling my plan to keep him close. "You and Jack Quinlan had a hit song, and no one knows?"

"Well, everyone on the show knew, and now you. Clem knows. You really can't tell anyone." I'm sitting up in bed now, and he comes and sits by my feet.

"So you must know him well?"

"I knew him for twenty-four hours and that was it." Dan's just sitting there, not nearly close enough, looking at me.

Dan shakes his head. "You pretend not to be funny and you pretend not to be a recording star. What else are you hiding?"

"I'm currently trying to hide how bad I am at tracking down celebrities." *And how much I wish you'd climb into this bed with me so I can smell you up close,* I don't say.

"I can't believe that was Jack. And I can't believe that was you." He gets up again and lies down on top of his covers with his hands behind his head. I lie back down and turn onto my side so I can run my eyes down the length of his body from the safety of darkness. He turns his head toward me. "Maybe it was you I was lusting after all that time."

"I doubt that very much," I say and roll onto my back so he can't see me smile.

We're quiet for a while. And I think he's gone to sleep. I am smiling at the ceiling in the dark, thinking of Dan, crammed in this room with his two brothers, dreaming of me.

CHAPTER 17

I ONLY BUY ONE MUFFIN ON MY RUN WEDNESDAY morning. I want to make Cormack's day, but I also don't want to start any trouble. Reenie makes waffles, and Brian and Finn and his kids show up like a dog whistle's been blown. We eat in the kitchen with the doors open to the backyard. Aidan, Paula, and Katie pull up a love seat and share it, sort of leaning into one another out of habit. It is so intimate the way they're sharing that seat, I have to stop myself from staring. Ruby comes and sits by me. We pass around a blue bowl full of strawberries and a glass bowl full of whipped cream. Words fly across the table—plans for the day's work, plans for the party. Under the noise, Dan and I sit side by side. He puts a spoonful of whipped cream into my coffee and watches me taste it. He smiles at my reaction and hands me his napkin to wipe the whipped cream from my mouth.

"What are you two doing today?" Reenie asks.

"Stalking a pop star," Dan says.

"It's not stalking if we never actually know where he is," I say and put a little more whipped cream in my coffee.

"And the plan is you're going to introduce yourself and ask him to write a song for your movie?" Cormack asks.

"Well, yes," I say.

"Is it that good of a movie?" he asks.

"It's a great movie, I think."

Cormack asks me, "Are you okay?"

"Yes, of course. Why?" I ask.

"You're gripping your chest like Reenie's finally done you in with all the bacon."

Everyone laughs, and I look down. My hand is actually on my heart.

Dan smiles. "It's a very heartfelt script," he says. "It's *The Notebook* meets *The Blair Witch Project*."

I shake my head. "It's not the stupid *Notebook*. And no one gets murdered in the woods."

"So what happens?" Reenie asks. "To bring them together at the end."

"He comes back for her," I say.

"He realizes she's the one who sees him as he really is," says Dan.

Cormack pushes away from the table. "Danny, are you having a heart attack now? Jesus Christ, Reenie."

Dan removes his hand from his heart and puts it in his lap. "It's a beautiful story," he says.

"It is," I say.

"Well, finally," says Aidan. "If that last script you almost worked on had been any good, you two would actually be dating." Paula elbows him, almost imperceptibly.

"Probably," says Dan without looking my way.

Brian asks, "Have you even gotten her on the water yet?" Then, to me, "I swear there's more to Long Island than Mom's kitchen."

Dan just shakes his head. "Did you guys get the boat in the water this year?"

Brian says, "If by 'you guys' you mean me, yeah, I cleaned it and moved it down to the beach before Memorial Day. Jane, want to go out today?"

"You mean with Danny," Cormack says, and it's definitely not a question.

"Well, yeah, if he wants to," says Brian. The look in his eyes is playful. The look in Dan's is not. "I mean, I think he's on record saying you're not his girlfriend, Jane."

"Don't," says Dan.

Reenie pats my hand. "They do this. It's nothing. And Brian knows how to be a perfect gentleman."

"Well, I'm coming anyway," Dan says.

The ensuing awkward silence prompts me to say, "Fun."

"It's going to be perfect weather for it," Reenie says. "Did you bring a swimsuit?"

"I bought Eleanor Roosevelt's childhood swimsuit in town, I'm all set," I say, and Dan laughs. I have to stop that.

DAN AND BRIAN don't talk as we drive to the beach. At least not to each other. They're both talking to me. They point things out, a park that has something to do with a tennis player, the tony area where they think Jack rented a house.

My mom texts me a selfie of her head collapsed on her work keyboard. I text back a video of the ocean as we drive. She replies: You win!

Me: How was Santa Barbara?

Mom: Dreamy

I send her a thumbs-up and close my eyes for a moment. This is going to end badly.

I follow Brian and Dan through the dunes to where the boats dot the beach. We are in a little cove that feels protected. The waves are smaller here. Brian and Dan leave their towels and phones in a mound on the beach and start pulling a catamaran into the water. Dan shows no strain on his face as he lifts his side, but the muscles in his arms flex with the effort. I am mesmerized watching this and also frozen with indecision about what to do next. I am in shorts and a tank top over my bathing suit, and if I wade in wearing my clothes, I will ride home entirely wet. If I take them off, I will be in nothing but this ridiculous bathing suit.

Dan decides for me. "Leave your clothes," he calls over his shoulder. I wait until he's turned back to the water and undress. I follow them into the small waves, polka dots and all. Brian is a more elegant version of the Finnegan boys. Where the rest of them are built thick with muscles, he's leaner. He's the sort of guy who would mount a horse in a single motion. He has the same movie-star looks, but instead of an action hero, he'd be an aristocrat working with Scotland Yard. They work silently, Dan pulling up the rudders and Brian hooking up the main sail. They each take hold of a hull from the front and pull the boat the rest of the way into the water. Once it's deep enough, Brian pulls himself onto the boat and lowers the rudders.

Brian takes off his shirt and tosses it beside him. The physicality of these brothers is staggering. Long, tan torsos covered in rippling muscles like they're descendants of the last of the great Irish supermodels, bred to pose in underwear on billboards. I flash back to Dan yesterday in the ocean and am glad he's keeping his shirt on.

"Want me to lift you up?" Brian asks me with a devilish smile.

"She's fine," Dan says quickly. He turns to me, hip-deep in the water, and his T-shirt is wet. Just the bottom half, but it's clinging to his stomach and I can see the outline of his muscles there. "Do you need help?" he asks. Clearly, I do.

"I'm fine," I say and hoist myself up out of the water onto the boat. I sit across from Brian on the piece of canvas that is stretched tight between the two hulls. This feels dangerously low-tech. Dan hops on next to me and immediately takes off his wet shirt. I do not turn his way.

I am staring at the wet shirt by my feet when Brian asks if I want to sit by him and steer.

"She's fine," Dan says, clipped. Brian smiles at him, like this is a game.

We start moving slowly into the open ocean, and Dan hands me a life jacket. I take it from him while still watching Brian like he's a two-year-old and I'm in charge of his safety. I can't be held responsible for what my face might do if I turn to look at shirtless Dan. Brian catches me staring at him and smiles. I have the feeling he's misinterpreted something.

"You're slow, old man," Dan says.

"Put your life jacket on, the wind's picking up," Brian says.

I hand Dan the life jacket that's by his wet shirt without turning his way. I don't let myself look at him until he's covered up.

"Janey Jakes all grown up. On my boat," Brian says into the wind.

"It's all of our boat," Dan says.

"When's the last time you chipped in for anything to do with this thing?"

Dan doesn't answer.

Brian shakes his head. "We have a history of fighting over women. Probably started with our mother."

"I won that one," Dan says. Then, to me, "I'm the clear favorite."

Brian laughs. "Because you're never around to piss her off." I want to know a million more facts about their history of fighting over women, including whether there's any validity to the fantasy I'm currently having that they're fighting over me.

"That's sort of gross," I say. "Have you stolen each other's girlfriends?"

"Not technically," Brian says.

"Once there's a serious interest, everyone sort of backs off," says Dan. "No one ever even flirted with Paula—Aidan was whipped from the minute he met her."

"Ah," I say and bump my bare shoulder into his. I mean it to be jokey, except the feel of our sun-warmed skin touching isn't jokey at all. "Insta-love. Your favorite."

"Yeah, except she didn't fall for him for a full year, so."

"That was truly pathetic," Brian says. "But I don't know, Janey. Dan keeps claiming you're not dating. Sounds like you're fair game."

He's kidding and he's not kidding. There's so much ribbing that goes on in this family that I'm not sure where the threads of truth lie. He's either flirting with me or trying to annoy Dan. Or both.

"I'm neither fair, nor game," I say, and Dan laughs. He gives me a sideways smile that says a million things, and I can feel in my body how much I like making Dan laugh. It's incongruous, really. I like making him laugh while I also want to run my hands over his chest. And the science of male-female interaction dictates that the more I make him laugh, the less he'll want to be touched by me. If I keep making him laugh, we'll pal around and have a million inside jokes, and then I'll be his wingman when he wants to go talk to Jennifer who's sitting at the bar. Jennifer is soft and speaks with an upward lilt at the end of her sentences. Jennifer thinks Dan's funny, and she'll be the one who gets to touch his chest. This thought makes me inexplicably annoyed, like I want to punch Dan and maybe Jennifer too.

The wind picks up, and we sail parallel to Long Island.

There are long stretches of waterfront homes and then a patch of trees where there's been no development. Beyond the trees, the beach is rocky and a huge bluff looms overhead.

"That's Queens Park Bluff," Brian shouts over the wind.

"It's beautiful," I say.

"I'll take you later if you want," says Brian.

"Okay, stop it," says Dan.

"Oh?" Brian is challenging him and I can picture the two of them as kids, fists up.

"Yes, stop it," he says again. The wind dies down a bit and we slow. It's as if someone's turned the volume down on the TV. Dan turns to me and rests his forearms on his knees. His hair is wild, swirls of black around his head in every direction. He looks like an ad for soap. Rugged soap that removes a day's worth of sweat and leaves you smelling exactly like you. His eyes are asking me a question. I don't know what it is, but I want to say yes.

"Tack," Brian says and pulls in the sail. Dan breaks eye contact and grabs my arm, leading me to the other side of the boat. It's not elegant, crawling across the canvas in a bathing suit and a life jacket, but when we settle in on the other side and Brian is across from us, we are moving fast again. The din of the wake we're leaving behind fills my ears, the ice-cold spray of the ocean mists my face, but all I can feel is the warmth of Dan's hand just behind my hip.

CHAPTER 18

~~~~~

I CAN'T EVEN IMAGINE WHAT MY HAIR LOOKS LIKE. I haven't blown it straight since I've been here—there's really no point. The humidity, plus the wind on the open ocean, must have it completely out of control. I'm in the back seat of Brian's car putting it into a braid, and I catch sight of myself in the window. It's mostly just the outline of me, but I recognize this person. She's younger; she's still a believer in fairy tales and true love. For a reason I don't understand, I smile at her.

Dan's on the phone. "No, that's a nightmare," he's saying. "She'll hate it. Okay, fine, I'll hate it. No. Fine."

Brian drops us off in the Finnegans' driveway. "Call me if you get bored later, Jane." He gives me a teasing look through the open car window. He is equally as handsome as Dan—the chiseled features and full lips—but I'm not attracted to Brian like I am to Dan. The pull is specific to him, the way he moves in the world.

"Fuck off, Brian," Dan says without looking up from his phone. Brian laughs and drives away.

"What am I going to hate? Or am I not the she?" I ask.

He looks up at me and holds my gaze for a second. "You're the she." It's not a proper sentence. It's practically gibberish. But it hits me right in the center of my heart. He runs a hand through his hair, which is nearly as wild as mine. "I might need a hat," he says.

"I might need a salon," I say.

"You don't," he says.

I think this is a compliment, and I don't know where to put it, so I look past him at the house. "So what am I going to hate?"

"A lobster boil. Tonight at the beach. With my high school friends. Aidan says it's going to be low-key, and I usually trust him on stuff like this. But still, we're going back in time, it will be a whole thing."

"Sounds fun," I say. "To see how you spent your time."

"That wasn't how I spent my time, unless Aidan or a girl forced me." His phone buzzes. "Huh. Guess who's at Chippy's Diner. Let's go."

"Jack?" My voice does a weird thing and I clear my throat to cover it up.

"Yep, let's go." He starts walking to where the bikes are leaning against the garage, and I cannot for the life of me understand how this is all so easy for him. My feet are cemented in the ground. And my hair. I just can't do this with this hair.

Dan wheels the bikes back to me. "Come on."

"Like this?"

"Like what?"

I grab the bottom of my braid.

"You look good, Jane. And this script is good. It's all good. Let's go."

He gets on his bike, so I do the same. As we ride, my mind races to tomorrow. Tomorrow Dan and I will call Nathan and tell him how well it went with Jack, that he's currently reading the script and brainstorming ideas. Nathan will say how good I am at my job. Dan will tell his family at dinner how calmly I handled things. He'll say I was a pro.

I do not engage with my reflection as we walk through the doors at Chippy's. I'm doing guided self-talk in my head: *I'm a pro.* The hostess tells us we can sit wherever we want as I scan the booths along the window.

Dan says to her, "Aidan said Jack Quinlan was here?"

"He was!" she says. "Left me a forty-dollar tip, which I guess he should have. Chippy let him leave out the back."

"When?" I ask.

"Like five minutes ago. You two want a booth?"

Dan turns to me. "Come on." I follow him to the back door, and we are in an alley with a dumpster, a Chevy truck, and no sign of Jack Quinlan.

"This is annoying," Dan says to the dumpster. He turns to me and reads the thoughts that are crossing my face. I try to hide them, to arrange my features so that they say, *I'm a pro. No problem.*

He reaches for my arm. "Do you need water or something?"

"For what?"

"I don't know, you look really stressed."

And I guess I am. I'm disappointed and relieved all at once. I want to make this movie and keep my job as much as I don't want to ever see Jack Quinlan again. I hate mixed feelings, and I hate when they all release at once. I look up at Dan with tears in my eyes, and he pulls me into his arms. Right there in the alley by the dumpster. His chest is as solid as it looks but also warm as he wraps himself around me. I rest my head against him and listen to the thrum of his heart as I breathe in the ocean-soaked smell of his shirt.

"This is all going to work out," he says into my hair. "We're going to make this movie, one way or another."

"How can you be like that? Just so sure." I look up at his face, and we are mere centimeters apart. I see that his eyes have a darker ring around the outside. My gaze moves across his mouth before I can stop it, and I tuck my head back down against him.

"I'm just sure. I know how something feels when it matters. Like *Star Crossed* wasn't it. I knew."

"I was so pissed," I say and look up at him again. "I mean, clearly. But you were right."

Dan takes a coil of hair that has sprung out of my braid and tucks it behind my ear. There is a miles-wide disconnect between how I know I look and how he's looking at me.

"We're going to see Jack on Saturday night at the festival

for sure, and he might write us a song. But if he doesn't, we're going to make this movie another way, one hundred percent guaranteed. It's that good, Jane. It's that true."

"That," I say. "That's the thing that made me want to punch you out. You're just so sure of what you think."

He smiles and says, "I know what I know." He lowers his forehead onto mine, and for a second, I know what it would feel like to have a guy like Dan feel sure about me. In that same second, I want desperately to know what it would feel like to be kissed by him. His arms are tight and protective around my back; his eyes are straight on mine. He would kiss me with intention, like it would matter.

"I think I need sugar," I say.

He lets out a breath and releases me. Among the tornado of thoughts in my head right now, the clearest one is that I do not want to be released by Dan. If I hadn't said anything, he'd still be holding me and I'd still have my head snuggled into the warmth of his chest. I am no longer a monkey starved for touch; I am a person starved for Dan.

"Let's get ice cream and I'll show you something good," he says.

WE HAVE CHOCOLATE chip cones in our hands as we bike to the end of town. This requires slow pedaling and extreme concentration on my part. Dan pulls ahead and looks back and smiles at me in a way that reminds me of *The Notebook*. I roll my eyes and let my legs stick straight out, mimicking Allie's ease and sense of fun for just a second.

We've turned right, away from the ocean onto a country road. Crops that might be wheat grow on either side, and oak trees dot the landscape. I speed up so I can ride next to him. "I see what you're doing," I say.

"What am I doing? Besides getting ice cream all over my arms." He licks the side of his cone where it's dripping.

"You're trying to sell me on *The Notebook* with this bike-riding-and-ice-cream montage. Like you've stuck me right into the movie. You're so transparent." I smile at him as I bike ahead. He catches up laughing.

"It does sort of feel like that, except you're not falling for me, and I'm never going to build you a house with my own hands."

"The plumbing would be terrible," I say. And please let him be right about that other thing. Dan is not Solid Partner material, and falling for him is a recipe for disaster.

We ride side by side for a while, and I ask, "Is it believable to you that Allie never got the mail?"

Dan laughs. "What?"

"He wrote to her every day for a year. I mean, in three hundred and sixty-five days, she never once helped her mom out and grabbed the mail on the way in? And she's waiting, expecting, to hear from the love of her life. You'd think she'd stalk the mailman."

Dan's quiet, considering this. "Okay, I'll give you that."

"I mean, if you meet 'the one'"—I risk letting go of my handlebars for air quotes—"you check your mail."

Dan doesn't say anything.

"I don't want to ruin your favorite thing. I was just

thinking about it, because I'm coming around to the ice cream and the bikes and the country-road montage."

We pedal around a bend, and there's a big red barn with three smaller buildings around it in the distance. He motions with his head toward the property. "That's actually my favorite thing."

I AM SO thirsty by the time we're inside the barn. Like dust bowl thirsty. Dan hugs a woman named Elana, and her husband, Claude, comes out with a big pitcher of ice water. I gulp down an entire glass before I am ready for polite conversation.

"Jane and I are in town for the music festival."

"You could have stayed here," Elana says. "We have your old room."

"Thank you," he says. "But we're staying with my parents."

She reaches out and takes his hand. "Well, wander around all you want. We have a tour starting in ten minutes, but you know where everything is." She gives his hand a squeeze, and they leave us alone. Dan's face is so relaxed in this quiet place, talking to these quiet people.

I pour a third glass of water and look around. The barn is full of large-scale paintings, oils and watercolors. All unframed.

"Your old room?" I ask.

"It's an outdoor museum—well, the rest of it is outdoors. I worked here and taught kids for a while during high school, and sometimes I'd just stay. They gave me a room over the barn, and I would sleep there if I was working on something late. They have a darkroom in the little building out there. After high school, for the two years before I moved to the city for college, I moved in. That was the first stage of my big rebellion."

"What did your parents think?"

"I'm not sure." We're walking around the barn, looking at the paintings. "I like this one," he says. It's a painting of a woman stretching. You can see the shadows between the discs of her spine.

"Your parents said nothing?"

"Yeah, so my dad just thought I was being lazy, putting off my life. My mom thought it was about a girl."

"Sounds consistent," I say, and he laughs.

"This is a place where it's okay to be quiet. I could spend a whole day, a week, painting something. And I had no idea what I was going to do, but I finally started to feel like I knew what I wanted." He shrugs, like what he said was a small thing.

"What was the next stage of your rebellion?"

"Studying photography. Then moving to LA. They did not approve."

We stop at a large watercolor painting of a forest. Dan takes my arm and pulls me away from it so that we can see the whole thing. "There's no limit to how many greens you can find in nature," he says.

I must make a face because he says, "Before you crack a man-bun joke, I just mean I like this one because it feels like a real forest, every single possible shade of green. Watercolor's just about how much water you add—it's simple and unruly, kind of like the forest." He reads my face again. "Okay, maybe too much? Is my gramophone showing?"

"No," I say. We're facing each other, shoulders squared, and I wonder if he can read my thoughts. I want him to say more things about the forest. Or about paint and the color green. I just like the way his face goes serious when he's talking about something that matters to him. Something that matters so much to him that he wants to teach it to a bunch of little kids at the pier. Dan's not chasing anything; he's inviting the rest of us to a secret place. Dan is that dangerous kind of person who can make you believe in anything.

"Want to try?" he asks.

I don't have a chance to answer before he's walking into a storage closet to retrieve a stack of watercolor paper and paints. "Come."

I follow him outside and up a grassy hill behind the barn. I regret my choice of the slippery-bottomed flip-flops that were adorable for our biking montage but are terrible for hiking. Yellow wildflowers welcome us to the top of the hill where a pond appears in the distance, a pale blue oval like an aquamarine. It's surrounded by tall beach grasses the color of wheat.

"Give it a try," he says. There's a breeze up here, and I like the way it's hitting the back of my neck and giving me a little relief from the heat. I close my eyes and turn my face to the sun, and I can still see the pond in my mind. The breeze makes tiny ripples in the water before it bends the grasses. I open my eyes and Dan's watching me, and it occurs to me that I don't know what time it is. It occurs to me that Dan doesn't care what time it is; he just knows what he knows. I look back up to the sun and guess that it's around four. "You seem exactly ready for watercolors," he says.

So I sit on the ground with the little paper flat between my legs. Dan has a thermos of water for paintbrush dipping, but he gives me a sip first. I take too big of a sip and a little bit spills out of my mouth and he laughs. I wipe my smile away with the back of my hand.

"You're a mess," he says. My shorts and tank top are dry but filthy. Dan doesn't seem to mind the mess. He's eyeing the loose curl he tucked away earlier, and I silently will him to do it again.

"Want to hear something crazy?" I ask.

"Everything you say is a little crazy, Jane. Doesn't bother me a bit anymore." He smiles with his eyes, and I wish he met one of my criteria for a partner, though I can't think of what any of those are right now. My only thought is that I want to climb on top of him and pull covers over our heads and stay there. I want to taste his bottom lip. I want to know what his hands would feel like on my skin, and I want to, just for a bit, feel what it would be to have his focus all over me. The force of this want has a pulse, and it terrifies me. These are thoughts that belong to someone like my mother. These are the thoughts of a woman who's about to get crushed.

"So what's crazy?" he asks and snaps me out of it.

I laugh a little and rest my head on my knees. "I think I might be relaxed."

"Perfect time to paint," he says and places the thermos cap of water in front of me. I dip the paintbrush and make an oval of blue, but the oval won't stay put, there's too much water mixed in and it starts to bleed. It's like the pond is leaking.

"Can I?" he asks. He has a bit of green on his paintbrush and he's eyeing my painting.

"Sure," I say. He scoots closer and our knees touch. He reaches between my legs to paint, his arm on my thigh. That delicious hug in the alley has broken the seal between us. We're allowed to touch now, and at every point of contact, my skin tingles like it's waking up. I steady my breath and watch him add vague, watery trees behind the pond. The bottom of the greenery blends into the edges of the pond, and instead of looking like a hot mess, it looks like we're seeing it from a distance. He rinses his brush and dips it in red, dotting the field with poppies while his forearm rests on my thigh. I watch his face as he paints, just inches from mine, his eyebrows knitted together and his lashes in profile. I feel like he's let me into his private world, the one where he is entirely in his senses. He turns and catches me watching. His eyes smile and mine dip to his mouth. He notices and leans in a breath closer.

"It's your turn," he says.

"What?" I think I'm holding my breath.

He releases my eyes and looks down at the painting. "Fill in the bottom, make it sort of earthy."

"I don't know how," I say.

The two inches beyond Dan's lips are like a vortex pulling me in. "That's the fun of it though," he says. "You get it started, and then the paint's going to do what it's going to do. It just sort of takes over."

"Like a laugh," I say.

"I guess. I was thinking of a kiss." He looks away, squinting against the sun.

"What?" I am sure I'm delirious and deeply dehydrated because I think he just said something about a kiss. Out loud.

"A kiss is like that. I mean, if it takes. Sometimes a kiss doesn't go anywhere. But sometimes it starts and makes decisions all on its own." He's looking at my mouth as he says it, and I wonder if he's imagining the same kiss I am.

"I'll take your word for it," I say and dip my paintbrush into the brown. "And I will admit, because I am relaxed and maybe sun-drunk, that the kiss in *The Notebook* was a great one. The one in the rain?"

"Oh, I remember it," he says. I'm looking at our painting, but I can feel his eyes on me.

"That movie came out when I was twelve, and I remember thinking, wow, I hope that's what kissing is." I turn toward him and his eyes are heavy on mine.

"And has it been?"

"Nope," I say. My heart is daring him to lean in, just a bit, and show me that kiss. But it's also beating like I'm about to jump out of a plane. My want and my fear are in their usual death match, and he smiles at me in the most tender way. It pulls at my heart and reminds me how easily I can be crushed. I turn back to our painting. The earth beneath the pond is too dark, so I add water to the brown to lighten it. Dan covers my hand with his and guides me to paint short brushstrokes to add texture to the earth. His fingers on mine, like they belong there, and the way he's inviting me to create something with him, it's all too much.

I say, "I think if I was from here, I'd stay." He takes his hand away, and I hate myself for breaking that moment. I rinse my brush and take a little yellow to add the grasses.

"You'd think," he says.

"So why LA? You could have worked in film in New York?"

"Yeah, I always thought I might go to LA at some point, but it all accelerated when Aidan got married." He gives me a long look, like he's not sure if he should go on. "I brought a girl I'd been seeing for a while to the wedding, and she decided right then that she wanted to get married. Aidan looked good in a tux, so I would too, she said. Like we were exactly the same."

I don't like this. I don't like this one bit. There is something coming over me that is both unfamiliar and unsafe. I'm feeling all the Jennifer-at-the-bar vibes. She got to touch his chest enough times to consider marrying him. "How old were you?" I ask, and turn my traitorous face back to the painting.

"Twenty-four," he says. "Suddenly I knew I had to get out of here to really start my life, separate from my family. I'm sure she'll be there tonight. She always turns up. And wow, actually, we need to get going if we're going to buy beer and I'm going to smell less sweaty." He stands up and offers me a hand. It's safe to say I've had too much physical activity today. A run and a boat ride and a long bike ride and a hike up a hill. That's probably what's making me delirious. That's probably why I keep holding on to his hand for unnecessary seconds while we stand there looking at our painting. I liked making something with him. I liked the feel of his forearm pressed against my inner thigh. I like the way I can't tell which strokes were his and which ones were mine. I hope we get to make this movie and that it's exactly like this.

"Thank you," I say. For showing me something new. For helping me get relaxed enough to make art.

"You're welcome," he says. We're just standing there looking at each other. "Let's get this home safely." He drops my hand, takes the painting from me, and places it in my bike's basket with exaggerated care.

We bike back to his house in silence, and I take a shower sitting down. That's how tired my body is. I wash my hair and brush it out and climb into bed for a nap. I have a missed text from Clem: Found him yet?

For a second, I don't know who she's talking about.

I reply: We almost did and I kind of freaked out. And Dan held me in an alley

Clem: Against your will?

Me: No like a hug. Then he touched my hair and we rode bikes and painted. I think I'm on a collision course with his mouth and whatever's on the other side of it

Clem: Ok, wow. That's his tongue

Me: I'm delirious. How's work? And have you seen the hiking guy?

Clem: Work's good, but no I realized we were hiking because he's cheap

Me: Ugh.

Clem: It's fine because I wanted to be home tonight to undo whatever you did to our bookshelves

Me: Yeah, that was a bad idea. Thanks

Clem: Love you. And it's okay if you're having fun. People do that all the time

CHAPTER 19

I WAKE UP LIKE I'VE BEEN DRUGGED, THE WAY YOU DO after a too-long nap. The room is dark, and what feels like the last of the daylight is coming in from outside. Dan has leaned our painting against the window, and the sight of it makes me smile. He is standing with his back to me, shirtless in jeans. I wonder how long he'll keep facing that way so I can keep looking at the way the light comes in and hits his shoulders and the way his Levi's grip his thighs.

He puts an arm through the sleeve of a white buttondown, and I ask, "What time is it?"

"Oh, hey. I didn't want to wake you up. It's seven thirty. Do you still want to come?" He's turned around, half shirted and half not. He's in the process of dressing, but my brain registers him as undressing.

I stretch my arms over my head. "Sure."

He sits on the bed, and I scoot toward the wall. "You don't have to. It's going to be a lot of idiots and Brooke, and it might be weird."

"Brooke?" I prop myself up on my elbows. "That's her name?" And the thought arrives fully formed in my mind: *I cannot compete with a girl named Brooke.* No one can. I've known plenty of Brookes, and they're all worse than Jennifer. Brooke's tall and plays competitive sports. Brooke looks great without any makeup. She has pretty things and they're monogrammed because it's not enough to get something for Brooke; you need to go the extra mile. That's how treasured Brooke is with her effortless hair.

"Are you okay?" To my absolute terror, Dan is reading my face.

"I slept too long. Give me five minutes to get dressed."

WE DRIVE TO the beach just as it's getting dark. Aidan and Paula have brought wine. Dan has a case of beer. We park and leave our shoes at the top of the path and walk down through the dunes to the beach. I'm in jeans and a white cotton sweater, and I can tell from the way the cool sand hits the bottoms of my feet that it's not going to be enough. Dan's next to me in khakis (rolled up just once to allow us a glimpse of the spectacle that is his ankles) and his now buttoned shirt, untucked and unironed. I wish I were responsible for all this rumpling.

Someone's dug a big pit and started a fire and put a huge galvanized steel tub in there. People are standing around the pit in the last of the evening light, and I have the sense that I am watching a commercial for something that I want to buy. There's an ease to the group as they stand around shoeless and talking. It reminds me of the scene of the first kiss in *True Story*, the one I'd been dying for through the first thirty-six pages of the script the first time I read it. It's at a party at the beach where their eyes find each other over and over again. I feel that newly familiar shift in my heart just thinking about it.

"Danny!" they call as we come into sight, and Dan puts up a hand in greeting. There are lots of backslaps and fist bumps, and I am aware that Dan is very aware of me. He introduces me as his "friend Jane from LA" and never once turns his back on me. If someone is speaking to me, he's watching my face to see how I'm reacting. When I smile, he does too. It's like we're at the prom and his mom has given him specific orders to be a thoughtful date. I am also aware that I am being sized up by his friends.

A guy named Charlie hands me a beer and says, "So, Jane, huh? What are you doing with this guy?"

Working. Hanging out. Relaxing for the first time in decades. "The Finnegans think I lost a bet," I say and they laugh.

Dan laughs, which is kind of a relief. I was trying to change the tone but might have overcorrected. He puts his arm around me and gives me a quick squeeze. "As you can tell, I'm still killing it with the ladies."

Laughs and the clinking of beer bottles. Most of his friends still live on Long Island; one couple is in from Boston. We take in the Los Angeles jokes: How do we decide if we're going to drive or rollerblade? Does our medical insurance cover plastic surgery?

"Do you come for the whole summer?" I ask the Boston couple.

"No," she says. "We wish. We're just here to see his parents and go to the music festival this weekend."

Charlie says, "Jack Quinlan was actually here today. Surfing. Really badly."

"Here? Like right here?" I ask.

"Yeah, I saw him around noon, and a bunch of girls were hanging out waiting for him to finish. They said he was here yesterday too."

Dan turns to me. "Sounds like we have our plans for tomorrow."

She arrives and there's no question in my mind that it's her. Brooke is wearing a gauzy maxi dress with a soft ivory fisherman's sweater over it, like her bedroom floor is covered in beautiful things and she just picked two of them at random and they happened to work perfectly together. Her eyes are light blue, and her nose turns up the exact right amount. Everything about Brooke is exactly the right amount.

The Boston couple hasn't seen her in a while, it seems, because there are hugs and compliments exchanged. I hear Brooke apologize that she's such a mess. She's been crazy busy. I would like to see the recording of how crazy busy she's actually been.

"Danny," she says and throws her ivory-sweatered arms around his neck. "I can't believe you're really here."

He hugs her back, more quickly than I've ever seen him hug anybody, but the hug takes him away from me for the first time tonight. I can feel the air next to me where he used to be. "Yeah, for the festival and my parents' anniversary."

"I'm coming to the party," she says.

"Oh, great," Dan says, catching Aidan's eye. "This is my friend Jane from LA." I should have a name tag that says that.

Brooke doesn't seem like a person who shakes hands, and I do not want to hug her, so I give a little wave that probably makes me seem like a kid.

"Hi," she says. "Fun." She falls into conversation with the Boston couple, and Dan guides me by the elbow toward the safety of Aidan and Paula.

Eventually we gather around a long low table, and the contents of that big steel tub are laid out in front of us. Buttery lobster, corn, and potatoes have miraculously been cooked to perfection in a hand-dug hole. Paula's brought little hurricane lamps, and the whole feast is lit up like a masterpiece. Dan sits first and pats the spot on the sand next to him. We're cross-legged but still close to make room for everyone. We have metal camping plates, and we just grab what we want from the middle of the table. Brooke is across from Dan, one seat down, with nothing on her plate.

"Like it?" Dan asks me. He's leaned in like it's a secret.

"Yes," I say and take another bite of corn. I am warm from the beer and the candlelight and the feel of Dan's knee against mine.

"Me too," he says. "I'm glad you came." There's something about the way he's looking at me that makes me think an impossible thing: *I am interesting and true and beautiful.* I like this thought so much that I have to look away.

"And they're not idiots," I whisper into his ear. I get very close saying this and can smell him, freshly showered and like cedar and Earl Grey tea.

"I guess they grew up."

A guy named Seth at the end of the table asks, "So, Danny, how's showbiz?"

"Good," he says. "Jane and I have a script we really like, so . . ." He trails off.

"What was the one you did last year?" Charlie asks.

"*Grapevine,*" he says and takes a bite of corn.

"Yeah, I looked for that in the theaters but couldn't find it," Brooke says. "But still it's good that you had work, right?" I could not dislike her or her false concern more.

"It was a great movie," Aidan says before Dan can respond. "Won an award at the Austin Film Festival."

Dan raises his beer bottle to Aidan and nods.

"That's great," Brooke says. "I mean the award. I wish we could have seen it, like a real movie."

"Well, maybe the next one," Dan says.

"It was definitely a real movie," I say. It's the first thing I've said to the table and my voice comes out too strong.

Paula says, "I loved it."

Dan doesn't seem to care that Brooke is diminishing his work. He says, "Jane thinks it was a little small. Or quiet?"

"That's so you," Brooke says with a laugh.

I wipe my mouth because I'm sure there's butter there. "It's quiet," I say with the total authority of a person who has seen the movie, which I haven't. "But not small. Dan was hired by Vinny Banks, who is a legend in Hollywood. He's in his sixties now and is super picky about the films he makes. So the whole thing was kind of a big deal. Not just the fact that Dan's an award-winning cinematographer."

Aidan smiles at me across the table. I grab a lobster claw and busy myself with it because I feel like I've talked too much. I do not like seeing a person diminished. And if that person is Dan, with artistic integrity for days, it turns out I absolutely hate it. Dan's leg presses harder against mine as the conversation continues around the table. The Boston couple has a toddler who they left with the grandparents. Charlie just bought a house in Montauk. Seth and his wife, Lucy, are starting a graphic design business together. I am reminded that we are at the phase of life where everyone is doing a thing. Brooke asks what Brian's been up to, and Aidan shoots Dan a look.

I have now had a beer and two glasses of crisp white wine and not enough potatoes to soak them up. I can feel it in the dizzy way the conversation flows down the table. The light is hazy coming from the hurricane lamps and illuminates all the laughing faces. It's forever before Brooke actually picks up a piece of corn and bites into it. Her eyes are on Dan and, oddly, so is my hand. My hand has moved to his shoulder. My fingers trace the seam of his white shirt, and they plan to keep it up until she peels her eyes away.

My hand has surprised him, and Dan turns to me.

"I hate her," I whisper. "Like for real."

Dan laughs and leans his head toward me a bit. My

smile is so tipsy wide that it could break my face. "You're getting under her skin too, I think."

"Because she's still in love with you and thinks we're together?" I'm whispering because we shouldn't be talking about this, but also because the softer my voice, the closer he has to lean into me to hear.

"No, because you're cool."

Words I have literally never heard before. This makes me feel so bold that I turn completely to face him and lean in like I'm going to whisper something in his ear. The smell of his skin and the brush of the stubble on his cheek make my body go hot, like it's been switched on.

"What?" he asks, just an exhale of a word.

"Is she watching right now?" I ask.

"Probably."

"Good," I say and lean in so that our mouths are a breath apart. "Because she's the worst."

"I thought I was the worst," he says.

We have both turned completely toward one another now, as if we have left the party and started our own. I can almost feel his lips on mine and taste the lemony lobster that got there before I did. This is as close as I've ever come to initiating a kiss in my life. I am acutely aware that this is all on me. I leaned in. I did the whispering. I am the one who turned her head so there's just the butterfly touch of his lips on mine. If he kisses me, this kiss will take.

"You're definitely the worst," I say.

Dan laughs, and the laugh pulls him an inch away. I can't help but think how I knew this would happen, my making him laugh actually moved him away. There's cool air between us and I want him to come back.

"Come back," I say so quietly that he leans back in to hear.

My eyes watch his mouth, the way I've been doing for days now. I just want to know what it feels like, just for a second. I think I might be ravenous for the taste of him. His breath is on my lips and I brush mine against his and liquid heat floods my body. It's barely a kiss, but his eyes go dark, like he felt it too. I could leave it there, a touch as casual as an arm resting on a thigh, but I cannot. I lean in and kiss him for real, tasting him for the first time, all salt and sunshine, and a current runs through my core with such force that I grip his thigh to ground myself. It's as though my hand on him is a starting gun, the signal he was waiting for. His hands are in my hair to pull me closer, and I pour myself into him. Dan parts his lips, and I see colors behind my eyelids, a sherbet sunset, a deep blue ocean. The kiss is explosive. He cups my face when he pulls away and smiles into my eyes. It should be raining and we should be standing in front of the house he built me. We're both breathing hard, inches apart, staring into each other's eyes as he takes his hands from my hair.

"Danny, come help with the fire," says the most annoying voice in the world.

Dan holds my gaze for a second. My heart is hammering, and my hand rises to touch my still tingling lips. He looks over his shoulder. Everyone's gotten up from the table. They're carrying bottles over to the pit where the lobster cooked. He offers me a hand, helps me up, and then releases it too quickly. "I think you got her attention," he says, as if that were the whole point of that life-changing kiss.

"Yes," I say. I am vulnerable, open and wanting in a way that is not safe. I feel a shifting of the earth beneath me. The words bubble up inside of me: *Kiss me again, a million times.* And this terrifies me. I want something too much, so much that it will burn in the fire of my want. I need to snuff it out. "Trained actress," I say. "You're welcome."

He narrows his eyes in a questioning way, but then turns toward the fire. "Right. Well done," he says.

CHAPTER 20

~~~~~

H OW LONG DID YOU DATE HER?" I ASK WHEN WE'RE
in our beds. I switched to water after my completely
unhinged effort at PDA. My body is exhausted from the
marathon day, but my mind is on high alert.

"On and off for three years."

"That's a long time," I say.

"It wasn't very serious. Not until she saw how great I'd
look in miniature on top of a wedding cake. It was a good
time for me to go and try to see myself someplace else,
where I wasn't part of the pack, you know?"

"I don't know, actually."

"I just mean my family. We all look alike, and when we
were little, my mom even dressed us alike. We were lumped
together, the Finnegan brothers, but I was the one who was
different. People always asked me what was wrong, why I
wasn't roller-skating in a toga in the talent show, doing keg
stands on a Fourth of July float. I grew up feeling like everyone was trying to fix me. I didn't understand why, because

I didn't feel broken. I knew I had to leave. I was afraid that the thing that made me different—the thing my dad thinks is a little off— I was afraid I was going to lose it."

I turn to look at him, and he's turned back to stare at the bunk bed above him. I wonder if he's scribbled "please, please, please" up there.

He turns his head to me. "It's like when you finally light a match on the beach and you have to cup it with your hands so it won't blow out. I was getting a sense of myself and wanted to keep it."

I can feel this. I think back to the light I saw in myself at fourteen and how quickly it died. "But how did you know? How did you know that the thing that makes you different was a good thing? It would have been easier to sort of blend in. Stay."

"Easier, but kind of awful." His eyes are serious. "Even when I was little, I knew that the thing that was inside me, that made me myself, was worth protecting. Aidan knew it too, which really helped. And honestly, Jane, it's all I have, besides a beat-up car with two hundred thousand miles on it. I have a point of view. I follow my instincts around because I know they'll lead me to something worthwhile. It's probably what you hated about me, that I don't want to just do the easy thing. I know people say it all the time, but I actually follow my heart."

The moment hangs between us. My heart is treacherous and historically wrong about everything, it is the weakest muscle in my body, but Dan and his family and our script are conspiring to whisper it back to life like it's an ember worth restoking.

"So when Brooke lumped me together as the exact same person as Aidan, I realized even she had no idea who I was. Like I was just another Finnegan brother, interchangeable."

His arm is outside his covers and the sleeve of his T-shirt is riding up just a bit so that I can see the light hit the top of whatever muscle that is. "I'm sure she didn't think you were interchangeable."

"She actually did. As soon as I left she tried to date Connor."

"Seriously?" I ask.

"No joke. She didn't love me, she just loved the idea of me."

"Gross, and tonight she was asking about Brian," I say. "That sucks."

"Yeah, she married and divorced the guy who owns the Subaru dealership in Montauk, so she's in the market for a replacement. Any Finnegan will do, I guess. And it was fine because I didn't love her, but it sort of proved me right. I left for LA right after. I needed to get away, you know?"

"Yeah."

"I'm sorry about *Star Crossed*," he says and turns his head toward me.

"You're about to take it back."

"I was, yes." He laughs. "I hated it. But part of why I hated it was that it gave me that feeling. They're attracted to each other and become a couple, but for no reason. They just sort of like the idea of each other, they see each other in broad strokes. And I think I hate broad strokes. Broad strokes and generalities remind me of when I was a kid and I was worried I'd disappear." He turns onto his back. I watch him in the dark, his arm flung up over his head. It's my turn to say something, but I don't. I'm not going to tell him why it feels so safe to play a role.

He closes his eyes and I guess that's it. We've been talking for the entire day, but I want to hear more.

"I was going to take you to Shanty's," he says from the darkness. "That Friday night we never went out. Have you ever been?"

"No."

"Me neither, but it's in the marina and I've driven by it. Always thought it would be cool to take a first date there. I wasn't totally sure about it, but then Aidan said to just risk it, and if you hated it, it could be something we'd laugh about later when we were a couple. Like the food poisoning you got on our first date or whatever."

He told his brother about me.

"That is seriously romantic." My eyes are closed, and I am picturing the two of us on a couch I don't own laughing about a disastrous but memorable date. He remembers what it felt like to hold my hair while I threw up at the gas station on the way home. I remember the way he wet a paper towel for the back of my neck. I have the strangest feeling that I would have acted entirely different on a date with Dan. I say to the ceiling, "I was going to wear jeans and my blue-and-white cotton blouse. It's a confident sort of blouse, and it hits at the right length so you don't have to worry about tucking it in." I can feel him looking at me, daring me to go on. I feel like we're playing a game, so I do. "I hate being on a date in a fix-it outfit, where you're adjusting your bra straps or pulling your top down so your stomach isn't showing. I usually wear a dress for this reason, but with you, I was going to wear jeans and a blouse. It felt cooler."

"I'm honored. That I was considered for the alternate outfit." I turn to him and he smiles at me in the dark. His mouth is in shadow now, but I can see it in his eyes. He turns back to the ceiling and I keep watching him. "I hadn't thought about what I was going to wear, but I was going to clean out my car. I actually walked into that meeting with Nathan stressed out because I thought I was going to run out of time and then you'd see that I was driving around in a big gym locker."

I laugh. "I don't love a dirty car, your instincts were good."

He turns back to me. "Thanks for tonight. And for hyping my movie to the haters."

I laugh. "That part wasn't even acting. Nathan's obsessed with *Grapevine*."

"And the rest of it?" he asks. His gaze is heavy on me, and I feel something change; it's the molecular composition of the air, thinner somehow. He's vulnerable asking this question.

"The rest of it?" I ask. The feeling of my mouth on his and the smell of the salt air on his skin return to me in force. I went way out of my comfort zone tonight, but I don't think anyone in the world would regret a kiss like that. He reaches out for my hand across the small space between us, and I take it. He has strong hands, and the little squeeze of his palm against mine moves directly to my stomach. I should say something now to affirm that the rest of it is a thing that I want. But I can't say it. I've already extended myself too far tonight, and I'm terrified of going any further.

"So tomorrow? We look for Jack at the beach?" I say. It has nothing to do with what's happening here between us. But I say it because the alternative is telling him how I feel. The alternative is climbing into his bed and risking my heart.

Dan's expression changes, like shutters pulling closed. "Okay, yeah," he says and lets go of my hand.

"Good night," I say and roll over toward the wall.

CHAPTER 21

~~~~~~

"NO MUFFINS?" CORMACK ASKS WHEN I SIT NEXT TO him in the backyard with my coffee. Ruby's up. She's wandering around the lawn in her Wonder Woman pajamas collecting leaves in a bouquet.

"I skipped my run. Did way too many things yesterday. But I could bike and get you some."

"No, but thanks. I don't think I'll be starving to death around here anytime soon."

We sit and watch the potato fields brighten in the sun. We watch Ruby perform some kind of dance for no one but herself. It mostly involves her stepping from side to side and swaying her arms over her head, like she's bringing the heavens down to earth. At regular intervals, she parts the air in front of her, like she's doing the breaststroke. It's mesmerizing, the magic of a six-year-old girl. Cormack reads the *Post*, and I watch the potato fields and replay that kiss behind my eyes. I can feel Dan's lips changing mine into something electric. I can feel the way that kiss wormed its way into my heart, making room there. I don't know how I'm going to see him today without begging him to kiss me again. I want this too much, and I just wish I hadn't insti-gated it. I want to go back in time and have him be the one who kissed me. And not because Brooke and her perfect hair were there, but because I want to know that I'm a per-son he was dying to kiss. The distinction shouldn't matter, especially based on how objectively successful that kiss was, but it does to me. If it were socially acceptable, I'd like him to present me with an affidavit stipulating that he wanted to kiss me as much as I wanted to kiss him, and that if I ex-press an interest in another kiss, he will not rescind his in-terest. It would be nice if it were notarized.

"Do you think dehydration can affect your brain?" I ask Cormack. "Like your judgment?"

"Sure. Probably why everyone in California is a little . . . you know?" He gives me a side glance. "They're a little more than three hours behind, if you ask me. No offense, of course."

I laugh. "Yeah, of course."

The sliding doors open, and I hear Aidan say to Dan, "Obviously."

"I saw the whole thing," Paula says, carrying both Katie and a cup of coffee. And to me, "Good morning. Muffins?"

I shake my head. I've really let everyone down about the whole muffin thing. Without thinking, I reach out to Katie, and she strains her little body in my direction.

"Please," Paula says and hands her to me. I don't look at Dan because I don't have a plan for what my face should look like when I do. I'm trying to remember what the right amount bored looks like. Katie smiles at me, and I think I'd like to know her long enough to give her a nonsensical nickname. Pickles, I think.

Dan takes the seat next to me. "Good morning," he says to no one in particular.

Katie has a clump of my hair in her fist. She's blowing bubbles with her tiny mouth, and she thinks it's hilarious. I look up at Dan and he's watching me over his coffee. His brow is heavy, and there's so much in his eyes that I have to look back down. Last night's kiss is still right there on his lips.

"You okay?" Dan asks me.

"Of course," I say, embarrassed. I'm not sure where we stand now, and I'm not sure what he wants. I need to be sure because falling flat on my face in this particular situation, with this particular guy, feels uniquely dangerous.

Katie's giving me a serious face, and I realize she's just mimicking mine. Ruby comes over and counts her toes. They both laugh when she gets to ten, and I am caught in the crossfire of their giggles.

We all move into the kitchen when called, and I keep Katie on my lap. I like the weight of her there, and I like having something to hold on to. Dan sits across from me and I can feel his eyes on me.

Cormack gets up to leave for work. "I know I said I wasn't working this week, but I've got to get to Montauk to give a bid on a new house." He kisses Reenie on the head and squeezes her shoulder. Just like it's nothing and also everything all at once. "What are you bums doing today?" He means Dan and me.

I feel Dan trying to catch my eye, but Reenie says, "Actually, Mrs. Barton at the library heard you were in town and called to see if you could come by today. She has that art camp going."

Dan at an art camp with a bunch of little kids. Dan knowing exactly what's inside of him and sharing it with them because his heart is so damn big. I am low-key annoyed with him right now for how much I like him. "You should go," I say and meet his eye.

"Come with me and we can grab lunch after?"

"Um, no." I say. And I don't mean to come off as clipped as I do. Fear is prickling in my heart; it was not safe to get this close to a man this good. Obviously. And kissing me back with those butter lips was just reckless on his part. I notice my hands balling up and put them under the table. "I think, if it's okay, I'm going to take a bike and scout out Whalebone Beach where Charlie said Jack was surfing. That's bikeable, right?"

"It is," Reenie says. "But if you wait, Dan can take you."

"Thanks, but I'm fine. GPS in my phone and I'm good. Right, Katie?" She's not buying it either.

I shower and put on my white cotton sundress that clings in the right places. It's the revenge dress I packed to wear in front of Jack, but for some reason, it's Dan who I want revenge against today. How dare he make me want something this much. I find Dan waiting by a bike in the driveway.

"Wow," he says, taking me in. His eyes run up the length of my dress and fix on the tiny white spaghetti straps on my shoulders. Heat flushes my neck. "You sure you know where you're going?" He's in shorts and a gray T-shirt with his good camera strapped across his chest. It makes me think of the first time I ever saw him and had the thought that he looked armed. He's dangerous all right.

"Yep." I try to temper the clipped sound of my voice with a smile, but I can feel how it doesn't reach my eyes.

"Jane."

"We should get going. You have kids to inspire." I give him what might be turning into my Brentwood post office murder smile, get on my bike, and go. He tries to ride next to me, and I slow down so that he's ahead. We turn into town, and he stops at the library. I wave and keep going.

I try to refocus on my mission as I pedal up Main Street. I'm going to find Jack and make my lie true. *Hey, it's Jane Jackson. Remember "Jump-Start Love Song"?* How hard could that possibly be to say?

I pull into the Whalebone Beach parking lot, and there's a G-wagon parked in two spaces. My heart drops into my stomach. For a second, I consider turning around and biking back to the candy store next to Chippy's, grabbing some malt balls, and calling it a day. There will be another movie—someone in Hollywood is probably writing a script at a Starbucks right now that's just as good. I picture that person, with brows knitted in concentration, an hours-old latte next to them. Except they don't understand love, the small acts of care that pile up to make it huge. They're writing a scene with a marching band and an explosion, and, God, I hate their script.

I get off my bike and straighten my dress. Another car pulls in, and a bunch of teenagers get out and walk through the dunes to the beach. I should follow them. I need to gather my thoughts. I need to summon my showtime energy. That song is a legitimate connection. It was a good song. And everyone's embarrassing at fourteen.

I say this out loud: "Everyone's embarrassing at fourteen." I repeat it under my breath as I start to cross the parking lot to the same narrow path in the dunes I walked through last night with Dan and his unironed white shirt. I rub my fingers together and remember what the fabric felt like, washed too many times.

At that moment, several twenty-something women emerge from the path, and in the middle of them is a head of hair I know from TMZ. My heart screams *Finally!* and *Run for your life!* all at once. This is the fire I need to walk through, but I wish I were doing it with thicker skin. That stupid kiss has me feeling like my heart is dangling outside of my chest.

I'm a deer in the headlights, my survival instinct kicking into high gear. I watch Jack, who seems to be on the phone, one earbud in as he hoists a surfboard on top of the car with the help of one of the girls. He's wiry verging on thin with the enviable air of a person who thinks they look better than they do. Jack laughs into the phone, and I'm just standing there at the edge of the parking lot on my cement feet. The sun feels too bright overhead, and there's a metal garbage can next to me, steaming with a week's worth of fast-food remains. I pull at my dress where I feel like it's riding up, and suddenly it's too tight. Everything is too tight actually, my chest, my skin.

I take a half step forward. "Hey," I say too quietly for anyone to hear me.

Jack is in the driver's seat now with his window down. He's nodding as if he's following the phone conversation, and he's backing out of his two parking spots. I need to approach the car, but my body won't do it. I notice that I have assumed Ruby's Wonder Woman power stance, my subconscious trying to convince my conscious that this is a thing I can do. *I can do this.*

From just ten feet away, I call "Jack!" in a medium-loud voice. He looks up but past me, and puts his car into drive. I yell "It's Jane Jackson!!" in an extra loud voice, and he looks right at me. The words don't register. I don't register. I could have shouted *Bananas have potassium!* to get the same reaction. And suddenly the red-hot shame that I've been carrying around for almost two decades turns into white-hot rage at being ignored and unworthy of remembering. He starts pulling out of the parking lot, and I scream "I'm Jane Jackson!" at the top of my lungs. His window is up, his left-hand turn signal is on, and my body, which had previously refused to cooperate, scoops up a discarded Super Big Gulp from the garbage and chucks it at his bumper.

I watch it explode against the back of his G-wagon, orange soda splattering. The car jerks to a stop, and the red of Jack's brake lights shifts my rage instantly to panic.

I turn and run.

Scenes of myself begging Jack for a favor after apologizing for a minor assault on his car flash through my mind as I run past the shocked faces of the young women and down the path through the dunes.

I am unhinged for real. Thank God Dan wasn't with me to see that. Jack, who deemed me a weirdo at fourteen, is probably calling security about me now. The old shame burns and mixes with my terrifying feelings about last night. My heart is being drawn to a foreign land that is famous for sinkholes and cataclysmic disasters. I don't know how to walk confidently into that place, and I don't know how to stay away.

I arrive at the beach and lie on my back in the sun. I barely give my heart a chance to settle before I text Clem: 911

She calls me immediately. "What happened?" I can hear gurneys rolling past her and the sound of voices bouncing off the hospital walls.

"I just saw Jack and threw a Super Big Gulp at his car. Orange soda."

Clem laughs. "You what? Let me guess—he stopped and immediately wrote you a song?"

"Drove off. Didn't even know it was me."

"Okay, kind of a nonevent then. What else? You sound panicked."

"We kissed," I say. "Dan and me."

"How is this a crisis?" She's whispering into the phone, and I feel like such a drama queen demanding she talk to me at work.

"Because *I* kissed *him*! Like a total maniac, like a crazed sex fiend." I'm covering my eyes as I say it.

"This I cannot picture, but also yay?" To someone else, "I'm just going to check the supply closet, back in five." A door shuts; then, to me: "I love this for you. This feels like good, loose behavior. How was it?"

I'm covering my eyes with my forearms, and I feel safe in the darkness with Clem. It's all so ridiculous. "It was like in *The Notebook*."

"So, terrible? You hate that movie."

"I know! I did! I mean, I do! But the kiss, it wasn't just like the kiss in the rain but also the whole time he carries her upstairs and they can barely wait to get their clothes off and she can't believe that's what she's been missing out on. All of that, in a kiss that lasted five seconds. I'm having feelings, Clem. I can't go back to the regular world after this."

"Do you have to? I mean, he must like you."

"Maybe. But I'm terrified. Like going-into-battle terrified. *I* kissed *him*, see? I'm the desperate one. I don't know if he meant it, and even if he did . . ." I trail off. *I'm easy to leave.* It's something that I know about myself, but right now it's more of a feeling than a thought, bubbling up uninvited to justify my fear. "Maybe it's just the sun and sharing a room and his totally absurd cheekbones. Maybe he feels sorry for me because I'm probably getting laid off."

"You just unpacked a lifetime of crazy right there, but that doesn't sound like a pity kiss."

"I hope not, Clem. I really like him. Are there patients dying because of this conversation? I know I'm being ridiculous."

"No, but I've got to get back to work. Can you just do me a favor? Don't do the thing where you assume you know what Dan's thinking and decide it's over."

"What's the alternative to that again?" I know what she's going to say, but I need to hear it.

"You can—wait for it—say how you actually feel."

"No."

"Yes. It's a thing grown-up people do. Brand-new, started on TikTok."

I laugh and it's a relief. "Love you, Clem. Go save some geezers. They're lucky to have you."

As soon as I hang up, my phone dings. Dan: I'm all done here, meet for lunch?

Just the sight of his name makes my heart race. I don't know what is happening to me, and I don't know how I'm going to tell him I saw Jack and choked.

Me: I'm at the beach

Dan: Want me to come there?

Me: It's fine. I'll leave soon and see you back at the house.

I splay out on the sand like a starfish for a while, feeling my chest burn under the thin straps of my revenge dress and listening to the ocean howl.

I get a text from "Dad," which is something I'm not

likely to get used to: There's a storm coming in. I'm headed back from Montauk. Are you still on a bike?

I look out at the horizon and see a patch of dark clouds.

Me: Yes, I'm at the beach

Cormack: Head home now and you should be fine

Me: What's the plan for dinner? Can I pick something up in town?

Cormack: Hang on

The clouds appear to be moving toward me, so I head back toward the dunes.

Dad: Reenie needs berries

Me: On it

It starts to get drizzly and then dark as I'm biking back toward town. I know there's a stand with a big wooden sign that says BERRIES right on the corner where I turn off of Main Street. As it starts to rain harder, I pedal faster, not because I don't want to get wet (I am already completely wet, and the great thing about wet is that you can't get wetter once you're saturated) but because I don't want to miss the berry guy. Something in me rebels at the idea of disappointing Cormack.

I'm pedaling through a thick sheet of rain, my white dress sticking to my legs as I go. When I reach the edge of town, a traffic light sneaks up on me, and my bike's wet brakes do not cooperate. Luckily, all of the sane people are indoors right now, so I skid into a fence rather than an untimely death. I'm at a park with a covered picnic area, and I wheel my bike to shelter and take inventory. The bike is fine. The tires are intact. My heart is racing. I sit on top of a wooden picnic bench and watch the rain pound the grass in front of me.

My phone, which has been safe inside the zippered pocket of my bag, rings. The rain is so loud that I can only feel it vibrate. "Tell me you're not on your bike," Dan says as a greeting.

"I'm not. I was, but now I am not."

He lets out a breath. "I'm coming for you. Are you still by the beach?"

"A park at the end of Main Street."

Dan pulls into the empty parking lot minutes later, steps out into the rain, and pops the trunk of his mom's wagon. I walk my bike toward him through grassy puddles, and the rain drenches the dress that is stuck to me like plastic wrap. I am already the temperature of this storm, so it just feels like diving under a wave when you've been in the ocean for hours.

He takes my bike, starts to load it into the trunk, and shouts over the rain, "Get in the car."

He's in a hurry because he's not soaked yet, but I'm not. I'm just standing there in the pouring rain smiling at the madness of this day. A streetlamp illuminates the spot in front of me where the silver rain is dancing against the blacktop.

"Are you about to laugh?" he asks.

"Yes, it's been a day. And now this. It's just like your dumb movie." I raise my arms at my sides to catch the rain. It lands warm and hard on my skin.

He runs his eyes down my body. "It's exactly like that, except Allie's dress wasn't quite that see-through."

My face flames and I cross my arms over my chest.

"Get in the car," he says again.

The front seat feels like the inside of a drum, dry and tight with a rhythmic pounding from the outside. The sky is dark, and while it's probably around three o'clock, it feels like midnight. Dan does not start the car. He reaches into the back seat and hands me a beach towel. I dry my face and wring out the ends of my hair. He just sits, turned toward me, and watches. I can feel his eyes on me and hear his breath go jagged as I dry the bottom of my dress, now at mid-thigh. I dab at my chest where my too-sheer strapless bra is serving absolutely no purpose.

"Your legs," he says.

"What?"

"What?" He's still looking at them.

"You just said something about my legs."

"I didn't," he says and meets my eyes. "Oh, they're wet, that's all. You should dry them." He turns his body back toward the steering wheel as if he's going to start the car, but he doesn't.

The air is supercharged. I can tell by the way he swallows that his heart is racing, and I'd like to reach out and touch his chest so I can feel it. That might be as good as the signed affidavit.

I don't look at him as I dry one leg and then the other, deliberately slow because I like what this is doing to him.

His breathing is altered, and the windows are starting to fog. When I'm done, I dry my neck and chest, aware but not really caring that my clothes have gone transparent.

"Okay, you're dry," he says, his voice rough. He takes the towel from me and drops it in the back seat, and I just sit there in my see-through dress not making a move. I am more aware of my body than I ever have been. It pulses under the surface, and I can feel his hands on me even though we're not touching at all. He narrows his eyes on the spaghetti strap on my shoulder, and it gives me goose bumps. In this dangerous foreign land, I am as sexy as he seems to think I am. Lightning cracks overhead. He doesn't blink.

"So, I . . ." he starts and takes my hand, then immediately cups it in both of his. "I'm sorry, you're freezing." This seems to jolt him back to reality, and he starts the car and jacks up the heat.

"I'm fine," I say. "What were you going to say?"

"I wanted to know if you were okay?" He looks at the rain on the windshield and back at me. "About last night. You've been weird today. And I thought we should talk about it?"

"You honestly can't imagine how weird I've been today." The words are meant to be lighthearted, but I'm staring at his mouth so they come out distracted.

He takes my hand again and entwines our fingers. "Is it because I kissed you?"

"You didn't kiss me."

"Jane. I was there. It was—" He makes an explosion with his free hand.

My smile is its own explosion—I cannot contain it. That kiss was exactly that, five seconds of fireworks.

"I just mean *I* kissed *you*," I say.

"Why does that matter?" he asks. His eyes dip to my mouth and then to my chest and down my legs, all of it somehow more naked for the thin wet cotton clinging to it.

Because I'm a little broken, I don't say. Lightning cracks again and I ask, "Are we safe here?"

He runs a finger over the strap of my dress and then watches as it falls off my shoulder. "Probably not," he says. He rests a hand on my thigh and I feel it everywhere, warm where my wet dress was cold. His eyes are on my mouth like he can already taste me. I want to kiss him again the way you want another breath of air when you're drowning.

He leans toward me, and I say "Yes" in response to a question he hasn't asked. His mouth is already on mine when I say it. His hand is moving up my thigh, and I reach for the sharp edge of his jaw. When he opens my mouth with his, it's an explosion again, and I am part of that explosion. My fingers claw into his hair and I lean into him, savoring the feel of his stubble against my chin. Dan kisses me like he wants to know every part of me. He's cracking me open, making me feel like it's okay to want something this much, and it's equal parts exhilarating and terrifying. *True Story* planted the seed, but now I can feel it: the reckless need to be close to him. His mouth is on my neck, and I'm gripping the front of his shirt, pulling him into me. This thing, for sure, has taken off and taken over. All I can hear is the pounding of the rain, the gasping breath that might be my own, and the intermittent vibrating of a phone.

"Your phone," I say in a voice that doesn't sound like mine.

"It's the mob," he says, breathless. "They don't stop, ever." He's kissing me again so deeply, and the rain is pounding the windshield so hard that I think I've misheard him about the mob. *Wait, the mob?*

"Dan." I hold his face in my hands because there's something I need to say, but the intensity of his navy eyes pins me in place, and his hand is lifting my leg, his thumb just under my knee, and I forget what it was and kiss him again. His phone vibrates, and I remember. "The mob?" I am nearly out of breath.

He rests his forehead on mine and touches my chin, warmth trailing his fingertips.

"It's nothing," he says. "It's the family group text." He lets out a breath and grabs his phone. "They'll text until you reply, and if you don't, they'll send the cops."

I cross my arms over my see-through dress. I don't want to be found like this. I don't want to be found ever, actually. I want to stay in this car, fogging up the windows with Dan.

He texts them back and says, "They were worried about you. I texted that I found you. They think we should be home by now."

"We have to get the berries. I told your dad."

He puts down his phone and moves a wet clump of hair

over my shoulder. His eyes graze my body. "We're going to stop this over berries?"

I smile. "He asked me specifically. I need to deliver the berries."

He looks at me for a beat, and it's not about berries. "When you smile at me, I feel like I want to capture it. But it's not the regular way like when I see something beautiful and I want to photograph it. When you smile, it does something to me, I feel it in my chest, and I just want to figure out how to get you to do it again."

I smile from the deepest part of my heart. Like this smile has been waiting for him. "That," he says and touches my lips. He presses his thumb to the corner of my mouth and I kiss it. "It's the best smile, but more than that, I just like thinking you're happy."

I wish I knew more about science to understand how the explosion that recently took place in my body has rearranged every single particle on this earth into something new and hopeful. This true and beautiful man is looking at what recently could have been described as a drowned rat as if she is precious. As if she is love. I want to say thank you, but instead I kiss him again, slowly, as if transmitting those words through my lips.

His phone vibrates with a rapid series of texts. I want to tell him to turn off his phone and repeat that whole thing about my smile a thousand times. "You should look," I say against his mouth.

He pulls away and checks his phone again. "Ah, there's a big debate about whether the berry stand is still there and what exactly the two of us are doing in a car in a storm. Connor has ideas." Dan shakes his head and rests it on the steering wheel. "This is hell." He looks at me again, up and down. "I'll be right back."

He gets out of the car and opens the trunk and returns, wetter, with a thick gray hoodie.

"Put this on," he says. "Sorry I didn't think of it sooner." He smiles and watches me put it on.

"That's better," I say, luxuriating in the feel of warm cotton on my skin.

He pulls each of my sleeves down to cover my hands and then pulls the hood up over my head. "Almost," he says and then pulls the strings tight so that he can just see my smile. "Perfect."

CHAPTER 22

W E TRACK AN OCEAN INTO THE HOUSE, AND REENIE doesn't seem to mind. I hand over the berries in their dripping cardboard boxes.

"Thank God you're okay," she says. "I thought Cormack was getting berries, but instead he decided to let a young woman pick them up by bike in a thunderstorm." I get the feeling this argument has been going on for a while.

"I'm fine, it was sort of exciting. And then Dan rescued me." My face goes hot when I see the smile creep across Reenie's face. Cormack looks down at his paper, but there's a hint of a smile there too.

"So what are these all-important berries for?" Dan asks, rescuing me again.

"I'm going to make a berry pie for dessert, Grandma's recipe." And then, to me, "You go take a hot shower and relax."

"If I take a quick shower, can I help you? Make the pie?"

I have a quick thought that the family recipe is a secret and that I've asked for too much.

She smiles at me, and I remember there are no secrets here. "Yes. Go. Then we'll get started. I'll make us some tea."

Locked in the bathroom, I text Clem: There was making out. In a car. Fogged-up windows and see-through wet clothing. He said a thing about my smile. What is this??

I SCORCH MYSELF in the shower and dress in jeans and a sweater to keep the heat in. It's about four o'clock, and Paula and Aidan are still out somewhere with the girls. Reenie's at the kitchen counter in an apron, holding a bag of flour expectantly. She has a pastry cutter and a bowl of cold butter cut into little pieces. She shows me how to cut the butter into the flour, and she lets me mold it into a ball. My hands are sticky and I have flour all over my wrists. Dan is sitting at the counter, reading something on his phone and also watching us. Every time our eyes meet, my face melts into a smile and I have to look away. I have completely lost control of my face.

"So I saw Jack," I say once the crust is chilling in the refrigerator. "I forgot to tell you. When we were driving." I feel myself blush. Reenie hands me a cup of black tea with honey and cream, and I bury my face in it.

Dan's smiling at me. "That's a big thing to forget," he says.

"Yeah, well, it was a bust."

"He said no?"

"No, he was mobbed by women and was also on the phone. I called to him, but he didn't recognize me. And he left." I don't tell him that I threw garbage at his car. Not my best moment. I give him an exaggerated *oof*.

"Okay, well, that's two almosts in two days," he says and holds my gaze. He means two run-ins with Jack, but I think of two run-ins between us.

"I think that math adds to zero," says Cormack over his newspaper.

I laugh. "Yes. Zero." And my eyes shoot back to Dan's.

Aidan and Paula come in with Ruby and Katie around five. Aidan drops a baguette and two packages of steaks on the counter. "Looks like we're cooking these inside," he says.

"Jane's making Grandma's pie," Reenie says.

"I am. It's my first pie, and so far it has not been easy. Seven more minutes in the fridge." We've already rinsed the berries and I've been instructed to cut the strawberries in half. I've tossed them with sugar and a teaspoon of cornstarch, and I'm keeping the bowl very close to me.

My mom didn't bake, and I've never seen a rolling pin in real life. I love the smooth feel of it and the messy way Reenie tosses flour onto the kitchen table so that the dough won't stick. I love flattening the ball of dough with my hand and then rolling it with the pin into a not-quite-right circle. I love lifting it and the way it breaks before it gets to the pie plate and how I can fix it by just pressing it back together.

"You're a natural," Reenie says, and I beam.

I pour the berries into the crust and put the whole thing

in the hot oven. I do feel natural here, I realize. My thoughts and words come out entirely unrehearsed. I can admit to not knowing how to do something and try. Laughter comes out of me as easily as my breath. It's a new feeling to be so much myself and to still be invited deeper and deeper into this family. Knowing their family recipe gives me a very specific and unnameable kind of pleasure.

"That's it," Reenie says. "Now we wait." She shoos me into the living room, where Dan's making a fire and Ruby's watching cartoons on the floor, chin in hands. He's on his knees stacking wood and balling up scraps of paper. I sit on the couch and watch him. In a matter of hours, everyone in this house is going to be going to bed, including us. The thought of it makes my chest pound. One breath closer to Dan, one single item of clothing so much as pushed aside, and I will come completely apart. I know it. Dan himself is the point of no return.

Dan gets the fire going, a little crackle and pop to start, and sits next to me on the couch. I can smell the woodsmoke on him. Woodsmoke and cedar and milky tea. My instinct to bury my face in his neck is strong.

"I like this storm so far," he says and puts his hand on my knee. I stare at his hand there for a second, considering the power it has to electrify me so casually, through denim, no less.

"Yes, I've had worse," I say and trail my fingers over his knuckles. We're just looking at each other and enjoying the crackle of energy that's alive between us. I wonder if they can see it from space. "You didn't tell me how the library was."

"So many topics we haven't covered today." He entwines our fingers.

The front door opens, and it's Connor and Marla with Sammy. The open door lets in the din of the storm. "Tree fell on the power lines on our street. Complete blackout," Connor says.

Reenie takes Sammy by the hand. "Well, it looks like we're going to have a big sleepover."

"Thank you," Marla says. She's brought a tray of chicken that she'd been about to cook and puts it in the top rack of Reenie's oven above my pie. Suddenly we are in a crowd. Sammy climbs on the couch between us. Katie is in my arms. Paula and Aidan are sharing an armchair. Marla has her feet on the coffee table, eyes closed and hands resting on her pregnant belly.

"So how are we all going to sleep?" Connor asks.

"I definitely need a bed," Marla says. "I can sleep with you guys."

"Great," I say and don't meet Dan's eye.

After dinner, Reenie invites me to cut my pie. The first piece is tricky, but the rest come out fine. Reenie puts her arm around me and tells me I did a great job, and everyone around the table says how delicious it is. My smile could crack my face, and Dan is watching me. I think of what he said in the car, and I wonder if I'll ever smile again without thinking of that.

WHEN I'VE BRUSHED my teeth, I find Marla asleep in my
bed, which I get. I wouldn't want a pregnant woman climbing up the ladder to the top bunk, and the bottom bunk
probably feels claustrophobic. I climb up the little ladder at
the foot of the bed and crawl up to the pillow.

Clem texts me back: What did he say about your smile

Me: Something really romantic, about how he likes seeing me happy

Clem: Jane

Clem: This is love talk

Me: Maybe?

Clem: Omg

Me: I know. I'm scared. He's just the most deliciously
no b.s. person, like all the way through

Clem: No b.s. is GOOD. You're scared because it's big.
That's okay! I've been waiting for this to happen. Never
thought it would be man bun Dan, who knew. You have my
full support

I'm still wide awake when Dan comes in. Standing, he's
level with my bunk.

"You're okay up here?" he whispers.

"Yeah." I turn on my side to face him.

"Okay." And he's not going anywhere. He just stands
there with his face by mine in the darkness. "Sorry it's such
a zoo here."

"I like this zoo." He takes my hand and I lean in toward
him. We are a right angle. I don't know how I'm going to

sleep if he doesn't kiss me good night. Beneath us, Marla turns over in her sleep. Dan lets out a sigh. "Good night," I say to keep myself from saying, *I really, really like you. So much that my chest hurts.*

"Okay," he says. He lets go of my hand and then holds his fingers up to mine so that each of them touch. It feels like a promise. He lets them fall away and gets in bed below me. I hear him pull up his covers, then pull them off again and get up. His face appears at bunk level, leaning in. "I really liked this day," he whispers. "Besides the time we weren't together."

"Same," I say.

He's locked in on my eyes, and he's daring me to say something more. I have too many over-the-top feelings spinning around my head to get a single one out. He reaches out and moves my hair off of my shoulder. The tips of his fingers trace my neck and then my jaw, and I let out a breath that comes from a place I didn't even know about. He says, "Tomorrow." Another promise.

~~~~~~~

CHAPTER 23

WHEN I WAKE UP, SAMMY IS IN MARLA'S BED AND
Marla is in Dan's. I get dressed for my run in the
bathroom and find Dan outside with Cormack, Paula, and
Connor. Ruby's dancing on the lawn.

Dan sees me and springs from his chair. "Hi. Here. Sit."
He motions to his chair, so I do.

"Why are you up so early?" I ask him.

"Sammy came in crying about something—I can't believe you slept through that." He drags another chair over
next to me.

"I can't either. I'm a pretty light sleeper."

"Not really," Dan says, and Cormack smiles.

"Not really what?" I ask.

"You were laughing in your sleep," Cormack says. "Dan
tells me you woke Marla up too."

"That is truly embarrassing," I say. I am not at all embarrassed. It surprises me so much that I scan my body for
the normal feelings—tight in the chest, hot in the face.
Nothing. I sometimes laugh in my sleep, and I love that.

Paula has a list. "So tonight's the party, of course. I need you guys there by five, just as an extra set of hands. I'm going to regret letting all the kids come, but that's how Reenie wants it."

Sammy wanders out and climbs into Dan's lap, nearly asleep still. He settles his cheek into Dan's chest and Dan rubs his little back and my heart does a funny flip.

Paula goes on. "Jane, you're in charge of managing this." She motions to Dan like he's a mess to be cleaned up.

"I don't need to be managed," Dan says. "I'm going to hate it, but I'll do it."

"That's the show of confidence we need," Paula says and shoots me a look.

Aidan comes out with Katie in his arms and hands her to me. I love that he does this. I am the holder of Katie, the getter of muffins, the baker of pies.

"Paula and I are both off today," Aidan says. "We were going to head to the bird preserve with the girls if you guys want to come."

"No," Dan says. It comes out so fast that it makes Aidan laugh.

"Okay," he says, with his hands up.

"Sorry, no." Dan softens. "Jane and I are doing other stuff today." He's not meeting my eye.

I say, "Well, we were going to go to the beach to find Jack."

Dan looks at me. The look says so many things so loudly that I'm afraid everyone hears. I smile at him, just with my eyes, over Katie's head.

"And then we've got a bunch of other stuff," he says. "So no birds for us."

Aidan and Paula exchange a look, and Paula says to me, "Okay, just make sure he shows up,"

"Tomorrow it'll all be over," Aidan says.

"And tomorrow we're all going surfing," Connor says. "Six a.m. I borrowed the Murphys' truck. You in?"

"Sure." Dan gives Sammy a squeeze and puts him down. "Fine."

"Let's go see if we can find Jack," I say. "Maybe we'll get pulled into a tug-of-war."

"Perfect," Dan says.

JACK'S NOT SURFING. The beach is crowded, and I suspect he either came, saw the full parking lot, and left, or decided not to come for fear of the crazy woman who threw a drink at his car. Regardless, I'm a little relieved. I don't have the purposeful focus I had when I got off the plane Monday. My mission to get this movie made at all costs has changed to a mission to get as close as humanly possible to Dan. I'll psych myself up to talk to Jack tomorrow, but today I just want to feel the way the sand heats the bottoms of my feet as Dan takes my hand and leads me down the beach.

I turn to him as we walk, and his eyes are asking if this is okay, holding hands in the light of day. I squeeze his hand in response. I get the sense that he's feeling as shy as I am about this new thing between us. For a second, I think I understand why they refer to the feeling in my stomach as "butterflies." It's fragile and new and unfathomably beautiful. I have never had butterflies before. "Butterflies on the Beach" should be a love song.

Dan lays out our towels on the sand, edges touching this time. He pulls off his shirt, and I take off my T-shirt and shorts. Dan lies on his towel and reaches a hand up to pull me down. In one movement, I am lying on my side next to him.

"You feel okay about the toast?" I ask.

"No," he says. He takes my hand again, and I resist the urge to roll over on top of him. I wish the salty air were a blanket I could pull up over us. "I have anticipatory embarrassment about how goofy the whole thing's going to be."

"The singing I can't quite picture, no offense. But let's say you fake your way through the song. What's the part of the toast you have to say?"

I regret the question because he has to let go of my hand to pull out his phone. He reads something and groans. "It's a poem. It all rhymes. God, I hate Connor sometimes. Everyone has a stanza about why they love our parents, my part's last. Probably so they can just end it if I can't get it out."

"Let me read it." He hands me his phone. It's very sweet. Brian talks about how they are so welcoming to people, Connor says they're hardworking, Finn likes their sense of humor, and Aidan loves the way they love to eat. "Okay, here's your part: 'And the best thing about our father and mother, we love how they love each other.'" We both groan at the same time. "I wouldn't want to say that either," I say.

He turns onto his side and runs two fingers up my arm.

I marvel at the fact that I can be simultaneously wearing this bathing suit and feeling this sexy. "For my brothers, nothing's too corny or too loud. The song will be over the top, guaranteed. And this horrible toast will go over like Churchill delivered it. People adore them."

"Well, that's good," I say, "If everyone loves the Finnegan brothers and their shenanigans, the stakes are low for this toast."

"Not for me." His fingers reach my shoulder and trace the strap of my bathing suit. He smiles at me and I know we're both mentally back in that car.

The answer to every question his eyes are asking is *Yes*, but I can't get the word out. I close my eyes and think of how fearless Dan is about saying what's in his heart. I turn to him with this in mind but am completely distracted by the way he's looking at me. I feel a shift, a total reversal of what my type is. What if my type is messy and good? What if my type is an unmade bed on a Sunday morning?

I cover my eyes with the back of my hand and refocus. "Your toast," I say. "Okay, try this. Don't be a Finnegan brother. Say your own thing. What's the thing you admire about your parents?"

"They're really in love."

"It's nice, the way they are together," I say.

"Yeah, on her birthday, he sings her this old song. It's terrible, but she cries every time. But it's more the everyday stuff, like the way they're always aware of where the other one is in the room, like they're each other's house keys. It's so many small things, but all together it's so strong. I guess they're the thing I aspire to be. I'd like to find that kind of love."

"What's that?"

"They're the thing I aspire to. I'd like to find that kind of love."

"Does that feel natural to say?"

"Yes, but it doesn't rhyme."

"Dan, you guys are too old to rhyme. Connor's trying to turn the Finnegan brothers into a vaudeville show."

He laughs and leans a bit closer to me.

"Just say the thing you want to say."

The air changes and he holds my gaze. "The thing I want to say?" His eyes are soft, and I feel like there's something he wants to tell me. "Wait, you mean to my parents." He looks over my shoulder and then back at me. "They're the thing I aspire to, and I'd like to find that kind of love."

"Perfect," I say.

"Okay," he says and then touches my cheek. I didn't know you could be starving for someone to touch your cheek, but I must have been. "Thanks."

"Sure," I say. He leans in and kisses me. He is sea air and sunscreen, and there's nothing in the world more natural than us together like this in front of all of Oak Shore. I feel the warmth of his mouth all over my body and I try to memorize the feeling. This thing with Dan is something I don't believe in, but it's growing inside my heart anyway.

CHAPTER 24

~~~

WE GO HOME AND I TAKE THE FIRST SHOWER. WHEN
I'm back in the bedroom and Dan's in the shower, I
think of my mom and how absolutely dreamy she'd find
Dan. She'd call him devastatingly handsome and close her
eyes as she described him to her friends. *Like a model, but
also a firefighter,* she'd say. And that wouldn't be too far off.
I'm smiling at this thought because it gives me a little perspective on what it would be like to be my mom, a believer.
To really let yourself get excited about big love. I think I
would like to be that brave.

I text her: I hate that I'm missing movie night.

She replies right away: No worries! I'm headed to the
Hollywood Bowl

Me: Well that's better than movie night

Mom: Nothing is

Which is exactly what I was hoping she'd say.

I dry my hair in the bedroom so as not to hog the bathroom. I'm not doing a complicated straightening thing be-

cause I'm sort of over it and the humidity will undo all that work the second I walk outside.

Dan comes in from the bathroom in just jeans, towel-drying his hair. His white towel covers his head and shoulders, leaving his torso on full display with no one there to stop me from running my eyes down the ridges of his abdomen. I keep drying the same clump of hair, hypnotized by the inch of skin just over his top button. Is there a zipper under that button, or is it buttons all the way down? I need to know. When he tosses the towel on the floor, his hair is standing straight up. He turns to me and tries for an *oof* face, knowing full well how crazy his hair looks, but he catches me staring. He gives me a smile that tells me he'd be happy to answer all of my questions about his zipper. I smile back, but the din of the hair dryer in my ear keeps me from saying anything. He sits down on my bed and pulls a blue T-shirt over his head. He doesn't speak, and neither do I. When I turn off the hair dryer, the room is completely silent.

We're looking at one another. I could take three steps forward and I'd be right in his personal space.

"You got your line?" I ask. No one kills sexual tension like I do.

"I do now, I probably won't when I'm up there all wrapped up in the chaos. I really hate this stuff." He runs his hands through his wet hair.

"Is that your date outfit?" he asks.

I look down, and I am, in fact, in jeans and the same blue-and-white blouse I'd picked out for our ill-fated first date.

"Yes."

"Probably would have gone well," he says. "Though I like that white dress too." He's picturing me naked—I can see it in his eyes. It's my turn to speak, something flirty, I think, but I have the sense of not knowing exactly where I am. My body is telling me that we are alone in this house and that one step forward would change everything, though inside my heart, I already feel like everything's changed. I am on a tightrope made of something as fine as a spider's web, and I want to be light enough to cross.

I say, "We should go."

CHAPTER 25

THE PARTY IS AN ACTUAL BLAST. FINN HAS SURPRISED
everyone by getting a guy with a guitar to perform old-
ies up on the little karaoke stage. There are definitely a hundred people crammed into the pub—Reenie and Cormack's
friends, the brothers' friends. All the kids are there, babies
passed around. We eat mini hamburgers with bacon butter
and pigs in a blanket. Irish nachos and spinach salad with
warm hard-boiled eggs. I'm drinking red wine from a jelly
jar, and it's delicious.

I talk with Marla and Paula and the guy from Chippy's
Diner and forget that Sammy is on my hip. He's resting his
head on my shoulder and gripping my waist with his legs.
It feels primal, like we're primates. When he goes heavy,
Marla takes him and lays him down in an unoccupied booth
in the back. She returns to us and jumps back into the conversation.

Dan finds us and places a hand on the small of my back.
It's something you might do when you approach a person in

a group. But it feels like something altogether new. I lean into his hand. "So the nightmare's about to start," he says, indicating the small stage.

"It'll be fine," I say. "Or at least quick."

The guitarist takes a break, and Cormack and Reenie take the mic onstage. Cormack tells the story of meeting Reenie on the beach in Oak Shore when she was dating someone named Wallace. He talks through the various underhanded ways he tried to steal her away while Reenie holds his hand and laughs. This feels like wealth, I think. This is the thing you save up for. You live your whole life so that you can be surrounded by too many people in too small of a room and tell the story of how it all happened. An old ache flares up in my heart, not for me but for my mom. I want to tell my mom that I'm starting to believe in love but that I think it's different from what she's described, that it's quieter and more powerful. But we've been lying to each other for so long about love, I would never know where to start.

Cormack raises a glass to the crowd but holds Reenie's eyes in his, and I feel the same shift in my heart that *True Story* gives me. It's a nudge from someplace buried, turning my head toward actual evidence of true love. I wish my mom were here, and I realize what I've wanted from *True Story* all along. I want to make this movie so my mom can see it. I want her to watch that love story and give up her tireless pursuit of the Hollywood kind. Love isn't a helicopter ride to Catalina; it's everyday care and treating the other person like they're your house keys. I want this movie to say the thing I can't say. *Mom, you're chasing your own lie.*

Dan comes up behind me and puts his hand on my waist. I want to tell him what I just realized about the movie, and I wonder if he loves it because it reminds him of his parents. But Brooke is walking toward us. She's in a short pink dress that feels both effortless and sexy. I turn around and watch Dan watch her.

"Danny!" she says. The greeting is too enthusiastic for a person you saw two days ago. She throws her arms around his neck, and I want to ask her—politely, not like a crazy person—to stop it. I see her bury her face in his chest and smell him, and boy, I do not like this one bit.

"Hey," Dan says, taking her hands and removing them from his neck. "You remember Jane, and do you know Finn's wife, Eileen?"

"Of course, hi," Brooke says. Eileen gives her a greeting that makes me think she's as happy to see her as I am. The music has started again, and Brooke is moving her hips in a way that suggests to me that she's a good dancer. Like she has natural rhythm and the confidence to follow it. "Dance with me," she says and takes Dan's hand.

"Still don't dance," he says. "Can I get anyone a drink?"

The music stops again and Connor has the mic. "Can my brothers please report to the stage." Everyone cheers.

Dan turns to me and I touch his forearm. It's not even subtle, and I kind of hope Brooke sees this blatant caress because I'm a total maniac now. "This is going to be totally fine," I say.

"Let's just hope for quick," he says. He makes his way to the stage and lines up with his brothers. Reenie and

Cormack are radiant with joy just seeing them all up there. The music starts, and they sing "Loves Me Like a Rock." Dan is truly the outlier. His brothers make a big show of fighting for the microphone to sing about how their mama loves them, as if they're fighting for her attention and that's part of the joke. Dan hangs back, and Brian puts his arm around him and pulls him to the mic. I see firsthand how much Dan's brothers don't want him to be different. They're a pack and they want him to fold in. And as Dan stands there, arms around Brian and Finn, letting them sway him to the music but not singing a single word, I understand why he doesn't live here. I understand how he loves them all fiercely, but needs space to be who he is. He doesn't want to be mistaken for someone he's not. He matters too much.

The crowd erupts with applause. Reenie has tears in her eyes, and Cormack has his arm around her. What a thing it must be to stay together for forty years. I wonder if there was ever a moment where they wanted to call it, walk away. I like thinking there was and that they stuck it out to get to here anyway.

Brian has the mic. "I want to wish our parents a happy fortieth wedding anniversary." Cheers all around. "We've written a little poem for you guys, just to prove once and for all that we all know how to read." Laughs. He starts with his stanza, then Finn, then Connor. I see Dan's face go serious when Aidan takes the mic. I'm standing off to the side by the bar, and I move toward the center of the crowd. Aidan hands him the mic and he doesn't say anything. When his eyes find me in the crowd, they lock on me. I put my hand on my heart. He nods and takes a breath, then smiles at his parents. "My parents are people I aspire to be like. And I hope to find love like theirs one day." The room is quiet and he turns to his brothers. "And, you guys, we're too old to rhyme," he says, and everyone laughs, raucous surprised laughs. My smile is so big that I have to cover it with my hand. Dan got up with his brothers, but didn't blend in. I love that he's used my joke. A bubbly kind of happiness floods my body as I watch him laugh with his brothers onstage. It feels good to want something for someone else, something that has nothing to do with you, just because you care about them. And I wonder if this is what love is. I rest my hand on my heart to feel if it's changed. I think it has. I have.

The music starts playing and the party resumes, people moving toward the bar, toward the bathrooms, to find a seat. I lose track of Dan as soon as he's off the stage. I'm just standing there alone with a giant grin on my face, so I make my way to the back booth to check on Sammy. It feels like fresh air being at the back of the room, far from the music. Sammy is lying on his back with his arms over his head, sleeping the sleep of the gods. I lean on the booth and take a breath, wanting to see Dan.

Just as I think this, he's walking out of the crowd toward me. He hands me a beer and says, "It was okay, right?" He's smiling too and I can tell he's a little revved up.

"You were great," I say. "Even a little joke at the end." We clink our beers and take a sip.

"I wasn't even trying to make a joke, but I remembered

you said that and it's true, so I said it. And they laughed. I can see why you like that. I mean, the singing was horrible." He takes a sip of his beer. "But the laugh was okay."

"It was perfect," I say.

"Thank you." He's looking down at me and his face is wide open. He is feeling something and he doesn't care if I know. He wants me to know. He's just laying it out there, right in his eyes. I would like to be that person for one day, just to see what it feels like. *This is who I am,* Dan says in everything he does. The power of that is overwhelming. I want to be able to take it in without changing the subject when I get nervous or scared. I reach out and take his hand, and he takes a step toward me.

A little hand tugs on mine, and I look down to see Ruby staring up at me. She's in an orange sundress and she's made a cape out of a white napkin.

I squat down to her without letting go of Dan's hand. "Love the cape," I say.

"It's time," she says. "For my dance. On the stage."

"Oh," I say. "I've seen you practicing."

"I wanted to. But I'm shy now." Her navy eyes fall. I look up at Dan for direction, but he hasn't heard any of this.

"How can I help?" I ask.

"I need the right music, and I don't know how to tell the man." She's on the verge of tears—that's the only thing here that's entirely clear to me.

"Okay, let's go together," I say and squeeze her hand. I stand up into Dan's personal space. We are once again too close, and the effect is not wearing off. My eyes go to his lips, which have parted the tiniest bit. "We need to go do something," I tell his mouth. "Ruby and me."

Ruby drags me through the crowd up to the stage where the guitar player is on a break. Ruby grabs my eyes and motions to him with her head.

"Hi," I say. "This is Ruby. And she has a song request, she's going to do a dance."

He smiles at her like she's the most adorable thing ever, which for sure she is. "Okay, great, let's see if I know it."

She whispers something we can't hear, so I squat down and give her my ear. "'Let It Go,'" she whispers again. This is a problem. There is no way this guy with a single guitar is going to be able to pull off that song.

I stand and act more hopeful than I am. "Any chance you know 'Let It Go'? Like from *Frozen*?

He laughs. "Not on my song list. Sorry."

I look down at Ruby, who is definitely going to cry. I can picture her now waving her arms at the potato fields in the exact rhythm of that song. It's clear that the breaststroke motions she was making to cut through the air in front of her are timed to the chorus. I imagine Reenie and Cormack in a state of complete heart explosion watching her dance on their special night.

"What if I download it on my phone? Can you connect it to your speakers?"

"Finn probably can," he says. "I'm going on a break anyway."

I nod at Ruby and give her hand a squeeze.

When Finn's hooked my phone up to the speakers, it's

just Ruby and me on the stage. "So introduce us," she says. Her voice falters, and she is worrying the knot of her napkin cape. I know that she's very close to backing out, so I do it.

I take the microphone. "Everyone?" I say. "Hello?" The crowd quiets and turns my way. Dan is leaning on the bar with Brooke by his side, but I'm the one he's smiling at. "I'm Jane. We have a real treat for Reenie and Cormack tonight. An original dance choreographed and performed by their granddaughter Ruby." The crowd cheers, and she looks up at me, expression still shaky.

I put the microphone back in the stand and cue up the song. I squat down to her and whisper, "Ready?"

"Sort of," she says.

"I'm never more ready than that," I say and she smiles.

I press play, and the song starts. I step off to the side, but Ruby doesn't move. Like not one part of her body is in motion, not even a twitch. She's actually frozen. Two hundred eyes are on us, and I can feel every single one. I know that a core memory is forming here, one way or another. She's either going to see herself as the kid who got everyone's attention and choked onstage, or she's going to see herself as the kid who absolutely made her grandparents' party. I don't want her to look back and feel shame; shame has been holding me back forever. I don't want her carrying anything but total appreciation for how brave she is. I stand off to the side and watch her, a statue, for the eternity of the first two rounds of the piano intro. Dan is watching in horror from the bar—it's like we are reenacting his worst nightmare for an audience. Cormack and Reenie are fine and probably have reasonable expectations of a six-year-old. I do not. I cannot let this happen.

As Idina Menzel starts to sing about the snow going white on a mountain night, I step onto center stage next to Ruby and try to get her to start to dance. I move my feet in the step-together-step rhythm I've been watching each morning. I take her hand and raise our joined hands high as they can go and then raise my other arm high in the air in the exaggerated slow motion that made her body look like dune grasses in the wind. Ruby starts doing the step-together-step in the tiniest way, and it is a relief, an actual lifetime of relief, for me to see her take a step past her fear. I smile down at her as the chorus is coming because I know I'm going to have to drop her hand. You can't do the swimming-forward motion holding hands. When I do, Ruby freezes up again. Her eyes go wide with fear, like I'm going to let her sink, and I need to show her that she won't.

I step up to the microphone and start to sing *"Let it go!"* over and over again, because there is no other option and because the message seems so completely on point. I haven't heard my voice in a microphone in decades, and it takes a few lines to warm up. I focus on the audience, but I can feel Ruby watching me. I want her to see that this is fun, that it's okay sharing a big part of yourself even when you don't know how it will be received. Even if some might say it's completely ridiculous. I sing the chorus again and breast-stroke my arms through the air. It feels good and comes from a place so deep inside of me that I can almost hear the voice of my younger self sing along with me.

That voice is actually Ruby's.

I stop singing, and her voice grows louder. *"Let it go, let it go."* She's moved on to arm movements that are more complicated than I had understood from across the lawn. I step to the side of the stage and watch. She is completely lost to the song, waving her six-year-old arms to bring the heavens down to this crowded pub. I catch Reenie and Cormack wiping tears. When the song is over, she bows to thunderous applause, and I am sure that was the best thing I've ever seen in my life.

Ruby gives me a look that I will never forget. *Yes*, it says, *I did that.* She hugs me around my hips, and I feel the ripple of her curls in my hands.

Paula makes her way to the stage and Ruby jumps into her arms. I am the only one on the stage now, and I look for Dan in the crowd. I think I see him standing too close to Brooke, but it's Brian.

"Wow." Dan's reaching up to help me off the stage.

"She was amazing," I say and take his hand.

The guitar man is back onstage, warming up with a slower song.

"That was—" Dan starts. "I don't know what that was. But it was my favorite thing. We'll always remember that."

Always. "Always" feels so good, as a word, as a concept. All ways. It feels like we are the only people in this room, and it's too much, looking at him. I turn around toward the stage and watch the guitar guy play but take Dan's hand in mine. I am not going to change the subject or mix up the message. I feel it now, the thing they write songs about.

"I like this one," Dan says. He's behind me and leans in as he speaks so that I can feel where his chest presses against my shoulders. I lean back into him in response, which probably speaks volumes but is the quietest conversation I've ever had.

"This is from the nineties," I say.

"Feels like a prom song."

"Prom song," I say and lean back into him.

"We should dance," he says and turns me around.

"You don't dance," I say. My face is at his neck level, and I raise my eyes to his, which are heavy on mine. He takes my other hand and then moves them up to his shoulders. He puts his hands around my waist, just barely pulling me toward him, and I move my hands inside the collar of his shirt. It's a small move, from his shoulders to his neck, but I can feel his breathing falter. We are moving, I think, more toward each other than from side to side, but we are moving almost imperceptibly.

"Maybe I do," he says into my ear.

"Yes," I say.

"I think we might have danced," he says into my hair. "On our second date, if we'd had one. Does that sound right?"

I like this game. I nod and lift my head so that I can feel his stubble on my cheek. "I would have accelerated my dress protocol for our second date. I think I would have worn a red one."

"I saw you in that dress." His breath is on my neck. "In the elevator." Then he pulls away and tilts my head up to him. "Is it possible that was just a week ago?" His eyes are black in the dim light of the pub.

"Seems impossible, but here we are dancing, so anything's possible," I say. I lower my head so that I can close my eyes and feel his cheek against mine.

"Would you have let me kiss you?" he asks. "On the second date. In the red dress."

"Kissing is for the third date," I say to his neck. "But probably. Yes."

He laughs and pulls me a bit closer. "Good."

The song's over, and we stay like this without any music at all. I love the feel of his hands on my back and his chest pressed against me, and if he's not going to make any move to stop, I'm not either.

CHAPTER 26

"WELL, TONIGHT WAS A BIG SUCCESS," FINN SAYS. We're seated in a booth at the back of the pub—all the brothers, plus Paula and me. "We got a live performance of *Frozen*, and Mom cried three times."

"Janey and Ruby let it go all right," says Aidan.

I raise my beer to him. We really did.

"And Dan with the ad-lib," Connor says. "You can write the next toast."

Dan shrugs. "Maybe I will."

"It's weird you all look so much alike," I say. I meet all of their eyes but not Dan's. He is sitting next to me in the booth, his leg pressed against mine, and I can feel the heat of those few inches of contact move through the rest of my body.

Connor leans forward, both hands on the table. "This is the part where you're trying to decide who to fall in love with. Janey, make your own decision, but you should know I'm the only one with money," he says.

Brian and Finn laugh, and Aidan chucks a balled-up napkin at him. "Slick. I'm pretty sure you're married."

"Doesn't mean Janey here isn't regretting her choices." They all laugh that comfortable way you do when you've tapped back into a running joke, and I think about love and how it might be real and how, if it is, I'm not sure it's a choice.

I half expect Dan to chime in with a barb or a happy family memory of one of the brothers stealing someone's girl. But he just shakes his head. "You guys never stop."

"He's just trying to force the issue," says Finn. They're all quiet for a change, as if considering the issue. It occurs to me that I might be the issue.

PAULA DRIVES AIDAN, Dan, and me back to the house. We take turns using the bathroom. I'm second, after Paula, so I go to the kitchen and get Dan and me each a glass of water after I finish. He likes it cold out of the refrigerator, and I like it room temperature from the tap. I sit on my bed in my shorty pajamas. The room still holds some of the charge from when we were here before the party. I stare at the space in front of me where he stood shirtless, and I almost reach out to touch the air where he was. I don't know how to get back to the wild making out we did in the car now that I am feeling all these feelings. It's all too much. I pull my knees to my chest and listen to the water run, the toilet flush, the door open.

"I got you some water," he says. "Oh, you did too,

thanks." He lines up the glasses, one cold, one not, by our painting on the windowsill between us, and sits on his bed. He's in his blue T-shirt and boxer shorts. His eyes dip to my legs. He gets up and turns out the light. The room fills with moonlight, and he sits back down on his bed. I rest my chin on my raised knees, and we're just looking at each other, not knowing how to cross the electrified space between us.

"Fun tonight," I say because I have to say something. The silence is too much.

"Yeah," he says and leans forward. He runs his hand down the back of my calf and wraps his fingers around my ankle. His thumb presses just below my anklebone and sends a current straight up the inside of my leg. It terrifies me that he can turn me to jelly with the press of a thumb. I look up, and he is watching me, gaze heavy. He pulls slightly on my ankle, the way your waltzing partner might press on your back, just a bit, to direct you. My body responds by going to him. I am up and on top of him, my arms around his neck as we fall onto his bed. Just like that, in one smooth motion, like I'm smoke rising from a blown-out candle.

We land side by side facing one another. He pulls me close and wraps his leg around mine. I'm overwhelmed by the feel of his bare leg on mine, his hair between my fingers, my chest pressed against him. We are braided together, on this thin stretch of earth where my skin is liquid and my breath has gone uneven.

"Finally," he says, so much want in his eyes.

"I think this is our fourth date," I say, sliding one hand from his hair to his shoulders, memorizing the trail of muscles down his arms. "This is the one where I find out what's wrong with you." His mouth is a whisper away from mine and his breath on my lips is deliciously warm.

"I'm broke," he says, unbuttoning just the top "Hug Me" button of my pajama top. We're well beyond a hug, and I shiver as we both watch his fingers trace my collarbone. I am dancing on the edge of something dangerous as I curve my hips into him. "I turn down work that will get me unbroke. My oven hasn't worked for six months, and I haven't called the super."

"What else?" I barely get it out as he undoes another button. "Kiss Me," I think this one says.

"I'm always losing my driver's license," he says, eyes back on mine but undoing a third button. "I spend half my life at the DMV."

"That's terrible." I run my fingers along that inch of skin between his boxers and his shirt that had hypnotized me earlier. He catches his breath, or maybe it's me. I grab the hem of his shirt and pull it off. His head emerges, gaze heavy on me. I keep my eyes on his as I run my hands over his shoulders, his chest, and down the ridges of his stomach, tracking when his lids flutter closed, his breath hitches. Everything that looked like marble is warm and buzzing with need under my touch.

"You really don't hate me anymore," he says, breath ragged as he undoes my last button and tosses my top to the floor. He takes a second to look at me, and I feel the heat of his gaze everywhere—I think I might be true and beautiful.

He runs a hand over my breast and smiles at the sound I make.

"I really don't," I whisper.

He rolls on top of me and kisses me, finally, and his mouth is an open door to the rest of him. Strong and sure and capable of undoing me. The liquid warmth of his kiss, combined with the weight of his chest on mine, sends a wave of sensation through my body that's almost unbearable. I wonder if it could kill me, the depth of this kiss and all that bare skin. He stops and looks at me, eye to eye. My heart is racing, and I feel embarrassed by how much I want him.

"You are just so . . ." he starts to say and then kisses me, even more deeply. My hands graze the soft stubble of his cheek. He pulls away, his lips the barest brush against mine, and all my nerve endings are suddenly in my lips. Heat pulses from where his mouth is on mine to where my hips can't stop pressing up into him. He takes a breath as if he's going to finish his sentence, but then runs his fingers down my neck and kisses me again, a claiming kiss. It finishes the sentence for him. I am so beautiful. I am so wanted. Inside this kiss I am all the things I have believed I am not.

"Do you feel that?" I ask.

"Yes," he says, mouth on my neck. "This feels like something I've never done before." His hands clutch my hips and my legs wind around his back. Another current moves through my body and I take a sharp breath. This feels different in every way. This feels like something there's no coming back from. He rests his forehead on mine, his breath jagged.

"You are just . . ." he starts again. "I had this feeling, the day when we fought about that stupid movie, that I'd lost something I didn't even understand."

"Stop calling my movie stupid," I say, tightening my legs around him.

"Well, it was," he says.

"You talk so much for an introvert." I keep my eyes on the place where his chest meets mine. I run my hands down the sides of his ridiculous stomach. He takes in a breath, and I feel wild with power from being wanted like this.

"Everything is different with you, Jane. I feel like I never shut up." My fingers curl inside the top of his boxers and his breath hitches. It might be my new favorite sound. His mouth grazes my ear, my neck, my breasts. My mind blurs at the sensations, his hands trailing up my legs, liquid heat everywhere. My pajama shorts are at my ankles, then someplace with his boxers, and there is no turning back. The want I am feeling has consumed me, and, like fire, it's turned me into something light enough to blow away. I forget to be terrified by how easily I'm slipping into this moment and how easily it can be taken away from me. Dan rests his forehead on mine and steadies his breath. I can feel how fast my heart's beating. His eyes scan my face and the length of my body like he's making a digital print, and tears prick the back of my eyes. I'm going to have sex with this intense, beautiful man, and nothing is ever going to be the same. He has been unstitching me since we met—my rules, my pretending, and now my heart. His eyes settle on mine. "You're just . . ." he starts again, but then kisses me so deeply that my mind gives up listening.

There's a condom just out of reaching distance and a moment when we nearly roll off the bed. He asks me if I'm okay as we right ourselves. I'm exceptionally okay and wonder if this is the first time I've ever been in bed with a man without my mask. I am unconcerned about how I look or sound; I'm just a mass of nerve endings, falling into this thing with Dan. Tonight I felt what it is to want someone else's happiness more than anything. I felt what it is to lend someone else your bravery and then to be brave yourself. I want to tell Dan that I think this is what love is. I want to ask him about it as we move our bodies together, but then my thoughts quiet and I am nothing but my senses. His hands gripping at my hips, cupping my backside, the softness of his lips against my ear sending electricity straight to my core. As the intensity builds, he whispers my name, and I feel as if the last stitch in my heart has been snipped, and I unravel in his arms.

"I'M TOTALLY PAST the fourth date," he says after. We're lying on our sides, facing one another, legs entwined. His hand makes a lazy path up and down my back.

"Let's see. We went to the beach, the crab shack, and then the museum. The party. Yeah, I think you made it." I reach out and try to organize his hair. It pops back in all directions, and it makes me smile. I have this thought bubbling up that I've gotten to the place I was trying to go, but without trying at all.

"Yeah, this was a good date. And you're acting exactly the right amount bored," he says, and I laugh. My arms rope around his neck and my leg creeps back up over his hip, in the place, it seems, it was designed to stay forever. I am having an avalanche of thoughts: that I've never had fun during sex before, that I want every moment of my life after this to be the same exact perfect mix of intensity and fun, that I understand why this is better than insta-love. It's the time spent digging that makes unearthing the treasure so satisfying. I desperately want this to be the end of the story. We feel like this and it just stays. I can't even imagine how awful it would be to lose a person like Dan.

And then I think of my mom. And all the pretending.

"What?" he asks.

"Are you reading my mind again?" I scrunch my face up to hide what's there.

He laughs. "Don't be conflicted, okay?"

"This just isn't a thing that I do," I say.

He runs his hands up my hip and along my side, and I shiver. "It is now."

"Don't take it back."

"I won't," he says.

CHAPTER 27

THERE'S KNOCKING ON HEAVEN'S DOOR. THAT'S WHAT I think when I wake up in Dan's arms and the first rays of sunlight creep through the little window. Dust particles fly around in the light, and I have a sense of being in the up-side down. I have spent a lifetime being on guard. I have worked so hard mastering how to be, and here I am flipped inside out. All of my raw bits are on the outside, and lying here with Dan, I am sleepy and sexy and playful. I rest my hand on his chest and memorize the rhythm of his beating heart. I have the strangest feeling that I want to protect him while also climbing inside of him for safety. It makes me think of Reenie and Cormack; it makes me think of *True Story*.

These are my thoughts as the knocking gets louder and the talking starts. It's the brothers.

"He's locked the fucking door," one of them says. Dan groans and tightens his grip on me.

"Knew it," says another.

"Well, obviously." Knocking turns to banging. "Danny, get up, we're going surfing. Ten minutes."

"He's totally whipped. He's not coming."

"Get your ass up, Danny." Banging. This sounds a little like Connor, but honestly, they all blend into one.

Dan kisses me. "I am in hell," he says. "They'll never leave and never shut up."

"Go," I say.

"You want me to go?"

"Never," I say. I want to take it back, it's too much too soon, but he smiles like he feels the same way.

More banging on the door. "Okay, I'll go. Will you sleep?" he asks. He's arranging my hair behind my shoulder like he's memorizing me. I run my fingers along his string bracelet.

"I'll try," I say.

He gets up out of bed, and it's the first time I've seen him standing and naked. I reach out to touch the side of his leg, all ropy muscles carved out of marble by an overzealous craftsman.

"Okay, assholes, I'm coming. Back away from the door and get me a coffee." He puts on swim trunks and a sweatshirt and kneels by the bed to kiss me goodbye. "Promise you'll be here when I get back."

"Promise," I say.

I fall asleep imagining them all in the borrowed truck, busting on Dan for our locked door. There is nothing about this week or this morning that I will ever forget. The periwinkle blue of his bathing suit, the seasoning on the kebab. The whipped cream in my coffee and the way he watched me drink it. The watercolors and the slow dance.

I WAKE FROM a deep sleep at eight and immediately re-member why I'm naked.

It's Saturday, the day of the music festival, and our last chance to track down Jack. I check my body for nerves and don't find any. I feel soft toward myself, and I wonder if it even matters if I talk to Jack at all. But it does; I owe a debt of gratitude to *True Story* for opening my heart to the waves of feeling that are running through me right now. It's like I've seen through a little wormhole to an alternate universe where this kind of love exists and I could have it. I want my mom to know this too.

I call Clem. "Are you up?"

"It's five a.m., you'd better be dead," she says.

"Sorry. I know. You're never going to believe who had sex."

"No!"

"Yes!" I let out a little squeal for emphasis.

This is obviously big news, and she must agree because I can hear her sit up in bed. "Okay, please tell me it was Dan and not Jack Quinlan, who you then proposed to after."

"Dan. And mean." But I'm smiling. I wonder if I'll ever stop smiling. "And it wasn't sex sex, it was like love sex. I can't even explain it, Clem."

"Wow. Okay, love sex. This is wow."

"Like fireworks but also talking and I like him so much I can barely function."

"See? A man-bun can be a good look on a lot of guys."

"I made up the man-bun. I was wrong about everything about him and I just had love sex and I'm losing my mind."

When her screaming subsides and we've hung up, I put on my running clothes and find Reenie and Cormack in the kitchen with empty plates and full mugs. They're sharing the newspaper. The ordinariness of it takes my breath away. Ruby's in the backyard singing to the potatoes.

"Good morning," I say.

"Jane," they say together and put down their papers.

"Sorry about those jackasses this morning," Cormack says. "I'm glad Danny gave in because that could have gone on for hours."

"I went right back to sleep," I say. This would have been fine to say yesterday, when I was sleeping in my own bed in my own pink pajamas, but now I feel like I've drawn them a picture of something sordid. While I feel the color rise to my face, Reenie gets me a cup of coffee and invites me to sit.

"That was quite a party," I say.

"It was," Reenie says. "Just perfect. And what's the plan for today?"

"I don't know about today, but tonight's the festival, so it's sort of mission accomplished or bust. I feel pretty good though. About that." *About everything.*

"It'll be fine," she says. "Can I make you some pancakes? Eggs? An omelet?"

"Thank you, but I can make myself something after my run."

"You don't want to miss breakfast," she says.

"Most important meal of the day, I hear." I hold my coffee in both hands and take a sip.

"Love happens over breakfast." Cormack smiles at Reenie. "If you want to know the secret to a happy marriage, that's it."

Reenie places her hand over his for just a second. And I wonder how much information transfers between them through a single touch like that after all of these years.

"What does that mean?" I say. "If you don't mind me asking. 'Love happens over breakfast.'"

"It's just something Cormack said when we were first married. Romance happens over dinner. The candlelight, the wine."

"Everyone looks a lot better than they usually do," Cormack says and laughs.

Reenie rolls her eyes. "Well, yes," she says. "That's the romance of it. But at breakfast everything's just as it is, in the light of day. No one wears lipstick to breakfast. And this is where you talk about your day and the part of the roof that might leak this fall. You bring your real self to breakfast."

"Warts and all," says Cormack.

"No one has warts," Reenie says and shakes her head. "Now how about you skip that run and I make you some pancakes?"

I think of the way she melts the butter and warms the syrup in that tiny yellow pan on the stovetop. And I decide not to run.

~~~

CHAPTER 28

R EENIE WANTS TO READ THE SCRIPT, SO I GIVE HER
my laptop. We're sitting side by side in the backyard
looking out at the potato field through the ivy arbor. Ruby's
brought out a box of beads, and we're making bracelets.

"You did a great job last night," I tell her.

"I did," she says. We are in full agreement.

She's stringing beads together in an order that can only
make sense to her. Blue, then blue, then green, then clear.
Mine is in an alternating pattern of three beads per color,
and I think of Louis from the pier with his string bracelets
that are nothing at all. And Dan wears them anyway, little
bits of nothing that are everything.

I watch Reenie out of the corner of my eye. I watch for
a smile on page nineteen when they meet. I watch for her
hand to grip her heart at the end.

The main characters in this script see each other for the
first time in a hotel lobby. Their eyes meet and there's a
spark between them. I think this spark will be conveyed by

a tight camera angle and a ping, some kind of music. It's insta-attraction, but not insta-love. I've never felt an immediate ping. I try to remember my first impression of Dan, and I just remember him being highly focused on photographing a hawk for no reason. He was handsome and disarming in his directness, but I did not feel the ping.

"What's funny?" Reenie asks.

"Did I laugh?"

"You did." She smiles at me.

"Dan's always losing his driver's license." I turn to her to see if I've given too much away, if she can see on my face that this is a piece of information I gleaned just before I had sex with her son. Twice. Her eyes give me an all clear. "I can't imagine doing that more than once. I mean, I'd just make a point to put it back in my wallet."

"You'd think," she says. "He's all heart. And I think that somehow his focus on the beautiful thing distracts him from the practical thing."

"Well, he's terrible at crossing the street."

"Oh, I know," she says. "Keeps me up at night just thinking about it."

I laugh, and she smiles at me.

"Grammy, can you help me tie this?" Ruby asks.

"I can help you," I say.

"No, but it's for you," she says. "You can't tie your own bracelet, you only have two hands."

"True," I say. My heart is in my throat. I want this bracelet like some people want a Tesla. Ruby hands the two ends to Reenie, who adjusts her reading glasses and ties it around my outstretched wrist. It's so quiet, I notice. Like a church kind of quiet where you'd notice someone clearing their throat.

Reenie snips the ends, and I admire the tiny beads of every color laid out in no order at all. "Thank you," I say to both of them.

Ruby climbs into my lap and adjusts my bracelet with tiny fingers. "You have to wear it forever," she says. "That's how these things work."

"I will," I say and mean it.

AIDAN AND DAN are back by nine, and I imagine they smell like sunscreen and salt. I turn around in my chair and see Aidan scavenging for food. Dan is standing at the open patio door. And I feel it, the ping, like a musical note you'd add in postproduction to emphasize how our eyes meet and how our hearts are about to explode. He smiles a little bit, and I can feel it all over my body. I love him. My heart is sending tiny bursts of energy into my body and out into the world. Centuries of songs and plays have been written about this moment. I feel strangely connected not just to Dan, but to everything. It's happening now, over breakfast.

Reenie jumps to her feet. "Feeding time at the zoo," she says to me. She walks into the kitchen and turns on burners and stirs pancake batter. Dan walks toward me and I get up. There would be nothing more natural in the world than to run into his arms at this moment, but I suddenly feel unsure about where we are in this relationship, and we have an audience a few yards away.

He takes my hand and entwines our fingers tightly. "Hi," he says. There's a huskiness to his voice that makes me feel sure again. "Did you run?"

"Nope. I ate pancakes and watched your mom read our brilliant script."

He laughs and takes a step closer to me. "How'd she like it?"

"She didn't say. How was surfing?"

He takes my other hand. "I thought about you the whole time while my brothers gave me shit."

This makes me smile so big that I have to look away from his eyes. He squeezes my hands.

"I got a present," I say and show him my bracelet. He runs his fingers over the beads, and there's something in his expression that makes me feel like he's as moved by it as I am.

"Romeo," Aidan calls. "Bacon's almost gone."

We walk into the kitchen not touching. I can still feel where his hands were in mine, and my urge to reach out and press the palm of my hand onto the back of his T-shirt is fierce.

Paula comes out in her pajamas with Katie in her arms and helps herself to a plate of bacon. "You guys are so loud," she says.

We sit around the table and the ride takes off. That's how it feels, like we are on Mr. Toad's Wild Ride, hands moving forks into mouths, plates being passed. Cormack is punctuating everyone's gripes with *"Let it go! Let it go!"* and this makes Ruby laugh. Laughter bounces around and it's impossible not to get hit by it. So I just strap in and feel it all around me. Dan's sitting across from me and catches my eye. *Ping.* There it is again.

Aidan gets up from the table. "Okay, I've got to get to work for just a few hours. Finn's going to text us if there's any sign of Jack during the day, right?"

"Yes," I say.

"Well, I'm reading the script," Reenie says. "I think it's lovely."

I smile at her. "Thank you."

"Are you two going to go to the beach today?" Cormack asks.

I look at Dan, who doesn't meet my eye. "I'm sort of beached out," he says. "I am going to need a nap first."

WHEN WE'RE BACK in the room, I am pressed against the closed door with my hands in his hair. It is impossible to get adequately close to him as I press my hips into his. We are kissing so deeply that he lets out a sound that I'm sure the whole house has heard. "Shhhhh," I say and he laughs into my mouth.

"Tomorrow we can get out of here and go back to civilization where we can be alone."

"Yes," I say. "I wish we could stay though. I know it's a lot here, but."

He rests his forehead on mine. "Yeah, it's always a lot, but this time it's perfect."

He reaches behind me and locks the door.

THE SUN IS pouring into the room, but neither of us wants to get up to pull the shade. It might be two. I am lying with my head on Dan's shoulder and my hand on his chest, pressing him in place. I'm not sure if he's asleep or just quiet. He runs his hand up my back and I look up to find him watching me.

He says, "I love your jaw. How weird of a thing is that to say, like from one to ten?"

"My jaw?" He runs his fingertips along it, from my ear to my chin. "Maybe ten?"

"I like the way it tenses when you're really mad. And the first time you wanted to murder me, I wanted to murder you right back, but also I was wondering what it would feel like to kiss you there and make you look happy again. Because when you laugh your jaw does this other thing that makes your face look honest. You're beautiful when you're having big emotions."

I smile and kiss his chin. I am certainly having big emotions right now. "That's completely nuts." He loves my jaw. It's not even my best part. "I'm glad I already know everything that's wrong with you," I say.

He laughs. "That was the tip of the iceberg. There's tons more."

"I doubt that. Tell me more horrible things." I run my

fingers down his stomach and think how I've never met a more flawless person.

"I take my clothes off inside out, so it's a pain when they come out of the dryer."

"That's fine. I wasn't ever planning on doing your laundry."

He laughs again. I like the sound of it and the way I can feel his chest vibrate under my cheek. "Okay. I don't like cozy mysteries."

"No."

"I don't. They feel like homework. Ten people, one dead guy, two knives, and some poison. It's like algebra, solve for X. Not relaxing."

"Wow, this is going to be a big problem," I say and pick up my head to kiss him like this is never, ever going to be a big problem. I love lying in Dan's arms. I love feeling him solid next to me. "What else?"

He examines my face before he answers. "Sometimes I worry my dad might be right about me. That I'll never really make it." His eyes soften in a sort of vulnerable way, so I pull back and wait for more.

When he doesn't go on, I say, "He's not right. You're so talented. The way you capture the beauty in things. You've already made it, the money will come."

He tightens his arms around my back, and we're quiet for a bit.

"What's wrong with you?" he asks. "Besides your spotty taste in movies." We are exactly nose to nose. He puts a piece of my hair behind my ear and watches it until he's sure it's stayed. "Tell me."

"Let me see. I have never lost my driver's license. Until recently I've been pretty conscientious about my work."

"Yeah, this is terrible," he says and kisses me, just the softest kiss.

"My closet is a total disaster, and I eat candy in it when I'm stressed." I rest my chin on my hands and look in his eyes. I really do want to be like Dan. I think of how I wish I could get inside his body and grab the part of him that's not afraid to say the true thing. To him, to my mom.

"There it is," he says. "I just saw you think something. What's so serious?"

I close my eyes. I have been in bed with this man for the better part of twenty-four hours. I feel like I've set my membrane to permeable and have taken him all the way in. "Okay," I say and open them. "It's not a small thing. It's more who I am."

"I think you're amazing," he says. He's looking right into my eyes when he says it.

My defenses are gone. I am naked, lying on a naked man. I am in love, all the way out on a limb with Dan, and I feel safe here. So I say it: "The thing about my dad dying? He did die. Three-car pileup on Highway 10. But, before that, he left." It's alarming how naturally it comes out of my mouth, the truth about my dad.

"Why?" he asks. *Brutal.* The word pops up in my head, uninvited, and I wince.

"Me. He didn't want to be my dad anymore." It's the simplest and most complicated truth of my life. He changed his mind. "Like he actually said so."

He tightens his grip around my back. "You didn't tell me that before."

"I've never told anyone, besides Clem. My mom doesn't even know I know."

"Then how do you know?"

"When I was fourteen, I had a really bad day. A boy broke my heart. My mom was still at work, so I couldn't go to her, so I went to her photo box. I went there sometimes for comfort, to flip through the old photos and relive my parents' love story. I think I was looking for clues as to who I was, who my dad was." I remember the pink envelope the birthday card was in at the bottom of the box. I'd seen it before and I don't know why I opened it that day. It was from her friend Carole and was dated a few months before my dad died. There was something written on the blank side about how she was better off without him and her friends would be there to support the two of us, and it made no sense. I raise my head to check Dan's eyes. He's looking at me with so much love that I feel brave all over again.

I reach around my back and take his hand in mine. I bring it up to his chest so that I can see this grounding thing, our hands woven together. "I found a card that led me to look deeper, and there was a letter from him—terrible hand-writing like mine—basically saying, sorry, I can't deal." *Brutal.* It hits me again. He actually used the word "brutal." Being my dad was brutal. That word, on that night, mixed with all the things Jack said earlier in the day—it all hardened like cement around my heart, my identity crystalized. For some reason, I was not a person to be loved.

"I can see why your mom would want you to just think they were happy and he died."

"Yeah. Even before that day when I found out, I always felt like I was missing something, being the kid without a dad. But at least that just felt like tragic bad luck. Something that wasn't my fault. When I found out he actually decided to go—like he was my dad for five years, he knew me really well, and then decided *no, thanks* and took off? It messed with me. I mean, I've known Ruby for a week and I'm going to have a hard time saying goodbye." *I was his daughter,* I don't say. It's a sentence I said out loud over and over again that night. *I was his daughter.*

Dan wipes a tear from my cheek. I never planned to tell this story, and here I am telling it to Dan, who I love. Every impossible thing is in this bed right now. He says, "I can't imagine leaving a kid. I can't imagine leaving you, actually." He's made me smile and I see the gratification in his eyes. "How does your mom not know you know?"

"I never said anything. I put the stuff away and pretended I'd never found it. She kept telling me the Disney version of their love story and I kept pretending I believed it. We are so close, really, but when it comes to this, it's like we live inside a lie. We're protecting each other, I think, but maybe holding each other back?"

"So why don't you stop?"

"Clem wants me to, but I don't know how. I don't want to call her out."

"For lying?"

"For lying about her own reality and mine. She wants me to feel like I matter." My voice cracks, a betrayal that comes from deep inside of me. That was too far, way more than I meant to say. I put my head down on Dan's chest so I can listen to his heart. "That's what's wrong with me, I guess."

"That you don't matter?" I don't want to look at him and I don't know what to say. He doesn't do the thing where he minimizes it and tells me that's silly. He just waits. I don't tell him how much I longed for a dad who would show up at a recital, give me a nickname, and worry about me when I was out late. But I've exposed the hole in me. The tiny paper cut in my heart that I keep trying to fill.

I keep my cheek on his chest and feel the rhythm of his breath. "It's not a logical thing, but that's basically it. So maybe, according to Clem, I obsess about my job and what people think of me so that they'll think I matter. I think I'd like to be worth sticking around for."

"Of course you are," Dan says. "I bet if he lived he would have looked for you when he got older. And he would have been so proud of the way you grew up—funny and beautiful with a gorgeous singing voice. I bet he would have loved you."

"I don't think so," I whisper. I feel a single tear overflow and roll down my cheek onto his chest.

"I find you exceptionally lovable."

I don't know what to say to this. My heart is wide open at this point, and Dan's just placed a gift inside. I roll off of him and onto my side, and he turns onto his so that we can be two heads on a single pillow. Those are beautiful words, I think: "exceptionally lovable." And also: "two heads on a single pillow."

"Why?" I ask. "Like, tell me three things that are lovable."

"The way you ball up your hands when you're mad. The way you want to protect me from seeming like a loser in front of my friends, which is a thing I don't care enough to do myself."

The smile that is about to overtake my face makes me want to cover it with my hands. "One more," I say, because the cracked-open version of me is greedy.

"I like how I can look at you and see a whole world inside your eyes, smart things and funny things that I'll get to hear if I'm lucky. I feel really lucky being here with you like this."

I don't know if there's room in my heart to take that in. I worry that those words will spill like water sloppily poured and seep into the earth where I can never get them back. I am not smiling now because I am so afraid of losing a single drop.

Dan takes my hand in his and moves them both up to his heart. "So. Now you know. You're lovable."

I smile. "Okay."

Dan wipes a tear from my cheek and says, "I'd like to be

the person who could take all of your sad things and make them happy. Like I'd hunt down each one and turn it over."

"I don't think anyone is that person for anyone," I say.

"I don't think so either. But I'd like to be that person for you."

~~~

CHAPTER 29

I T'S THREE O'CLOCK WHEN I SNEAK FROM OUR ROOM
into the shower. I turn on the water and catch myself in
the mirror. I am different. I am beautiful in a way I never
thought possible, like all the way through. My hair is wild,
and it looks like it was meant to be like that. I am the star of
my very own love story, and the entire hair and makeup
team has conspired to make me glow. I dress in jeans and a
black top, sandals with a little heel to give me a boost. I rest
my hands on the sink and lean in toward the mirror. I am
having a moment; I feel happy. I push down the automatic
fear that this will be pulled from me, that I'll be happy and
the world will take it back. I can see myself just under the
surface, this whole version of Jane who can be strong and
funny at the same time. This version who can be completely
herself and still be called lovable. I remember what Dan
said about his budding sense of self being like a lit match on
the beach; mine feels precarious too, and I want to protect it.

I need to bring my strongest, best self if I'm going to ask Jack for a favor. This loose, open version feels like my best self. I smile at her in the mirror. "Nice sideburns, Elvis," I practice. It actually feels good.

I text Clem: Okay this is it. Tonight we actually see Jack, pep talk?

Clem doesn't reply.

Aidan and Paula drive us to the Owl Barn. Dan is holding my hand in the back seat, and I am trying to imagine the warmth of him coating my body like armor. I turn to him and he's already watching me.

"You ready?" he asks.

"I guess. Last chance." I give his hand a squeeze. I am absolutely not ready, but I am happy and raw and in love, I think. There has to be some power in that.

The parking lot is full when we arrive, so we park on a residential street and walk to the Owl Barn. People are milling around everywhere, lining up to get in and buying merch from guys with pushcarts. Finn's left word with security, and we all get in through the side door. Dan and I stand just offstage with the half-baked plan that we will catch Jack as he comes in. Dan's behind me with his arms around my chest as we listen to a band warm up. His head rests on my shoulder.

"I feel like I met a girl on vacation, but I get to take her home with me tomorrow," he says.

I am dying to get from here to tomorrow. I don't necessarily want to leave Long Island, but I do want to get to the other side of this Jack thing, one way or another. I want to move forward with everything, Dan especially, and stop looking back. Telling Dan about my dad has me feeling vulnerable, like someone pulled up the shades and you can see right into my wobbly heart. But there's something about him that makes me think I can wander onto the high wire and be okay.

I turn around so I can see his face. There's so much love there, like he's happy he gets to look at me. "I'm glad this isn't going to be long distance," I say, playing along.

"We'd have to write letters."

"And my mother would hide them."

He laughs. "I have total faith that you'd go to the mailbox for me."

"I would," I say and wrap my arms around his neck. I think what I want to say is *I'd do anything for you.* I can picture him at my house with Clem and me. It's not a daydream kind of scene. We're not sipping champagne under the bougainvillea. We're rinsing dishes in my tile-countered kitchen and laughing. I imagine him pulling sheets out of the dryer. I have never felt this way before, and I want to tell him, but I don't know how. I've never read a script where the heroine tells the hero that she wants to do chores with him.

We stand offstage and watch as four bands come and go. I am relaxed in my body and feel oddly sure of who I am with Dan's arms around me. We are quiet inside the din of the music. His hands on my hips, his lips brushing my cheek. So when the ground starts rumbling, I am surprised, but I immediately know what it is. Jack has bypassed us somehow and has walked onstage, where he is taking his time tuning his guitar. The crowd is frantic, and from where I stand, I can see the calm on his face, like he knows the world will wait any amount of time to hear him sing. This isn't one of those times when you haven't seen someone in twenty years and you're surprised at how much they've changed. I see Jack all the time. Music videos, magazines, TMZ. That time I threw an orange soda at his car. In fact, I've seen his grown-up rock star face many more times than I ever saw him at sixteen, pre-whiskers, pre-anything. He turns his head, and I see that he's shaved his sideburns. I'm entirely unarmed. Our half-baked plan is already half failed, and this is my last chance to try. I wipe my sweaty palms on my jeans.

"He must have come in the other side," Dan says. "Let's stay here. Finn will stall him if he leaves that way."

It's hard to describe the screaming that erupts when Jack starts playing. It's easier to describe the effects of it— the ground I'm standing on starts to shake, my head fills with the color red, and I can feel where the roots of my hair meet my scalp. I squeeze Dan's hands.

He sings "Purple," his newest release, and I can feel the beat of it in my chest, competing with the rabbit's beat of my heart. I am not nervous in my mind the way I can be at meetings or before dates. I'm nervous at a cellular level, like every atom of my being is desperate for him to write us a song. He sings "By My Side" and then "Coconut Girl." As the last song ends, the crowd roars, and two security guards escort him toward our side of the stage. He is walking directly toward me, and the breath leaves my lungs as if I've been kicked.

"This is it," Dan says. "You can totally do this. You're totally worth writing a song for." Tears burn in my throat at this. It's like he's seen the hole in me and wants to fill it.

"Thank you," I say. He puts a gentle hand on my back to push me ahead.

I take a step forward to block the exit and my mouth goes dry. I open it and close it twice before I say, "Jack."

He looks me right in the eye. "Good night," he says. Polite. Neutral. He has no idea who I am. He doesn't even seem to remember that I was the same nut who chucked a soda at his car. His security guards place themselves between us before I can say anything else, and he walks out the door. I feel like I've just dropped my keys down a sewer grate—there's no getting them back.

A guy who seems like the right age to be Jack's uncle is following them out, and I have absolutely nothing to lose. "Lyle," I say, and he stops. "I'm Jane Jackson, we spoke on the phone." He shows no recognition at all. "Jack and I recorded 'Jump-Start Love Song' together when we were kids.

He smiles. *"Pop Rocks?"*

"Yes, we did the duet together." I do not pause long enough for him to walk away. "And I'd really like to talk to him, like for five minutes about a movie I'm making. Can you help me out?"

"You were the one with the braces?"

"Yes! That was me! Great memory. We really had a great time with that song. Can you get me five minutes?"

"Hang on," he says and walks outside. He leaves the side door open and there's a limousine waiting. He taps on the window, it lowers, he says something and nods.

"This is good," Dan says and takes my hand. "You're sweating like crazy. This is going to be fine. A favor from an old friend."

Lyle turns around and motions for me to come, and I walk outside without a word. My chest is in my throat. I am aware of my position here, the smaller person asking the bigger person for a favor. I take a second and try to imagine myself as a lit match on a totally still night.

Lyle opens the limousine door for me, and as I step in, I notice that I am in jeans and a black top, the same thing I wore the day I met Jack. This throws me off for a second. I want to explain that it's a coincidence, though Jack would never remember that day the way I do. That quick thought is another gust of wind on my precariously lit match.

Jack is on the left side of the black bench seat with a tiny cup of espresso in his hands. I try to imagine performing for a huge crowd, indoors in August, and then hydrating on three sips of espresso. He hands his cup to Lyle and leans forward to give me an awkward, half-sitting hug. He smells of scotch, coffee, and mint gum, and the combination makes me even queasier than I already feel. "Janey Jakes! Of course I remember you!"

I read his face for a clue as to what color that memory is in his mind. You remember seeing a dolphin family surface

during a beautiful sunset, and you also remember the noro-
virus. There are a million shades in between. I'm sitting
across from him with my knees pressed together, and my
hands folded so that I can contain all of my energy in one
place. Lyle is sitting next to him, and I sort of wish I had
someone sitting next to me, a backup person.

"I know you must be dying to get out of here," I say,
though I think I might be talking about myself. "So I'll
just get to it. I'm a creative executive at Clearwater Studios
now, and I've just acquired a really beautiful script, it's a
love story. And we—"

He interrupts me. "Remember we went to Studio City
for like an hour and then you said you loved me?" He turns
to Lyle. "I swear to God."

Okay.

There it is.

I feel it in my chest, simmering. Lyle laughs, though I
don't know if he thinks this is funny or if it's his job to laugh.

Lyle looks me up and down and says, "That tracks."

"Beverly Hills," I say after a quick intake of breath.
"And yes, I did say that. I was fourteen." Now that I've said
it, I think the phrase "I was fourteen" should be a blanket
explanation for every stupid thing everyone did that year.
No one should be held responsible for the things fourteen is
capable of. Jack and Lyle are both smiling. I roll my shoulders back and take another breath. "So we need something
big to make this film commercial enough to be green-lit,
and since you're on the radio every single time I get in my
car, I thought of you." I toss my hands up in a theatrical

ta-da and then backtrack and squeeze them together. "Just one Jack Quinlan song for the soundtrack and I can almost guarantee you an Oscar. That's how good this script is."

They're both looking at me, and Lyle has a smirk on his face that I want to rub off with my fist.

"I remember you now," Lyle says. "From like a week ago. I called you back. You sounded a little desperate. It was cute, and it sounds like nothing's changed."

Jack shakes his head and smiles. "Love that."

Hearing how consistent I am about being desperate takes me back to that night where I was desperate for love but was told that I was too weird and gross to have it. Humiliated, I turned to the comfort of my parents' love story, only to find out that Jack was right.

That little pink envelope, then the letter, the word "brutal" written so casually in that sloppy handwriting, a throwaway word. A throwaway girl. I was crazy to unearth these details today, and now they're out, swimming inside me and opening the darkest door in my heart. It's where I carry my essential not-enoughness. It's where I know that my mom knows too, and that she's lied to me my whole life to keep me from finding out that I'm not worth it. This old, old pain forms a lump in my throat.

"I'm not at all desperate," I say, punctuating each word the way a desperate person might.

Jack slumps back in his seat and turns to Lyle. "She was kind of hot," he says. Lyle nods, and I have this feeling that I am not here. That I've dissolved or that Jack thinks the world is a big limo and he can put up the partition anywhere he wants. "But then also kind of ridiculous? I don't really remember. Perfect Janey Jakes." He doesn't laugh, but Lyle does.

"Yes, that was my job," I say. I can feel myself shrinking. My hands are clasped so tight that I worry one of those tiny, tiny bones might snap. There's a burning at the back of my nose that feels like betrayal. This pain has nothing to do with Jack, I realize. Jack is just tied up in that day, the way an old song can take you back to a kiss. Sharing the truth about my dad with Dan and then seeing pompous Jack has left me uncomfortably exposed for what I am. I don't know how to lock that tiny door in my heart, but I do know that I finally have my audience with Jack Quinlan and I am probably going to start to cry.

"So you're telling me now you want me to do a song for your movie?" Jack asks.

"Yes? But you can read it first? To decide?" I don't know how to stop the question marks in my voice.

"I don't have time for that, Janey. But seriously, it's hilarious to see you again. *Do do do do do do,*" he finishes with the familiar riff.

Lyle takes that as his cue to get out of the limo and hold the door open for me.

"I could just send it to you and you could consider reading it?"

"Oh my God, Janey. Stop. You're embarrassing yourself." The words feel like a slap. I can normally take a verbal slap—I work in Hollywood—but not today. I am too raw already.

"Yes," I say. That's what I need to do. Stop.

I move to get out of the limo, and Jack says, "Wait." I pause for a second without turning around. My body is telling me to keep going, get out and run. My ambition to get this movie made tells me to turn around, so I do.

"Yeah?"

"It was shitty that they didn't give us credit on that song."

"Yes, it was," I say and wait for more. I glance up at Lyle, who's as interested in where this is going as I am, probably because he's the one who agreed to it on Jack's behalf.

"I mean, I understood about me, I wasn't even on the show. But they could have let you sing it for real. I hate that they were so hung up on looks and charisma and whatever. We were kids." He gives me the smile that a serial killer practices in the mirror to feign compassion.

I am at a loss for a response. I think he's just told me that I was unattractive and uncharismatic, but that's not possible. People don't say things like that to each other. "It was fine," I say finally, my favorite lie. "We got paid."

"Yeah, I know. I just wanted to say I felt bad for you. It had to hurt."

Lyle says, "It made sense to me, Hailey was so compelling."

"Compelling?" My voice cracks.

"Oh, no, sorry," Lyle says. "I don't mean that as an insult. God, no. I just mean they knew Hailey was the sort of person an audience would keep coming back for, she'd hold their interest. It was a business decision and it worked out. They ate that song up."

I have never heard a word resonate with so much clarity. Compelling is the exact thing I am not. It's been a feeling I've had for decades, but I've never been able to name it before. Thank you to Lyle, the namer. I am uncompelling, unable to hold interest. You could be watching me and turn the channel. You could be my dad and decide not to be. This absolutely tracks.

I need to get out of this limo. "Yes, well, it all worked out. Thank you for the time." Jack didn't even connect that I was the one who threw a soda at his car—that's how unmemorable I am. I keep my head down as I step out of the limo. I am dangerously close to tears, and I don't want anyone looking at my face.

Dan is standing in the open stage door, waiting for me. Music is blaring behind him and he walks down the steps. "No? Your face is telling me it was no."

"It was no."

Dan takes me in his arms and I'm a little too numb to feel it. "Let's get out of here," he says into my hair.

We walk for a few silent minutes before he stops me and asks, "So what happened? Did you have a chance to pitch the movie or did he just shut you down?"

"He shut me down all right."

"He remembered you though. He had to."

"Yep," I say. "He remembered me exactly right." I have never been described so precisely. "I don't want to talk about it."

I start walking. I wonder if a nervous breakdown feels like having every thought you've ever had all at once. I am thinking about that night and the cold feeling in my heart reading the words "I do love you, Terry, but fatherhood is brutal." I think of the next time my mom told me their story and repeated the *Notebook* thing that stupid, believing, younger me had come up with, and how alone I felt seeing the lie on her face. I think of Hailey making it and Jack making it and even Will selling real estate for a camera. I can feel it bubbling under my skin, a smattering of rage cross-pollinating and growing. I knew this already. I am not compelling enough for love. I am not worth sticking around for. And all of this has to stop. Jack is a total douchebag, but he was right about that.

"I don't know why you brought me here," I say. And I mean to Long Island and into his bed and into this place where I have big feelings and a bracelet and believe in unicorns. Of course this isn't going to end as a big happy thing.

"Well, you asked me to," he says and takes my hand.

I stop and take my hand back. "I didn't have that much of a choice."

Dan looks completely calm. "This is going to be fine, we'll find another way to get this made."

I look up at his impossibly handsome face and the way he's looking at me like he loves me. It's so cruel to look at me that way. It's just because he's only known me a week. He'll understand soon enough. This might actually be our fourth date. A sadness washes over me, a fresh cut on an old wound, and then the rage starts to surface.

"Maybe you're going to be fine, Dan. With your big

perfect family and your weird quiet projects. But I'm not fine." It hurts a little coming out, but it's the truth so I say it again. "I'm not fine." I start walking again, so he does too. "I don't know what happened here, or even what we were trying to do. But this is so stupid, it's just a story. It's bullshit."

"What's bullshit?" he asks. He takes my hand and stops me. "What are we talking about? Don't say us."

"All of it. You want a list? This script. Me finally making a movie. Me and you together. Standing with you in the rain. Some shitty watercolor. It's just too fucking humid here, that's all."

He pulls me into his arms and holds me tight. I listen to his beating heart. I smell his quiet smell. I know this is the last time, so I just take a second, like a fading dream. I am awake now.

"Okay, that's enough," I say, pulling away. "Sorry for the little meltdown and sorry for all of it. Let's get back to your parents' house and just put this behind us." I start walking, maybe rudely fast, and he's walking alongside of me.

"Jane. Talk to me. You're really upset. This isn't another thing you can gloss over." He grabs my arm.

"Another thing?" The words shoot out of my mouth like a bullet. "I don't gloss over things."

"You do. Like with your mom. She's been lying to you this whole time, but you're lying right back."

Literally how dare he. I stand there and look at his wide

Batman eyes, and I feel a hot burning in my chest. "So I'm a liar now? And you're an expert on my relationship with my mom? Just want to be super clear here."

"No, of course not. I just want to know what happened with Jack so we can talk about it. Like, let's face it and move on."

"Face it and move on" enrages me. It's an oversimplification of the dumpster fire of my feelings. Of my dad leaving and my mom not wanting me to know I was never enough.

He takes my hand. "I know you're angry right now—can we just go back to when I was telling you why you're lovable?" He reaches to touch my clenched jaw and I step back.

"Oh, stop. Quit trying to turn everything into a love story. Everything isn't always about love. We're just people on a trip. It's called a fling, Dan. Look it up."

He stops walking and I turn to see him, recoiled like he's been slapped. "Those are some pretty broad strokes, Jane," he says.

We are at a standoff here under the old-fashioned street-lamps on this stretch of road unimaginatively named Main Street. I could reach out to him now and apologize—it's clear that I've hurt him. I've taken something that felt specific and once-in-a-lifetime, and I've turned it into a weekend at Club Med with a guy named Bruno. I should take his hand and tell him that he is it for me, that I want to go back to LA and turn him into forever. But I am too small for big declarations right now. The part of me that can get up and be brave has retreated through the gaping hole in my heart.

So I say, "Right?" It means nothing. It's too light, and the nothingness of this comment feels mean.

"What's happening right now? Don't you dare take this back," he says.

"Good one," I say. It's my post office voice—that's how small and mean I am. I feel like I've let someone convince me there are unicorns, only to find out they were kidding. I am in free fall here, but I know one thing: there are no unicorns, especially not for me.

I start to walk again, through town and toward the house. The streets are quiet because the festival is still going on and I can hear his footsteps maybe ten feet behind me. He's giving me space, which I appreciate, but he really has no idea how much space I'm capable of giving him.

CHAPTER 30

~~~~~

RUBY IS CONKED OUT IN A SLEEPING BAG IN THE LIV-
ing room. Cormack and Reenie are on the couch
watching *Seinfeld* reruns. There's a little sunflower throw
pillow between them, and their entwined hands are resting
on it. I wonder if they even know that they're holding hands
after all of these years. I wonder if it ever surprises them,
this need to be so close, or if they just thought this is what
marriage is. I am awake enough to feel like their casual
hand-holding is obnoxious.

"How did it go?" Reenie asks.

"Not so great," Dan says before I can. "I think we're
going to go sit outside for a bit."

"Actually, I think I'm going to go to bed," I say. "But
you go ahead." He's looking at me like he doesn't recognize
me, like I'm not the person he woke up with this morning.
Which I'm not. At all. "I'm going to rebook myself on an
early flight tomorrow too. So much regrouping to do. But
thank you both for having me this week." Ruby turns her
head, and her black curls wiggle and then rest. The thoughts
I've been entertaining about forever and a little girl with

Dan's coloring and my curls sit sour in my stomach. There's another sentence I should say about the kids and the pie, but I can't quite get it out.

Reenie and Cormack get up to hug me. Reenie takes me in her arms and I feel like a rag doll. I think of my mom, the fragile feel of the bones in her back under my hands in a lifetime of hugs and mistruths. This hug with Reenie is a new thing that suddenly feels dangerous, a window into something that I don't get to keep.

"Well, we hope you'll be back in the fall," she says. "Or anytime. You're always welcome. But the fall is lovely and less crowded."

"She'll come back when she wants," Cormack says and pulls me into his arms. "I really hope you do."

Dan's got his hands in his pockets watching for my next move. I cannot believe I let myself get in this deep in the world of fairy tales and true love. It's like I got drunk on that script and the din of Dan's family. The warmth of his hand in mine.

I'm fiddling with Ruby's bracelet, every possible color in no particular order, and I shake my head. "Well, good night. I'm going to head to bed. Thank you for everything."

I lie heavy under the covers. My body feels like lead. I have a missed call from Clem and a text: Just checking in to see how it went? Did you see him and seal the deal?

I don't even have the energy for Clem. I don't want to hear what she's going to say about my anger. I don't want to tell her there's no happy ending. So I turn to the wall and try to sleep.

CHAPTER 31

I LAND AT NOON AND GO STRAIGHT TO MY MOM'S house. I haven't called Clem back because I know what she'll say about all of this. I'm not ready to come clean about just how completely I've fallen apart; I'd rather be in a place where I know how to pretend.

My mom's street is Sunday quiet. I have a key, but for some reason, I knock. My mom opens the door in her yellow duck pajamas, just like any other Sunday, but today there is a man in her kitchen cooking something in a pan.

"Jane!" She takes me in her arms. "I'm so happy to see you." She pulls me into the apartment, which feels and smells different with this man here.

"Gary," I say as he's walking toward us.

He extends a hand. "So nice to meet you finally."

I shake his hand. "Thank you. Hi."

They're smiling at me like this isn't the weirdest thing ever. My mom gestures to me. "So come sit. I thought you were coming in later. Didn't you say dinner?"

"I'm making omelets," Gary says. "I've just caramelized the onions. Can I make you one?"

I blink. He's a nice-looking fifty-year-old guy. He's Gary who caramelizes things, and my mom is as light as a feather. "No, thank you," I say.

Gary goes back into the kitchen, and we sit on her old sofa. I have never once in my life seen a man cook something for my mother. Not in thirty-three years. I take in her apartment as if for the first time, because we are in a new reality where my mom is living in the false paradise I've just run out on. The missing thing is not missing. I have a feeling in my body that I know is jealousy. Feeling jealous of my mother, whose life I ruined by being too brutal for her true love, is a new low.

She makes big eyes at me. "What do you think?"

"I think he's caramelized you." I'm trying for a joke, but I am so angry and hurt that it comes across sarcastic.

She puts her arm around me. "Tell me about your trip."

"Why do you look so good?" I ask her. She looks how I felt just yesterday, sort of glowy and light.

"I'm happy," she says and looks at her hands.

"With Coffee Bean Gary."

"You can just call him Gary," she says. "I think I might be in love."

"Mom, stop," I say. It's not the silent *Mom, stop* I've wished every time she's thought she was in love. It's coated in anger for how long she's set me up to feel the way I do today. Love may be a real thing, but it's not for us. Just stop. Gary's going to leave. At least I was smart enough not to try.

"I feel like myself with him and I want to touch him all the time," she says.

"Oh my God, stop," I say.

"He's asked me to move in with him, and I'm going to."

"And you're just going to do it? Give up your home and run blind into this thing and ride off on a goddamn unicorn?" My voice is jagged. My anger is razor-sharp, and I cannot reel it in.

"What? No." She pats my hand and I pull it away. I'm just so sick of her happy stories, and I'm so sick of pretending to believe. "Why would you say that?"

I start to cry. The tears start in my chest and burn my eyes as they flow. Gary walks into the room with omelets and immediately retreats to the kitchen.

"Jane, what's happening?"

It's time. I know that. I can hear Dan telling me to face it and move on, and this makes me angry all over again. It's nearly impossible to break a dynamic that's been choreographed between two people for decades. You protect me; I protect you. We're both liars.

"This is big for me," she says. She thinks I'm crying about Gary. "It's important. He's important to me. I love him and I want to share things with him."

"Great," I say, wiping my eyes. "Good for you, I'm glad you can share things with somebody."

She looks at me as if she's been slapped but doesn't know with what.

"What does that mean?" she asks.

I let my face fall into my hands. I don't know how to

untangle my thoughts and memories. I don't know how to reach into the mess that I am and pull out the easy version.

"Is this about the movie? What's happened to you?" she asks.

I felt it. I know what love is now, and I remembered that it's not for me. "I'm just really angry." At myself for believing I could have the fairy tale, at her for never owning up, at Dan for lifting the curtain and showing me what I can't have.

"About Gary and me?"

"No." I look up from my hands. "Maybe. This thing you're feeling, it's a daydream. I know better. And I think you know better too."

Silence hangs between us, and the normal next step would be to reveal what I know to be the truth about my inherent unlovability. I could just open my mouth and tell her I know she's been lying to me about who I am my entire life. But it's too raw and I'm too angry. One more cut and I will bleed out.

~~~~

CHAPTER 32

I GET INTO MY CAR TO HEAD HOME, AND THERE'S A text from Dan: Landed. Did you make it home?

Me: I did.

Dan: Are we going to talk about this?

Me: Probably not

I send that text and the pit in my stomach deepens. I'm crying again, and it doesn't feel like residual crying from before. I'm crying because I can feel myself doubling down.

Dan: Jane

That's all he says, but when I read it, I hear it in his voice. The way he says my name, the way he whispered it in my ear, into my neck, my mouth. I hate the way I let myself start to believe in this thing.

Me: Just stop. It's over

My finger hesitates for a second before I hit send and turn off my phone.

I drive to Venice Beach and order a plate of potato skins that I don't eat. I try to reconcile the passage of so little time. It was eight days ago that I sat here with Dan and agreed with him about the quiet things being the things that move us. It was five days ago that he put his hand on my mouth for the first time. I will not deny the thing that *True Story* helped me know: permanent, beautiful love is alive and well in the world. But it is not for me. I was better off before I felt it. A week later, I'm right where I started, still in danger of losing my job but also freshly heartbroken.

I start to drive home and am relieved when I remember that it's Sunday and Clem will be at Grifters until eleven tonight. The last time we talked, I was telling her about love sex. I need to catch her up on my recent cycle of humiliation and rage, and I just don't have the energy for it tonight. The best thing about Clem is also the worst thing: she knows all my truths. And I think she believed in this thing with Dan too.

I see her car on the street before I notice her on the porch swing. I slow my steps because I know there's no hiding from Clem. The ocean of sadness in me is rising, and if I let it out, it could drown us both. But when she stands and opens her arms to me, I fall into them. The part of me that's tired of being angry and tired of lying needs Clem more than anything.

"Why aren't you at work?" I ask.

"I called in sick. I had a bad feeling when you ignored my text."

"I don't deserve you," I say into Clem's shoulder. Clem, who's not leaving. Clem, who's happy to laugh and cry whenever I need her to. I sat with Clem while she mourned her marriage. I brought her tacos and cranberry seltzer, an odd but frequent request. But that felt like a wound worth tending to; this feels pathetic. It was only a week.

"Bad?" she asks.

"Yes." I hug her again and start to cry. I am tired from so many things.

"Maybe we should sit out here for a bit? I'll get you something to eat."

She goes into the kitchen. I sit under the bougainvillea and listen to the cars drive by. There's a bit of sunlight hitting the street, and I watch the stripe of it roll over cars as they pass. I close my eyes and imagine the sound of the cars is just the confusion rolling around in my head.

Clem comes out, sits next to me, and hands me a hot mug of soup.

"Soup?" I ask. It's August, not exactly soup weather.

"I don't know, I just thought I should bring you something, and spaghetti seemed cumbersome. Take a sip, it's tomato."

I rest the soup on my raised knees and give her a sad smile. "Thank you."

"So you lost the perfect guy and the perfect movie?"

"You're great at this," I say.

"Drink your soup."

I take a sip, and it tastes like comfort, warm and thick. "Jack laughed at me and said no. He also reminded me that I'm not compelling."

"Compelling?"

"Yep. Also, not attractive. But it was the compelling thing that took me down."

"Because you believe it."

"It doesn't matter if I believe it if it's true. They kept me in the background on TV. When it was my voice they needed, they knew the song wouldn't be a hit if I was attached to it. They knew before I did."

"This isn't about *Pop Rocks*," Clem says.

I take another sip of my soup. It's the only thing I've eaten today, and my stomach wakes up and rumbles.

"I know," I say.

Clem turns to me. "I'm going to say it out loud. Okay?"

I nod.

"You ruined your mom's life by not being compelling enough to love. That's it, right? That's the whole story you're stuck on."

I don't say anything.

"You've been fostering that story as long as I've known you, tending to it like a pet. It controls so many things about your life, and I have a feeling it's torpedoed your chance of love. And the only reason that story has this power is because you keep it chained up inside. You've got to talk to your mom, stop all this bullshit. I bet the truth about your dad's leaving is more complicated than you not being the world's most compelling five-year-old."

I rest my head on her shoulder because I really am so, so tired. Tired from travel, tired from crying. I'm tired from staying up all night with Dan.

"I don't know how to talk to my mom about this. I feel like it would break something between us. It terrifies me."

"I know."

"I blew up at Dan."

Clem gives me a tight-lipped look like she's trying not to say something.

"What," I say.

"The movie was a long shot. But the Dan thing sounded real. What did he do?"

"Told me to face the truth." I let out a hard laugh.

She raises her eyebrows but has the grace not to say anything.

"I hold on to a lot of shame," I say. "Like it sneaks up on me."

"Yes, you hold on to it really tight, like it's your identity."

I feel that sentence right in my heart, like a sharp, quick fist.

"In other news, Mom's in love again, so." I take a sip of hot soup.

"Sometimes love is totally illogical."

"Yeah," I say. I don't say more because I don't want to hear the sound of my voice talking about how it was with Dan, how relaxed I got and how happy I felt just pedaling a bike by his side. I could be funny or quiet or bad at watercolors, and it was all the same to him. And I think about my Manifest a Solid Partner project and all the guys who I just couldn't get into a natural rhythm with. It wasn't necessarily something wrong between us—those guys never even met me. They all felt like cardboard because I was cardboard with them.

"There's a version of me that's better than the version of me that I show the world," I say after a while.

"It's the version I see," says Clem. "The first time we met, remember we couldn't stop laughing? I saw who you were right away. And now, I mean, you put on your costume and get in your Lexus and chase a life that you think is going to make everything okay. And the truth is that one day the hostess at the Ivy is going to know who you are, maybe she'll even escort you to Scorsese's table, and it's still not going to change the fact that your dad left." She puts her arm around me and pulls me close. We're quiet for a while and watch the fireflies. There's a palm tree in the backyard of the house across the street. It towers over the neighborhood on its impossibly thin trunk, the secret of its deep, deep roots below the ground.

"Do you want to talk about Dan?" she asks after a while.

"The whole week feels like a dream now. The kind you wake up from and slam your eyes shut so you can go back again."

"So you're going to go back? It all sounded pretty great."

"I was myself with him, like it was so easy. I just said the first thing that popped into my head. And I was funny. For some reason, that was okay." I take a sip of my hot soup. Clem's watching me because she knows there's more. "But there's so much of me that's broken. It's a matter of time before he sees all that and bolts anyway."

Clem gives my shoulder a squeeze. "Ah, your favorite story," she says.

CHAPTER 33

~~~

MONDAY MORNING ARRIVES IN A MORE PAINFUL way than it usually does. It's six a.m. and I've barely slept. I am raw. Raw and empty. I've scheduled a meeting with Nathan for noon and I plan to come clean. I have both Dan and Clem in my head telling me I need to face things head-on. I'm not ready to face everything, but this one is unavoidable. I have lost so much in the past few days; I cannot lose my job too. I've run through the story a bunch of different ways, but the only one I can easily tell is the truth: *I lied. I totally made it up.*

"There she is," Nathan says when I've been announced. "Come, sit. Tell me everything."

I stop before I sit, just to feel this. It's what I've been hoping for all along. Nathan thinks I've caught a tiger, that I've jumped through the hoops to make the big thing. Nathan is finally looking at me like I'm a player. And I realize that Clem is right. It changes nothing. I am not better or worth more in these few minutes that Nathan believes this.

"Everything," I say and take the seat across from his desk. "Everything would really be a lot."

He laughs. "Tell me about Quinlan."

"I saw him and we spoke about the movie." I reach down to arrange my skirt over my knees in that way I do to buy time, and I see that I am in jeans. "I'm in jeans," I say out loud. "What a weird thing for me to do."

"Are you all right?" Nathan asks.

"Yes, sorry. So I saw Jack and he's a no. He's not going to write us a song, wants no part in the movie. Honestly, I was a little desperate to get this green-lit and exaggerated the extent of our relationship. So it was probably never happening." I pause and wait for some sort of admonishment. When I get none, I go on. "I have racked my brain and can't come up with anything that makes this commercial enough for what you need, so I guess that's it."

Nathan sits back in his seat. "Fine. Let it go."

"What?" I feel Ruby's hand in mine, and my heart squeezes at the memory of her arms swirling through the air and the sweet sound of her singing voice. I spin the beads on my bracelet.

"The option, let it expire," he says. "Find something else."

Find something else. Like that's an easy thing to do. Fly first class and then spend the rest of your life riding the bus. Meet a one-in-a-million guy and then get back out there and swipe for a partner with dental insurance.

"Are you all right?" Nathan's asking me. "You seem a little out of it."

"Do I? Sorry." I look right and left and run my hands over my jeans. "The next script I bring your way will be chosen with an eye toward tigers and explosions." The emptiness spreads inside me. This is not the work I want to be doing. Creating a bunch of nothing to try to get something.

"All right. Sounds like you get the assignment," he says.

"I do." I get up and head to the door, but stop and turn around. "Did you love the script?"

"I did." He's holding a sharpened pencil with both hands.

"Do you wish someone else would make it?" I ask. "Because I do. I'd just like to see it. Like it's a movie I'd want to watch with my mom."

"Our option's expiring in a couple of months. Maybe someone will pick it up."

CHAPTER 34

I GO BACK TO MY OFFICE, SHUT THE DOOR, AND SIT under my desk. I rest my head on my knees and feel the soft cotton of my jeans. I breathe in for five. It's over. I breathe out for five. I breathe in for five again and take inventory. I spent a week in an alternate reality and, as payback, this under-desk reality is my future.

I have my copy of *True Story* on my knees. I'll keep this copy forever, I think. There are notes in the margins and big exclamation points next to dialogue I've circled. I start to read the first scene so that I can see it play out in my mind.

The Finnegans' world seems a million miles away. The orderly chaos. The way they all know each other and no one hides from who they are. The ribbing, gentle and not; the way Dan just says the thing without fear of recrimination. They tell the embarrassing story; they bully you into admitting you like the girl. I close my eyes and picture myself seated around their garden table, tethered to my seat by a sleeping baby and laughing over her heavy head.

I sit like this under my desk and eat two mini Krackel bars and read the rest of the script. At the end my hand is clenching my heart and my eyes are wet. I thought this movie was going to be my ticket to success, but really it was the key to another world. It's a world where someone would know me anywhere, at any time. He'd know me with his whole body. I've banished myself from this world, but it was just a matter of time anyway.

The door to my office opens and Mandy says, "Jane?" Perfect.

I have no choice but to wipe the chocolate off my face with the back of my hand and crawl out from under my desk. "Sorry," I say, getting up. "Just dropped something."

"Okay?"

"So what's going on?" I ask, wiping the back of my hand on my jeans.

"That's what I was going to ask you. Good to see you taking a casual day."

I look down at my jeans and don't tell her that I forgot to get dressed.

"Yeah, so we're not moving forward with *True Story*."

"I'm sorry," she says.

"It's fine. I mean, it's not fine. But . . ." I'm not sure what I'm trying to say. It's as if I know this thing is dead but I'm not willing to bury it. "It drives me crazy to have this idea in my head of how that movie would be and how it would affect people and then not have any way to get it out."

"What does Dan Finnegan say?"

"He doesn't know yet."

"Did you ever watch his movie? *Grapevine*?"

"No." I want to roll my eyes, but they won't roll. I just stare down at my desk.

"It's beautiful. I know he's the worst, but he's talented."

"He's not the worst," I say to my desk. "I think I'm going to go home."

I'M IN BED with my laptop watching the closing credits on *Grapevine*. A good cry is a lot like a good laugh, I realize. It starts as your head connects to something in your heart and just sort of takes over. The wet eyes, the snot. This movie is so Dan—quiet and warm, like you want to climb right into it and stay forever. The small things are the big things. It's the thing that happens at breakfast.

I have done everything wrong. I went in search of a prize, and when I didn't get it, I turned on the prize I already had. I don't deserve Dan—I know this—but I miss him in a visceral way. It's been one day, and I am already desperate to hear his voice. I could call him and test the waters. I could tell him that I loved his movie—everyone likes compliments. He'd say thank you and then there would be an open line between us again. I don't want to rip myself open and show him how ugly things are inside me, but maybe we could talk about this movie or Ruby or the forest. And maybe I wouldn't feel so desperately empty anymore.

I call him before I have a chance to talk myself out of it. It goes straight to voicemail. I text him: Loved your movie

It doesn't go through. He's blocked me.

I had the open line. I could have said anything. I could have told him how I felt and that I was scared and ashamed. I didn't.

Clem knocks on my door when I'm in the middle of watching it a second time.

"Is this a nervous breakdown or the flu? Because I'm out of soup."

I pat my bed. "Get in," I say.

She climbs into bed next to me, still in pink scrubs, still coated in the stress of the day. "This doesn't look like *Bridget Jones*."

"Shh," I say, and I can feel her relax into the movie. It's the way the light hits the vineyards and the way the heroine is backlit by the sunset. It's the small details that attract your eye, the Dan-ness of it all, that make this movie great.

"Okay," she says. "It was beautiful. So are you going to pine over this guy forever?"

"That's my current plan, yes."

She smiles at me.

"I called him an hour ago."

"From your closet, I assume."

"No, from right here."

"Wow."

"Yeah, I'm a real badass. But he didn't answer. I sent a text and it didn't go through. I think he's blocked me, so. Probably for the best."

Clem lets out a breath. "Remember when Nick was pulling away and I kept saying he won't give me what I need? Remember what you said?"

"Stop it."

"No, say it."

"Whatever it was, I just saw it on Instagram or something," I say.

"You said I should stop waiting for someone to give me what I need."

I roll my eyes. "Yep, I'm like Yoda. Please soak up all of my wisdom."

She doesn't laugh. "I know you don't want to hear this, but you need to come clean to your mom. Like now. All the heavy lifting you thought this movie *True Story* was going to do for you, showing your mom something true, opening up a conversation. I think you need to do that for yourself."

ON TUESDAY I go to work and text my mom from under my desk.

Me: I'm really sorry. I was horrible. I'm happy for you and Gary

Mom: It's fine, and thank you. I know you're having a hard time

Me: Movie Friday?

Mom: Yes please

That small bit of forgiveness loosens the knot in my chest, but the pressure there still feels unbearable. Even if Dan hadn't blocked me and I could apologize, I'd still have ended up here under my desk eventually. Because even if he forgave me and there was love talk, it would have ended, and I'd have been back down here eating mini Snickers and hiding the wrappers.

On Wednesday I sit through an internal strategy meeting and stare at Nathan's cavernous left nostril. I watch it expand and contract as he speaks, but I don't hear a word he says.

On Thursday I call in sick. I lie in my bed and watch my ceiling fan spin. I don't normally use it and I don't ever dust it, so I watch it fling particles of death around my room. Dead skin and nails, the dust of things that were never meant to last. I close my eyes and hear a car pull into my driveway. I imagine Dan getting out and knocking on my door. I imagine myself jumping into his arms. He'd reel from the impact but smile at me and pull me close. Stubble scraping my cheek, lips catching my ear. I hear the car pull away, and I know it was just someone turning around. Dan doesn't even know where I live.

On Friday night I am in a dark, overly air-conditioned theater watching a loud superhero movie with my mom. The other choices were love stories, and I know she was being thoughtful picking this one, but it's backfired. There's no getting away from thinking about Dan. I take in every scene and feel how much he would have hated it. I long to see the way he would have shot the scene when the villain climbs out of the junkyard in the moonlight. I run my fingers over my jaw, where he spent an entire day planting small, breathy kisses and saying my name. There is no getting away from him; I have been infiltrated. I can stop going to the movies, maybe, but I cannot get away from my own jaw.

"Sweetie," my mother whispers. I hadn't realized that I was holding her hand. And crying. "Do you want to go?" she asks with a squeeze.

I think about the offer. We could go to my happy place, her apartment with the old patched couch. We could order moo shu pork and experiment with liquid eyeliner. But my jaw would be there. And my raw, aching heart, turned inside out so that all of the hidden bits are exposed. I'm going to bring myself wherever I go now, and I'm going to have to get used to it.

"I wish I could go back and do everything differently," I whisper, finally. A car explodes in the background to thunderous effect.

"I do too, Jane." She squeezes my hand. I rest my head on her shoulder in the dark as a seven-foot-tall man kicks in a steel door on the screen. I think of *True Story*. I think of Reenie and Cormack and the way she looked at him during his toast. I even think of Gary making my mom an omelet. And offering me one, like that was a thing I deserved.

We walk outside into the warm, dry August air. It's wildfire season. I can feel it as I stop under the fluorescent light of the marquee. There's something restless in the air, and I think of how fires lead to mudslides and how everything that happens on this earth was caused by something else. People jostle us as they exit the theater, but my feet are planted firmly in place.

My mom says, "Well, that was a terrible movie," just as I say, "I know about my dad."

It surprises me almost as much as it surprises her. She cocks her head a bit, but doesn't say anything.

"When I was a kid, actually the same night I humiliated myself with Jack Quinlan, I found the letter. I know that he left us before he died. And that it was because of me." The words come in fragments, like I'm forcing them out. The tightness in my chest burns up through my throat.

She narrows her eyes at me and then looks at my feet. "That's not how it was."

"Please stop lying to me," I say, my words steadier.

"Should we go home?" she asks.

"Let's do this here," I say.

She takes a breath and straightens her shoulders. "He was young."

"I know."

"We were broke."

"I know. And I know you lied because you thought the truth would hurt me. But I found out anyway, and honestly, the lying made it so much worse." The tears come; they rise from my chest with a sob and just flow. People are still trickling out of the theater, and I don't move my feet. I'm going to stand here and cry until my tears run out.

"Oh."

"We could have just agreed he was a big jerk and moved on. That it was a shitty thing for him to have left. But the fact that you lied made me feel like it was something to be ashamed of." I wipe my face with the back of my hand and it barely helps.

"I don't see how that makes a difference." I don't blame her for being defensive. This must feel like a sneak attack.

"It makes a difference to who I am. There's a difference between being a person whose dad died and a person whose dad left. It's the difference between being unlucky and unwanted." She starts to say something but I interrupt. "And don't say of course he wanted me. I read the letter, he didn't."

She looks down at her hands. "He didn't."

The truth hangs in the silence between us. It's so ugly, hanging there.

"Thank you," I say.

"Well, I'm sorry. That I lied, and that you've been carrying this for so long. The truth is I did love him, but in this he was selfish and immature, and he just couldn't handle it. It was on him to stay, it wasn't on you to make him."

All the fantasies of what I could have said or done to make him want to stay flash behind my eyes. And I'm not even sure those fantasies have stopped; they've just changed into fantasies about what I might say or do now to be loved by the bigger world. By a date, by Hollywood, by the hostess at the Ivy.

"I never understood what it was about me," I say. "All the kids with their dads showing up for things. Or worrying about their daughters' curfews or interrupting kisses under porch lights. It's a universal thing, fathers treasuring their daughters. I watch TV, Mom. I know things." My mom smiles, just a little bit, but I can't stop. "Remember that movie with Robin Williams where he loves his kids so much that he dresses up like their nanny so he can spend time with them?"

"*Mrs. Doubtfire*," she says, so quietly.

"Yes. That movie wrecks me. I've never gotten over that, how much he wanted them."

She pulls me into a hug and runs a hand over my dad's curly hair. I sob into her. I've started and it just won't stop. After a while, she pulls back and looks me in the eye. Her eyes seem clearer than usual.

"I think I never gave up on love because I wanted you to see it. Not even for me, but for you, Jane. I wanted you to see a Hollywood happy ending and know you could have that too. And I know it was hard for you to see me fall apart every time it didn't work out. I know it was a lot of times." She gives me an apologetic smile and I take her hand. "Every time, I felt like I let us both down."

"I never felt let down," I say, "because I never believed you were going to find that happy ending. I was lying to you as much as you were lying to me." The pressure in my chest is loosening, but I still feel the weight of unsaid things there. "And I don't think it was good for us, the lying. Every time you told me your happy story and I acted like I believed it, it put distance between us. Can we just not do that anymore? You're the only family I have. I want it to be different." My face is wet with new tears, and now that I've said it and the world didn't end, I don't know why it took me so long. Old hurts are buried so carefully.

She squeezes my hand. "Why are we talking about this now? You've been carrying this around forever."

I wipe my eyes on my sleeve. "I think I might have fallen in love? And it's more beautiful than you described. But I wrecked it before it could wreck me."

"Why?"

I let out a breath and shove my hands in my pockets. "Because I can't actually believe someone would stick around for me. I mean, besides you and Clem. It's Dan, by the way. Dan who I don't hate." I laugh a sad laugh. "I guess I panicked and left before he could see the part of me that's so easy to walk away from."

My mom's heart breaks—I see it behind her eyes. They're wet with tears. "I'm so sorry you've been feeling this way for so long. Let's figure this out before it takes anything more away from you."

"I liked it," I say. "Falling in love, like actually falling. It's sort of effortless, you know?"

"I do." She smiles.

"But also terrifying. If I got any closer to Dan and he changed his mind . . . I don't know how people recover from stuff like that. Now that I've felt it, I can't believe you were strong enough to keep trying."

"Trust me, you're stronger than I am. The little girl with the power to support us both with the sheer energy of her smile."

Of course I think of Dan. Dan, who feels my smile in his chest. Dan, who is always at the tip of my tongue, the ends of my fingers. All he has is his talent, his ability to follow his heart. What's inside of me is all I have too, the good and the bad.

"Can we start over?" she asks. "I loved your dad, was so in love with him. But if he'd stayed, we would have broken up eventually. He was all about himself. We wouldn't have died in each other's arms like in that stupid movie."

"I love that movie," I say, wiping tears. I ache at the thought of standing with Dan in the rain in a see-through dress.

"Thank you for telling me this," she says.

"It was nothing," I say and laugh. It was everything.

"If we're being honest, your dad was a lot like the rest of the guys I dated. Big fun and then gone when it stopped being easy. It's a type. But not Gary."

"He made you an omelet."

"I know!" She loops her arm in mine, and we start walking back to her apartment. "It's a totally different kind of thing."

"I really wish you could have seen the movie I'm not making."

CHAPTER 35

LABOR DAY WEEKEND COMES AND GOES. CLEM MAKES me hike in Topanga Canyon on Sunday but lets me stay in bed on Monday. I wear jeans to the office again on Tuesday. I do it on purpose this time. I even let my hair air-dry in the car, so that by the time I get to the elevator, it's a big mass of curls. I run my hand over it, and I like the way it feels, full and free. "Okay," I say out loud. The elevator dings and the doors open and Dan is not standing there. I have no idea why I thought he would be. I cannot will him into existence.

I sit at my desk, not under it. I am no longer hiding from anything. I pull up the treatment for a new script and read it straight through. I feel nothing. No laughs, no tears, no quickening of the heart rate. There's a helicopter chase in which the propellor of the villain gets caught in the landing skid of the other. Who cares.

I lean back in my chair and swing my legs onto the desk. I'm in flip-flops at work, and suddenly "dress for the job you want" takes on new meaning. I almost feel like I woke up this morning and put on a costume to dress up like myself. I wiggle my toes. A helicopter fight is so noisy. It'll sell tickets and make for a great trailer, but we won't laugh or cry. We won't learn anything about ourselves. We'll just be hiding in all that noise.

I have the watercolor Dan and I made together in my desk drawer. I swiped it from the windowsill before I left the house. It's sloppy and dotted with little bursts of beauty, a bit of a blur, like the week we were together. It bothers me that I don't have a photo of us together. I don't know why I would, but it strikes me as strange that I would have had such an intimate relationship with someone and have so little evidence of it. That last part's not true. The evidence of my time with Dan is in how clear I feel for the first time in decades. I don't know anything about what's going to happen in the future, but I know that I have spent a lot of time lying in the past, pretending that I didn't want to get invited to the ball because I never thought I could be invited. It wasn't Dan who showed me who I was, but I got quiet enough around him to see myself and just live in my body for a while. I have a truer version of myself back, and that's what I can see clearly. Who I am, what I'm capable of, and where I've been terribly afraid to trust my own instincts. I also have this bracelet, which feels more concrete and shows no sign of disintegrating. I roll the beads between my fingers, and I can feel Ruby there, or at least her sense of certainty.

I take out *True Story* and read a few scenes for comfort.

Those characters show up flawed and fall in love anyway. Their connection is the kind of love I never understood, the kind where the love is the reward for being yourself. It's *This is who I am* followed by *I'll take it!* When I was with Dan, I jumped in without a mask or a script or best-practices bullet points. I was vulnerable with him, if just for a little while. I felt what it was to be loved, and I don't know how to turn away from that.

I pick up the phone and do the thing I've been dreading. The last step in shutting down *True Story* is telling the writer. Kay picks up on the first ring. There's no pretense to Kay, and it's a little contagious. The first time we met, she told me that *True Story* was loosely based on her relationship with her late husband, and I cried. It was the first time I'd ever cried at work, and I think it's why she sold it to me.

"I've been thinking about you!" she says.

"Me too," I say. "How are you doing?"

"Good," she says. "I'm working on another script. It sort of came out of nowhere, and now I'm up at dawn and walking around my house talking to myself in crazy voices. It's such fun."

"I'd love to read it when you're ready," I say.

"Oh, good," she says. She's quiet on the line, and I remember that I'm the one who called.

"So I have some bad news. Clearwater isn't going to move forward with *True Story*." There's a little hitch in my voice as I hit the last few words.

"Well, that is disappointing," she says.

"I know, and I'm sorry for both of us. I tried. I did a lot

of stupid things to try to make it happen. I really wanted to see that movie made."

"You will, Jane. Don't worry. The option's up in six weeks, and I had other people interested. I thought you were the right fit. I still do, just maybe not Clearwater."

"Yes," I say and sit up straighter. "I am the right fit. I have some ideas, a few of which are totally reckless. But I think that's what I'm about right now, so please don't resell the option without giving me a chance."

Kay laughs. "I knew it, you're brave."

We're quiet on the phone for a second. Then I ask, "Was it love at first sight? With your husband."

"Oh God, no," she laughs. "He was wearing this awful bowling shirt and smelled like old cigarettes. I only went out with him because my roommate blackmailed me."

"And then what happened?"

"Everything," she says.

This makes me smile because this is a thing I'm starting to understand. Everything. A look, a kiss, whipped cream in my coffee. Standing on a hilltop together looking out at a pond. His hand possessively behind my hip on a catamaran because he wanted me to be his. A little girl dancing for her grandparents. It's everything.

"Why do you ask?" Her voice sounds wistful, like my question has taken her to another place.

I think of how strong my mom is to have kept trying again, over and over. I think of how afraid I've been for so long, hiding behind my own fear and a carefully chosen ro-tation of dresses. I believe in love now; I've felt it and cannot unfeel it. It's an imperfect thing, and it changes and breaks and heals the way people do. I could have had love like that, or at least I could have tried.

"I fell in love, and I chickened out," I say.

"Oh, Jane. Don't let that be the end of your story. You're braver than that."

CHAPTER 36

~~~~~

A N HOUR LATER I AM SEATED UNCOMFORTABLY ON top of the DON'T GIVE UP billboard in West Hollywood. It's directly in the sun, including the metal ladder on the back that scalded my hands as I climbed up. This feels like hijinks, something Janey Jakes might have thought up and something Dan would never, ever do. But Dan is a once-in-a-lifetime person and I am having once-in-a-lifetime feelings. I know how much I hurt him. I broke this beautiful thing, and I might not be able to fix it, but I want to try. Or at least explain. So I sit on a small platform on top of the billboard that is surprisingly not covered in hawk crap. I'll stay here as long as I have to, even though it's hot in the sun and soon I'll have to pee.

I spent the drive over here debating whether this was the best or worst idea I've ever had. I cannot accept the fact that this is over. Every night I imagine myself back in the cave of that bunk bed with him. And then I imagine him in my house, walking around my kitchen. I want him to look up at me from my dishwasher and smile at the way I'm smiling at him. I want him to experience the contrast between my made bed and my candy-wrapper closet and love me anyway. I picture him standing in front of the bookshelves I painted robin's-egg blue last summer, picking something out to read because we have all the time in the world. I miss a thing I never even had.

I watch his apartment building now from my perch, and I imagine what it's like in there. I bet he hasn't called the super about his oven. I've seen him load a dishwasher, and while I was processing a lot of other thoughts and feelings at the time, I did like the orderly way he did it. He's a visual person, and I bet everything in his apartment is something he likes to look at. He's a visual person, which is why I'm counting on him to look out the window and see me here, waiting. *Don't give up, Dan.*

I watch the traffic roar by on Sunset Boulevard. The ridges of the platform press into my rear end. I shift a little to get comfortable. A teenager with a dog stops and looks at me for a second. He shakes his head and walks away.

I sit and breathe in the foolishness of what I'm doing, the complete absurdity of my plan. I don't even know if Dan's home. And if he is, he could sleep all day or leave the house without ever looking out his window. But I know that Dan likes to look out a window. He likes to see anything through the confines of a frame or the rectangle of his camera lens. And I also know that I don't care about looking stupid anymore. I am lovesick. I am putting myself out there, for him. I know what it feels like to have something wonderful, and I want it back. I give a half-hearted wave to a couple who are looking at me curiously.

They stop, and the lady asks, "What are you doing up there?"

"I'm trying to get someone's attention," I say.

"Well, it worked," the man says.

"No, I mean someone in particular. He lives across the street." They turn and look at the pink building, and a few more people stop to see what they're looking at.

"Someone in that building," the lady says. "She's trying to get his attention."

I am so awkward as they watch for my next move. This is hard enough, stalking someone who's blocked your number so you can profess your love. I know I am giving all the *Dateline* vibes here, but I need to sit with it. I am not going to make a joke. I'm not going to entertain these people. An older man gives me a thumbs-up and keeps walking. No one else makes any move to leave. I am ridiculous, but it's worth it. Only Janey Jakes could have come up with this scheme.

"Do you love him?" one asks.

"Feels a little like stalking, but less threatening," says another.

"I'm just trying to make a point," I say.

"And you can't call him?" asks the lady.

"He's not replying."

My phone buzzes, and my heart stops. It's Dan: What are you doing?

Me: Trying to get in touch with you

Dan: For what?

Me: Can I come talk to you?

Dan starts to reply and then stops.

Me: It's hot and I have to pee.

Dan: Fine. Pink building, apartment 5

My heart rate speeds up. I climb down the back of the billboard and cross Sunset Boulevard (at the crosswalk). His building has a little courtyard, and apartment five is on the second floor. I take the stairs too fast, and I'm out of breath when he opens the door.

"Crazy," he says. He's in sweatpants with a tear in the knee and a slightly too-small white T-shirt. His hair is a rat's nest. He looks perfect. I want to rewind back to before I let my worst self break my best thing so I can jump into his arms. I have a million unrehearsed things to say.

But first, "I really have to pee."

He steps to the side and lets me in. His apartment is entirely white, like a big canvas. White walls, beige jute rug. White slipcovered sofa. "Right there," he says.

I go into his bathroom and take it in. This feels personal, sitting in someone's bathroom after having arrived unannounced. His towels are white; his soap is Dove. He has shampoo that cannot be bought at a big-box store. *I knew it!* Over his toilet is a small ink drawing of his family, the boys all still smaller than their parents. Cormack has his arm around Reenie. Aidan is looking straight ahead. Dan is looking down at a dog.

I come out of the bathroom, and he's standing in front

of the couch. I smell a hint of darkroom chemicals in the air. There are two jars of water on the glass coffee table. His hands are in his pockets and his face is inscrutable.

"Who's the dog?"

"The what?" he asks.

I walk over, and we both sit on the couch, a continent between us.

"In the drawing of your family."

"Sparky, he died when I was ten."

"I'm sorry," I say.

"Is that why you're stalking me? For pet stories?" There's no humor in his voice. It's hard and biting.

"No, but I am sorry."

"About the dog?"

"Yes." I'm looking at my hands. "No. About the rest of it. The way it was when I left."

"What are you doing here, Jane?"

I turn toward him and pull my knees up to my chest. The words swim around my head, and I pick some. "I don't want to give up. Like the hawk said."

"I didn't give up. You're the one who lost her shit and left. Is that a thing you do? Because it's not totally shocking that you haven't had a long-term relationship."

"That's just it. It's not a thing I do. I don't do any of this. I smile nicely and wear exactly the right thing." I scrunch up my face a little. "I talk about my work, but just a little so guys will feel comfortable if they want to pay for dinner. I'm five minutes late and the tiniest amount bored.

I am kissable but not overtly sexy. That's what I normally do. It's a whole thing."

Dan shakes his head. "I don't even know that person. You don't even bring a bathing suit to the beach."

"Ha, see? Even my pajamas were wrong. And I talk about my work constantly, and I had sex with you almost immediately. I'm a disaster with you, Dan."

"I think we're on the same page then." God, he's infuriating.

I get up and walk to the window. I need to refocus, because I don't know when I'm going to get another chance to explain myself. This would have been a great situation for a script. "When I auditioned for *Pop Rocks*, I got the part because I'm a lot like Janey Jakes. I'm loose and funny and my face shows exactly what my heart feels. That's who I actually am. I stopped allowing myself to be that person a long time ago, but I feel kind of unleashed with you, you know? Like I don't need to contain myself."

He still says nothing, but he's looking at me like he agrees that I am entirely unleashed. I have no place to hide, so I just keep going.

"And it's funny that I'm such a mess with you and that you actually liked me. Because when I date, I have all these rules about how guys should look and act and how I should look and act. I basically lie to them so they'll think I'm Reese Witherspoon. And I'm not Reese Witherspoon, Dan. That's the thing I know now. And that's the thing I think you were okay with."

I stop and take a breath and sit back down on the couch, my legs crossed under me. Dan runs his fingers through his hair and crosses his arms over his chest.

"So," I say, "I think I should have started with this. I'm really sorry that I blew up and shut you out. Jack said some things that made me feel that old sense of worthlessness. And I walked out of that limo so small and there you were so perfect. I thought I had to be the stupidest person in the world to think you might love me."

He meets my eyes, and I should take back the love thing. It's too strong of a word to use, but it's the word I mean. I really did feel like he loved me.

"So rather than saying, hey, Dan, this feels scary, like a normal person who's been to therapy, I blew the whole thing up."

He nods. "You really hurt me." I can see the hurt in his eyes and I marvel at it, that a person like me could hurt a person like him. "Is that it?" he asks.

My need to be close to him is like a hunger. I am starving for his arms around me, my head on his chest. And I feel terrified, an actual chill through my body, that he is going to ask me to go.

"I brought you something?" I say. I reach into my bag and hand him our watercolor.

He takes it with both hands. "You thought it was shitty," he says. "So, thanks?"

This isn't going the way I saw it going in my head. He's not seeing the painting the way I do. He's not accepting my apology and taking me in his arms.

I take a breath and look down at my hands. I am on the verge of begging for something from him, and that's not how I want this to go. "Okay," I say and get up. "Thanks for hearing me out."

I pick up my bag more slowly than necessary. When I am on the other side of that door, I will actually have lost him and I'm going to fall apart for real. "Okay," I say again.

Dan follows me to the door. He's going to open it, I'm going to walk through it, and he's going to close it. That's how doors work.

I turn to him and his eyes don't meet mine. "I forgot to say, the movie got canned."

"I'm not surprised," he says. He puts his hands in the pockets of his sweatpants, signaling that he's not going to hug me goodbye.

"I'm probably going to quit my job," I say. "That's a whole other thing, and I know you're trying to get me out of here. But maybe we can talk about that later?"

He steps toward me, reaches for the doorknob, and opens the door. "Sure," he says.

Tears prick the backs of my eyes. I am so sad to lose him, to have let my bottled-up pain wreck this beautiful thing. The pink courtyard of his building is inviting me out, and I just don't want to go.

I've broken my own rules about overtalking and being overeager. I have done all the talking in this conversation. Still, I don't want to stop. "The thing about the painting, Dan." My voice catches and I know it's starting. My throat burns and I wipe my eyes with the back of my hand. "Is that it's kind of a mess, you know? I loved making it and I love how you stepped in with your fancy flowers and spruced it up. And now that we're back here and I don't get to see you anymore, I see everything about us in it. The way I put too much water in the blue and you helped me fix it. The way I didn't know what I was doing and you just made me try. It's messy. You know what I mean? It's not technically good. But it's beautiful. That's the whole point, and it makes me so mad that you don't see it. Maybe I'm actually the worst. And maybe you're a snob about movies and can't fix a toilet. But being with you was the most beautiful thing that's ever happened to me."

His face softens, but he doesn't move.

"And I love that you follow your heart around looking for beautiful things. I love that you're quiet, because when you do say something, it's perfect. I love that you want to make things that matter. I love that you know how much you matter."

He takes a step toward me and I reach for his hand. I close my eyes for a second, just to feel his palm against mine, his fingers closing me in. When I open them, he's watching me. "You know that thing you said about my smile?" I ask.

He nods imperceptibly.

"No one else has ever said a word about my smile. I think I only smile like that when I'm with you."

"You're not smiling now," he says, his voice thick.

"Yeah, well." His eyes are intense on mine. It gives me a quick hit of hope, because at least he cares. "I'm sorry. I wish I could unhurt you."

His face opens a bit more, warmth returns to his eyes. "How would you do that?"

"I could write you an apology letter every day for a year?"

He smiles the smallest bit.

"I'd drop them off here, slide them under your door, to make sure," I say. I risk a tiny step closer to him.

"What else?" He takes my other hand, and it's heaven. I have shared my entire body with Dan, but there's nothing that's ever made me feel closer to a person than this offer of a second hand.

"I'll buy you gifts," I say. "Shampoo that's never been tested on lemurs. Goatee cream."

He smiles a real smile and pulls me into his arms. I rest my head on his heart and breathe him in. The laundry smell and the cedar, hints of photography chemicals. He runs his hand down the back of my hair, permanently curly now. Everything about me that I thought needed to be fixed is just right when I'm with Dan.

I look up at him and his eyes are wet. "I really missed you," he says. "I've been kind of a mess."

We've stepped into something. It's the thing in *True Story* where they're flawed and they screw up and they come back closer, broken hearts wide open to each other. I could do this a million times and then die in his arms. I'm not unhinged enough to say so, so I just say, "Same."

Dan takes my face in his hands and looks at me like I'm the truest and most beautiful thing he's ever seen. He kisses me, a crashing desperate kiss, and the roaring ache in my heart quiets. I have been starved for this, and I have to keep myself from swallowing him whole. His hands are on my neck and then clutching my waist and then under the back of my shirt. I grip the top of his sweatpants, my knuckles against his stomach, such a familiar place. I would know Dan anywhere, at any time. I know him with my whole body.

My back is up against a side table, and something that may be house keys digs into my hip. A glass of water spills, and I feel the wet of it on my sandal.

"Bedroom," he says, still kissing me.

"Yes," I say. It's my favorite word now, I think.

We fall into his bed, and it's my personal heaven—crisp white sheets that smell like Dan. He undresses me, and I lie there more naked than I've ever been because I have said everything. It's all out there—how I feel, what I want, where I'm damaged. I understand now what it means to have everything to lose. He hovers over me, and I trace a finger along his shoulder. I never thought I'd get to touch him again this way. We make love without taking our eyes off of one another. We are a tangle of limbs and sheets, our hard selves dissolved for good. We are boundaryless; he's gotten to every part of me. I have tears in my eyes afterward. I don't know how to explain it to him, but he's not asking me to. I've shared a lot with Dan about my broken parts, but actually apologizing to him has me more vulnerable than I've ever been. *Here's my heart,* I'm saying. *Do what you will with it.* He wipes a tear from my cheek.

"Sorry," I say. "I don't know what my problem is." We're nose to nose on a pillow.

"I've been crying all week," he says and pulls me closer.

I wrap myself around him and wipe an imaginary tear from his cheek. "I'm sorry that makes me feel so good."

He smiles at me. "Happy to help." He arranges my hair like he's going to photograph me, each curl in the right direction.

"I'm probably going to quit my job," I say. "I'm going to do it before I've even thought it through. I have a million ideas I want to talk to you about, like professionally."

"Fine, but I refuse to get dressed," he says and pulls me close.

"I refuse to let you."

"I missed you," he says. "Every minute."

"Same," I say again and nuzzle into his neck.

"I know there's a way you think this stuff is supposed to go," he says. "And I don't even know what date we're on. But you were right, what you said before. I am in love with you."

I raise my head so I can see his face. I scan his eyes to see what's there. He means it, and he's not afraid of it at all.

"I knew it when we were together," he says. "And it nearly killed me when we were apart. I just wanted you to know. Because I know how much you like being right."

"Yes," I say.

"Yes, what?"

"I don't know. I keep saying that." Dan is looking at me with absolutely no expectation. He knows what he knows. "I love you too," I say, my hand on his heart.

CHAPTER 37

~~~~~~~

IN THE EVENING I TAKE DAN TO MY HOUSE. I DON'T
want to show it to him as much as I want to see him in it,
standing there next to the tile counter of my kitchen. Pulling a pitcher of cold water from my fridge. I want him to
meet Clem and my mom and know how much I have, even
though I have so few people. He stops short at the end of
my walkway when he sees the bougainvillea growing along
my porch.

"I'm going to film something here," he says.

"Like what?"

"I don't know." He turns to me. "Maybe I'll just take a
million photos of you."

He likes the robin's-egg blue of my bookshelves and
the way they seem moody in the amber light. He picks up a
photo of my mom and me in my bedroom and says I have
her eyes. I don't tell him that I sobbed in my bed watching
Grapevine twice. There's plenty of time to rehash the past
few weeks, and right now I want to move forward.

We make turkey sandwiches with big tomato slices and

take them onto the porch swing. We drink ice-cold beer and watch the fireflies. His arm is around me, resting perfectly over my shoulder in a way that makes me want to keep brushing the tips of my fingers across his. It should be strange to have him here, Dan Finnegan, who I love, but it's not. It feels like he was always supposed to be here.

"I should call Aidan," he says.

"Okay," I say.

"He's been a little worried. They all have."

"I'm going to have to explain this to them, aren't I?"

"I don't think so."

"They must think I'm kind of . . ." And I gesture *so-so* with my hand.

He laughs and pulls me closer. "A perfect pair." We're quiet for a bit. "He actually called yesterday, my dad. And I was looking at the phone thinking someone died. My dad never calls me."

"What did he say?"

"He was so awkward, it was sweet. He didn't really know what to say. He was driving and rambling on about the traffic in the summer and how expensive freon is getting and how it's good to apologize when you need to."

I smile up at him. "He thinks you did something dumb. Can we just keep it that way?"

"My dad's not keeping score."

"I love your dad," I say. "So he'll be happy about this?"

"Ecstatic. Actually I should tell them." He pulls out his phone and then drops it on his lap. "I really don't feel like breaking this quiet."

"Maybe we should send them a selfie," I say.

He smiles and kisses me. "This is going to shock you, but I'm not a big selfie guy."

"Do it," I say.

He reaches out and takes a photo of our sheepishly happy faces. We look like we're embarrassed to be this happy. He sends it to the group text called "The Mob." There are ten people on it—his parents, his brothers, their wives. He texts: all okay now.

And we watch as his phone blows up.

Aidan: OH THANK GOD

Brian: Knew it

Connor: The day the crying stopped!

Cormack: Don't feck this up young man

Marla: Bring her for Thanksgiving

Reenie: Danny, you look so happy!

At that, he puts his phone down. "This could go on for a while." I put my head on his shoulder, and he wraps me tighter in his arms. I want to talk to him about the movie we need to figure out how to make. I want to tell him about Kay and her husband's ugly bowling shirt. But I like the way our breathing synchronizes in this silence. I like focusing all of my attention on the spot where my forehead rests on his neck. So we sit like this in silence and watch the world go by on Montana Avenue.

Clem comes home and finds us like this. "Is this . . . ?" she asks.

"Yes," I say.

"Finally. Hi, Dan." She drops her bag on the porch and

waits for us to scoot over. She wedges into the empty space. "We might need a bigger swing."

"I'll put it on my list," I say.

We sit and swing for a few beats. I know Clem has ten thousand things to say to Dan, and I'm wondering where she'll start.

"So the whole billboard thing went well?" she says finally.

Dan laughs. "In the end, yes."

"I want to take credit for it because it was really inspired. But I just told her to go to your building and bang on doors. I'm not an artist." Clem gets up and sits on the porch railing so she can see us together.

"So you're a nurse and a bartender?" Dan says.

"Yes, full service," she says, and he laughs.

My phone rings on the kitchen counter, and I get up to get it. I like the way the two of them look sitting on my porch, like everything I need is in one place. I picture Dan living here with us, and I want to follow that daydream to its full completion, but my phone is ringing.

It's Barry Nielson, my old agent, returning my call. "Good call, Janey. That NDA expired five years ago."

"Okay then," I say. "Go ahead and spill it."

CHAPTER 38

~~~~~

EIGHTEEN MONTHS LATER

MOST DAYS DAN AND I ARGUE ALL THE WAY TO THE set, and most days we hold hands all the way back. There's a rhythm to it that I like. We wake up; we drink coffee on my porch. I eat a Pop-Tart, and he gives me a hard time about it. Clem sides with Dan, though she's not around as much as she used to be. She's met a guy named Whit, and Dan and I like to say that together their names sound like a bunch of people clearing their throats.

We think we're hilarious.

In a sure sign of the apocalypse, my mom and I invited Dan and Gary to Friday movie night with us. It was her idea, an effort we could make to open our circle and let love all the way in. This happened just the one time. Gary finishes his popcorn before the previews are over. Dan likes to sit in the back row. One of them pulled out a pack of Twiz-

zlers, and I almost walked out before the movie even started.
Some things are sacred, carved so deep in our hearts that
they need to be preserved as they are. I am a card-carrying
member of the true-love society now, but only six nights a
week.

My mom has moved on from the smoky eye to a full
range of pastel shadows. We go back to the house she shares
with Gary now, and I stay with her later because we have so
much more to talk about. We're both in love, yes, but also
we're honest about it. She doesn't feel the need to go on and
on about what a gem Gary is; she can share what's not perfect. I tell her about the set of house keys I gave Dan that he
lost an hour later hanging off the pier to photograph a pod
of whales. I appreciate her in a new way, how hurt she must
have been by my dad and how hard she worked to make it
okay for me. We both have a new way of living, and our Friday night check-ins matter more than ever.

There is so much laughter in my house and in my life.
Not always sidesplitting, snot-making laughter, but sometimes just this light feeling that something good and true
could happen at any moment. I look forward to everything.
Interestingly, I no longer laugh while I sleep; I actually
sleep like the dead. Curled up inside Dan, his arm over
mine in that way that seems both ordinary and like a mira-
cle. My funny dreams are happening out where people can
see them now.

Today Kay is on set for the first time. We're filming for
the second to last day at the Santa Monica Pier. I quit my
job two weeks before Clearwater's option expired, and Kay

sold it to me right away. The people from Wallflower Pictures connected to the story like Dan knew they would, and the filming has been beautifully low-tech. Dan has a knack for making a low budget work for him, as if without all of the bells and whistles, the other things in the frame have to work harder. Vinny Banks agreed to sign on as director, mainly because he liked the script but also because he likes working with Dan. Of course I'm the producer.

I like to say that out loud in the shower or sometimes under the covers with Dan. I raise my eyebrows in mock surprise, but he is not at all surprised.

"Jump-Start Love Song" is paying my bills again, just like when I was a kid. It took three hours for word to spread that Jack Quinlan sang the vocals on that song, along with the geek from *Pop Rocks*. It's one of the only songs in history to hit the *Billboard* Hot 100 chart twice nearly two decades apart. It's now the song that's on the radio every time I get in the car. But besides the astounding royalty checks, it hasn't affected my day-to-day that much. A person like Jack takes up so much space, requires so much light to shine on him, that there's not a lot left for the person standing next to him. I find that I like standing in the background where I can hear my own thoughts. This is the best of all possible outcomes for me—Jack absorbing the noise while I create something of my own.

A simple call to my agent asking him to leak that tidbit, and dominoes are falling every day. *Pop Rocks* is making a cultural comeback, in a campy kind of way. It's been out in syndication for two months, and they've started selling merch—backpacks and cordless microphones. Dan and I watch it some nights, and when we do, we laugh. I'm sure this isn't a relatable experience, watching your childhood played back to you on TV, watching your body change and your delivery improve. It's all contained right there in the too-bright studio light that they don't use anymore, but it's different now that I'm not looking at it through the veil of my memory. The truth about Janey Jakes is that she was funny. She had impeccable comedic timing and worked hard at her job. I feel a fondness for her that I wasn't quite expecting. I like the way her eyes dance when she's about to make a joke. She has a habit of worrying the bottom of her sweatshirt with her forefinger and thumb when someone else is talking, something I don't ever remember doing. Her posture seems deliberately terrible. She's not perfect, but she's certainly brave, and I find myself watching her with respect. She put herself out there at such a young age and survived. It's like moving a mountain to change the way you think about yourself, yet it can happen in an instant if you're ready.

It's Ruby's favorite show. She watches it after school, the same episodes over and over. She refers to Hailey as the pointy one, and I'm Aunt Janey. We're going to visit for a week around the New York premiere of *True Story*. We plan to reserve a whole row of seats for the Mob. I can't wait to hear what Reenie and Cormack think of it. I wonder if it will touch them the way it's touched me or if they'll just think that's what everyone's love story looks like. Complicated, resilient, and constant.

ANNABEL MONAGHAN

My mom's coming too, and I'll reserve seats in the fifth row on the aisle for the two of us. I won't miss a minute of watching her watch this movie. Maybe we'll have Chinese after.

It's the end of the shooting day, as we're starting to lose the light. I'm standing at the end of the pier with my back to the sunset watching the chaos wrap up. Dan's walking toward me, looking through his camera. He smiles at whatever he's captured and then at me. "Perfect," he says and puts his arms around my waist. It hasn't gotten old, the feel of his arms wrapped around me, my head lost in the warmth of his chest. Sometimes I watch him reading by the amber light in my living room and try to imagine what it would feel like to be tired of him, to stop wanting to reach out and find him in the middle of the night. So far I cannot. The longer I know him, the deeper I want to dig, the more he matters, like both the giant love of my life and my house keys.

"Tomorrow we shoot the ending," I say. "You ready?"

He laughs because I have my hand on my heart. I keep it there. "I love you too," he says.

I smile my widest smile. "Did I say something?"

"Not out loud," he says and pulls me toward him.

"I love you," I say, like I always do.

He kisses me, which is probably workplace inappropriate, but I don't care. Dan feels like the place from which I've launched and the place I want to keep going home to. We walk hand in hand back down the pier to where Kay is nose to nose with Vinny Banks. They're arguing about something, I can tell by the pitch of their voices, but their body language is telling another story.

"Well, that's interesting," Dan says.

"Are they meeting today for the first time?" I ask.

"Yes, and he has some new ideas about the ending." Dan shoots me a look.

"Sounds like we're in for a stormy romance."

"The best kind," Dan says and squeezes my hand.

We get in my car and "Can't Find My You," my solo hit, is on the radio. That's another domino that's fallen. It's climbing the charts again too, and I hear it maybe twice a day. I lean back in my seat and take Dan's hand and picture myself the day I recorded it. I was alone in the studio where I'd kissed Jack two days before, no longer sure of anything at all. I was heartbroken over the new story that had been laid out for me, and you can hear it in my almost-fifteen voice. I was a thing that had been just about to bloom, but so much stronger than I gave myself credit for. None of it matters because I'm blooming now.

"What's that smile about?" Dan asks, reading my face.

"I was just thinking about my first kiss," I say.

He laughs and squeezes my hand. "Who is he? I'll kill him."

"He's not that easy to track down. I'll tell you over dinner," I say. Dan's actually going to love that story, the completely goofy, wide-eyed optimism of a girl who didn't know any better.

"Fine," Dan says and turns up the radio. "Want to sing me home?"

And I do. I pull into traffic and sing quietly. One hand on the steering wheel and one in Dan's, in my out-of-practice, newly retrieved, grown-up voice. It's a good song, and it feels good to sing again. The air comes into my lungs and comes out as music. Something out of nothing, and also something out of everything.

ACKNOWLEDGMENTS

I started thinking about Janey Jakes after I read Jennette McCurdy's memoir, *I'm Glad My Mom Died*, twice in two days. I was captivated by her story and hypnotized by the writing, and my mind stayed in the world of kids growing up playing their assigned parts, reading from scripts. Everyone does this in a way—living out the roles we've been assigned—but the way it impacted Jennette absolutely grabbed my attention. If you know her, tell her I say thank you for sharing her heart and her story with us.

Thank you to my editor, the genius Tara Singh Carlson, who has infinite patience and is able to say *This makes no sense* in a way that sort of sounds like *You're doing a great job*. Besides my marriage, ours has been the most satisfying collaboration of my life.

Thank you to my wonderful agent, Marly Rusoff, who continues to cheer me on with so much kindness.

Thank you to my team at Putnam—Ivan Held, Lindsay Sagnette, Katie McKee, Molly Pieper, Nicole Biton, Molly Donovan, Aranya Jain, Claire Winecoff, Jazmin Miller,

Alexis Welby, Ashley McClay, and Sofie Parker. You are the hardest-working, most kick-ass people in publishing, and I am so grateful to have you in my corner. Extra special thanks to the PRH salesforce for their enthusiasm for my books and everything they do to get me on the shelves.

Thank you, again, to the super-talented cover designer Sanny Chiu for the vibrant way she brings my stories to life. Thank you to Mary Beth Constant for the much-needed copyedit, and to Ashley Tucker, the interior designer who made this book feel so crisp.

I know only two people in Hollywood, but they're both bighearted bigwigs who continue to baffle me by taking my calls. Tim White and John Carls—thank you both so much for answering my simple questions in granular detail. And thank you in advance for overlooking how I have overlooked so many of those details for the sake of my story.

When I had a first draft of *Nora Goes Off Script*, I called two of my writing friends, Karen Dukess and Lynda Cohen Loigman, and said, "I think I might have written a book. Can you check?" That's the nature of this job, you make something up, straight from your heart, and then you hope it's got legs, but you don't really know. They were the two who declared, "It's a book!" Thank you, always, to my writing friends for being these people for me. I have true friendships with writers I know only online and hope to meet in person someday. And I have writing friends with whom I get together and share ideas and feelings about what it's like to have a job where you show the world your heart and hope for the best. Particular thanks to Karen Dukess, once again, who did a last-minute eagle-eyed read of this book. I feel especially cared for by this community.

There are a few characters in this book named for actual people. Paula is named for Paula Schaefer, who paid big bucks to benefit the Watershed Literary Festival and won the raffle to have a character named for her. Reenie is named for a reader who attended a book signing in Larchmont, New York, and stole my heart. My Instagram friend, Sarah Miller-Adams, sometimes goes by Peanut, and she is exactly the kind of wonderful person who deserves a nickname like that.

Thank you to the independent booksellers and the librarians who work so hard to connect readers with the right story. I have seen firsthand how you stop and listen and then place the exact right book in your patrons' hands. Thank you for welcoming my books onto your shelves and welcoming me into your communities. Continually working to open doors and minds is seriously heavy lifting—please keep at it!

So many things I never dreamed I'd have (TSA precheck, a zucchini spiralizer, an interest in football)—the happiest surprise is that I have readers. Thank you to every reader who has taken a chance on any one of my books. Thank you for telling your friends, for sharing your stories with me, for taking the time to show up at my events, for writing detailed reviews. Thank you to those of you who are creating on Instagram and TikTok—videos, collages, hand lettering, cakes, and pencils. Ours is the most positive and whimsical corner of the internet, and I am so grateful that my books are involved. A million thanks to Super Reader Annissa Armstrong, who always shows up, and who was willing to sneak dental floss into an event when I needed her to.

Thank you to my sons, Dain, Tommy, and Quinn, for your loving support of my writing and for continuing to grow into the best versions of yourselves. The wild pack of brothers with Irish names in this book have nothing to do with you. I swear it's all made up, including the mother who over-prepares breakfast, but who does not make lunch. Tom, thank you for moving mountains this year so that I could write a book about a quiet, perfect man who knows his own mind. I swear it's all fiction. Really.

A CONVERSATION
WITH ANNABEL MONAGHAN

What inspired you to write *It's a Love Story?*

Just after I finished writing *Summer Romance,* I read Jennette McCurdy's *I'm Glad My Mom Died* twice in two days. It was the writing that grabbed me and made me want to reread it, but also the fact that my kids grew up watching *iCarly* and *Victorious* constantly. Those actors feel like people I know, and I couldn't stop thinking about all the different ways their lives have gone. Jennette wrote this amazing book; Ariana Grande is a billionaire. It made me think about the rest of the child stars I grew up watching, and how people tend to measure their own success against the success of the people they started out with. We are a keeping-up culture, social media makes sure we don't forget that, and I wanted to write a book about a person who was trying to keep up with what she thought she should be doing relative to her peers. I also wanted to explore what it might be like to grow up on camera being told where to stand and what to say, and what it might feel like to start listening to your own voice.

Throughout the novel, we see Jane struggle with self-worth and missteps from her past. What interested you most about exploring such struggles?

By the time we're adults, most of us are just walking, talking versions of the stories we tell ourselves. Some of those stories are the ones we're told over and over as children, while others are stories we concoct to try to understand the things happening around us. I'm not a professional, but I think an important part of our life's work is untangling some of those stories to see what's actually true. Are you lazy because someone said so? Are you worthless because someone tossed you aside? Oftentimes, as Jane discovers, those stories that we've let define our worth are about someone else's issues, not ours.

In order to inhabit Jane's mindset, I forced myself to sit with some of my own closely held and not-so-true beliefs about my worthiness. It's uncomfortable, invisible work to abandon emotional habits, but boy, does it feel good when you can see yourself through a more compassionate lens and let that stuff go.

How would you describe Jane's project, *True Story*, in your own words? What do you think makes it so important to her?

I was thinking yesterday that it would be fun to try to write *True Story* as a novel, like novelize the script I've been imagining. It's a tall order, but maybe a fun idea? It's the story of a couple who meet and fall in love and make every mistake. They let each other down (the way we all do in real life) and come back together each time with a stronger sense of who the other is. I think Jane connects to this script because it's funny and funny is her thing, but also because of the way the characters can be so imperfect and fail so miserably and still find their happy ending. Jane works really hard to hide her unpolished self, her anger, and her vulnerability. She even tries to hide her sense of humor, which is the dating kiss of death. The idea that the things she's been hiding might make someone love her even more is completely earth-shattering, given her sense of the world.

Jane gets a lot of support from her best friend, Clem, throughout the novel. Are any of her characteristics inspired by your own best friend(s)/ support systems?

I have wonderful friends from so many different phases of my life, but there's a feeling I have when I'm with my friends from high school that does remind me a bit of Clem. I was not cool in high school, that should be stated somewhere on the record in case you can't find photos, but my friends loved me anyway. They were my friends before I learned it was best practices not to say all my feelings out loud. They are friends who remember the house I grew up in and helped trim the burned edges of my perm. When I'm with them now, I relax into my most authentic self because putting up a front would be futile. Like Clem, they're a safe place to regroup.

What was your favorite scene to write, and why?

I loved writing the scenes where Jane loses her temper. I loved taking her from a controlled person who strategically plans her outfits, to a foot-stomping, name-calling toddler. I loved making up a story in her mind about the kind of person Dan is and then watching her run with it. Those scenes and the ferocity of her rage had me typing so fast that I imagined steam coming from my laptop. And seriously, no offense to anyone who went to Brown. I have no idea where that came from.

The Finnegan clan is one of the highlights of this novel. Did you always know you wanted Dan to come from a big family? Do the Finnegans bear any resemblance to your own family, or is any spe-

cific Finnegan inspired by someone from your own life?

I have three sons with Irish-adjacent names. When everyone's home, I feel like I live in a big, beautiful junkyard packed with friendly, but starving, dogs. Besides that, my family isn't quite like the Finnegans. I think the Finnegans are an exaggerated compilation of big families I've known over the years. These are families where there are too many of them to be accommodating of food preferences, and no one walks on eggshells. They temper a hug with a friendly insult. "Nice shirt" accompanied by a yikes face and a big laugh. There's something so unexpected and unemotionally charged about the way they engage. I wanted to write a family where no one holds back, where every embarrassing story is told and retold to the point that it loses its power. I love this part of the Finnegan family culture—everything is laid out on the table and everyone is loved.

Reenie and Cormack Finnegan are a wonderful example of true, long-lasting love. What inspired their relationship, and what were your favorite elements of their marriage to write about?

There are definitely elements of my own marriage in Reenie and Cormack's. I have been married for a thousand years, and what I've learned is that real love is not like it is in that Tiffany ad where she's in her best dress and he's in a tux hiding a blue box behind his back. That has literally never happened to me. In my life, love actually happens over breakfast. It happens during our morning dog walk, where we talk through our plans for the day and laugh about something we saw on TV a decade ago. It happens in line at the DMV and in hospital rooms and over texts from Costco. I've found that long-lasting love is about just showing up for the other person, giving them the benefit of the doubt, and treating them like they're as important as your house keys.

The watercolor Jane and Dan create together becomes a bit of a symbol throughout their relationship. What do you think this moment signified for each of them?

The original problem with these two is that they have totally different creative views on how a film should be made. They seem to have different views on everything—Dan looks within for approval, Jane wants approval from the hostess at the Ivy. When they sit down to paint, Jane is completely out of her comfort zone and needs to be vulnerable enough to do a bad job, to just give it a try and see what happens. Dan steps in to help and what they create together isn't a masterpiece, but it's an effort at the messy act of collaboration. I think this is when Jane loosens her grip on her idea of the perfect guy and starts to rethink what kind of partner she might want.

Without giving anything away, did you always know how this story would end?

Well, given the genre, yes, I knew we'd end happy. I did not know how we were going to get there for many, many drafts. It took me a while to get to know these characters, and as I got to know Jane, I understood just how broken she was. She has a lot of issues simmering. They felt like a powder keg about to blow, so as I neared the end, having her behave the way she did started to make emotional sense to me.

What's next for you?

I am working on a novel about a woman with a full-time job and three side hustles, who falls in love with the CEO of the largest shipping and logistics company in North America. He has a really nice boat.

DISCUSSION GUIDE

1. What was your favorite scene, and why?

2. Have you ever told a big lie and gone to great lengths to cover it up, like Jane has with Jack Quinlan's song? If so, what was the lie?

3. As Jane spends more time with the Finnegans, she desires a sense of belonging among the family. Why do you think she feels this way?

4. Do you have any special traditions with anyone in your family, like Jane and her mom have with Friday movie nights? What are they and how did they come about? What do they mean to you?

5. What do you think about the embarrassment Jane felt around her past with Jack? Was it justified?

6. Jane is especially touched when Dan's niece Ruby gifts her a bracelet she'd made. Why do you think this had such an effect on her?

7. Have you ever felt like you needed time away from your family, like Dan has with "Dan time"? If so, what does "your" time look like for you?

8. Jane's final meeting with Jack Quinlan grew intense rather quickly. What do you think about how Jane reacted to him? What would you have done in her shoes?

9. Have you ever had a *True Story* in your own life? Something you were so passionate about that you'd be willing to risk it all to make it happen?

10. What did you think of the ending? Is there any character you wish you could have known more about?

Benefits of a summer romance: It's always fun, always brief, and no one gets their heart broken.

Ali Morris is a professional organizer whose own life is a mess. Her mom died two years ago, then her husband left, and she hasn't worn pants with a zipper in longer than she cares to remember.

No one is more surprised than Ali when the first time she takes off her wedding ring and puts on pants with hardware—overalls count, right?—she meets someone. Or rather, her dog claims a man for her...by peeing on him. Ethan smiles at Ali like her pants are just right— like he likes what he sees. He looks at her like she's a younger, braver version of herself. The last thing newly single mom Ali needs is to make her life messier, but there's no harm in a little summer romance. Is there?

1

SOMETIMES YOU JUST HAVE TO THROW SHIT IN THE pantry. Flour, garbanzo beans, Oreos. Just throw it in there and shut the door. Sometimes your kids are fighting or there's a capless Sharpie sitting right between the dog and your one good couch, so you don't have time to unpack your groceries according to a system. Sometimes you just need to wing it. These are words I never say to my clients. I truly do believe in the mindful storing of food, according to activity. Are you baking? Are you snacking? Are you breakfasting? But over the past few years, I find that I'm doing all of those things at once. In a dirty pair of sweatpants. I'm starting to think there aren't enough labeled glass jars to contain the mess that is my life.

It's no secret that I'm more than a little stuck. I'm in a holding pattern, like a plane trying to land in too much fog. I am here but also not here. Married, but also not. Instagram thinks I need to engage in some serious self-care to get me back to living my best life. They're obsessed with my cortisol levels and the depth of my meditation practice, but I'm pretty sure this is a job for something bigger than the magnesium foot bath they've been putting in my feed all week. Today is the two-year anniversary of my mother's death, which makes it the one-year anniversary of the day Pete announced he didn't want to be married anymore. In fairness to Pete, he's never been one for remembering special dates.

I woke up that morning thick with grief. The calendar shouldn't have that kind of effect on us; there's no magic to the passing of three hundred and sixty-five days. It could have been a leap year and I would have had a whole extra day before I fell apart. I decided the night before that I'd make my mom's oatmeal chocolate chip cookies for breakfast. That's the sort of thing she'd do all the time: break up the monotony of life by doing something fun and unexpected. I was going to show my kids that fun doesn't die.

I left the butter on the counter to soften overnight, and I got up at six to start baking. It was late June, like it is now, and the sun was already up. I moved my teetering stack of unread mail into the sink to make room for my mother's mixer. I creamed the butter with the sugars and combined the flour, baking soda, and cinnamon in a separate bowl. I was crying by the time I added the three cups of oatmeal, wiping my tears with the sleeves of my pajamas. It's really unbelievable how much oatmeal is in this recipe, and for some reason that made me miss my mom even more.

This is how Pete found me. Crying into the Costco-sized box of oatmeal with my back to a sink full of un-opened mail.

"Jesus, Ali," he said. Of course, he said this all the time. But his tone wasn't angry like when he couldn't find a clean shirt or when one of his dress shoes had been filled with Cheez-Its and zoomed under the couch. And he wasn't sarcastic like when he waved his hand over the Leaning Tower of Paper and asked what I did all day. It was a soft, "Jesus, Ali," as if he'd run out of the energy to ever say it again.

I didn't usually react to Pete. His exasperation was sort of white noise in the background of my life. I sidestepped these comments and turned to the kids or the dog. Or my mother. But she'd been gone for a year, so I stood there crying. About the oatmeal, about the way Pete was looking at me and also not. And about the big chunk of my life I'd spent married to a man who would not cross the width of a kitchen to comfort me.

"I want a divorce," he said. When I didn't say anything, he said, "I don't want to be married anymore."

"That's what divorce usually means," I said. It was sarcastic and didn't even really sound like my voice. I felt pressure on my chest and a ringing in my head, like maybe I was going to leave my body. I have a memory of having had this feeling before, but it was when a doctor's voice put a time limit on my mother's days on this earth. Twelve to eighteen months. And I wanted to say, *Why not nineteen?* I was enraged by the arrogance of his specificity.

Pete left that night, and it's been fine. We act like we're

on a reality show called *America's Best Separated Couple*. We
are civil, almost warm, in front of the kids. He comes to get
the girls for their Tuesday night soccer practices and Saturday games and takes them out for ice cream after, Cliffy in
tow. Cliffy does not like team sports in any way, a fact that
Pete will not acknowledge, so he brings him to be his assistant coach. Cliffy packs crayons and a notebook. During the
fall and spring seasons I go to the games, of course, and
then we have an awkward goodbye in the parking lot during
which I act like I'm in a hurry to meet a friend to do something outrageously fun.

I don't. Instead, I get in my car and talk to my dead
mother. This is a new practice of mine, and I find it oddly
therapeutic to lay it all out for her and just let my words
echo off the dashboard. I wait for her to jump in with her
red lips and wide smile to assure me that it will all be absolutely perfect in the end. But she doesn't, and I miss it the
way you miss a lie. I miss the quick fix of her materializing
at my door with a tray of chicken and the insistence that
home life is easy and fun. It must be me, I would think,
because I am finding this neither easy nor fun. The actual
time with the kids, hunting stones in the creek out back or
singing show tunes in the bathtub, was always easy and fun.
But the rest of it—the house and the lawn and the appli-
ances that take turns breaking and the plumber who says
he'll come but doesn't come and charges my credit card
anyway and the waiting on the phone and the explaining to
the bank that yes, I had a broken toilet, and that yes, it is
still unfixed, and then the explaining to Pete why he still

has to use the kids' toilet in the middle of the night and his looking at me like, truly, I am capable of nothing. Neither easy nor fun.

But when she was around it was easier because I had a partner. She kept me company on Saturday afternoons, when Pete really should have been stepping up but needed to get in a thirty-mile bike ride. She was the one who helped me potty train and found the pediatric dentist that took our insurance. She was the one who caught my eye and smiled every time Cliffy said "angel muffins" instead of "English muffins." If I sounded stressed on the phone, she'd drop everything, pack a picnic, and take my kids to the beach so I could clean out a closet in peace. She was the only person alive who fully understood how restorative cleaning out a closet is for me.

My kids called her Fancy, because her name was Nancy, and it suited her. She was not a person whom I would describe as fancy; a lot of her clothes were hand sewn and she drove the same Volkswagen for twenty-five years. But she was prone to acting on a desire or a whim, anything easy and fun—a passing fancy. Sometimes her name plays tricks on me. A passing fancy. Fancy's passing. Cancer struck my Fancy. I am now Fancy-free. What I really need to do is Fancy myself.

Which is why this morning I tried the cookies-for-breakfast thing again. I did not cry as I added that extraordinary amount of oatmeal, and when my kids came downstairs to the smell of butter and sugar, they were tickled in a way I haven't seen them be in a long time. I felt like she was right there, with her long chestnut ponytail, dyed to match mine, and not a stitch of makeup besides her bright red lipstick, hatching an idea for an outing to the park or a science experiment called Baked Alaska. She'd clap her hands, bracelets jingling, and say, "You know what would be fun?" And this was rhetorical, because she was always the one who knew what would be fun. It's taken two years, but watching my kids eat those cookies this morning, I felt a bit of the heaviness lift. Just an easing in my chest that has given me the energy to hire my own services and tackle my pantry today.

I open Instagram on my laptop so I can see all of my posts at once—my clients' pantries look like they could belong to serial killers. Equidistant glass canisters labeled in my signature font. The images give me a quick dopamine rush. Bringing order to their homes satisfies a need in me that is so deep that I'm sure it's innate. As a child I wouldn't leave for school until my bed was made and my stuffed animals were arranged in order of size. My bedroom, my desk, my set of seven pencils. All of it washed me in stillness. The great thing about being an only child is that, at the end of the day, you find everything right where you left it.

I find it hard to believe that I was ever that person as I reach for the third nearly full box of cornstarch and place it at my feet next to a dozen open packages of crackers and stale tortilla chips. There is so much stuff on my floor that I fear it will rise up and engulf me. I will be swallowed whole by the Costco-sized box of granola bars that no one likes but I just can't throw out. Ferris rests his head on his paws, waiting for some of this bounty to come his way.

You have to make a mess to clean up. I'm always chipper when I tell my clients this. They're overwhelmed as I take every item out of their cupboards and spread them out on the floor. I am never overwhelmed in their houses. I talk as I go, and there's a forward-moving energy to my voice. "Now, we have everything out. Let's choose the items you use most often for breakfast!" In this way, I calmly guide them through the parts of their day, dividing their shelves into categories with pleasing storagescapes. Or I should say storagescapes™. It's a word I made up as an Instagram handle, and I'm trying to make it a thing. As I stand here in front of my pantry looking at all that cornstarch, I realize the calm I feel in those situations is because it's not my own mess. I don't resent the man who bought someone else's big jug of protein powder. I don't miss the mother who brought them that jar of Christmas chutney. My clients' messes are simple; my own mess is fraught.

I find a fourth box of cornstarch and it takes me down. I use one teaspoon of cornstarch once a year to make a pecan pie for Thanksgiving. How have I become a person who doesn't have the time or energy to check the pantry before she buys more cornstarch? How is it possible that I am a professional organizer who doesn't even make a grocery list? I ask myself this question and hear it in Pete's voice. He's asked me this before, and I can't remember how I explained it to him. You'd have to be here. You'd have to sit through a whole day of my life, right inside my head, to understand how that's possible. I'm not sure I understand it myself.

I give up and shove everything that's on the floor into a garbage bag. It's time to go get my kids anyway. It's the last week of school, and I just want summer to start already. Summer happens outside, and the mess of my garden is a much happier mess to be in. I find my keys under the camp T-shirt order form that was due last week. I find my phone under a buttered piece of toast. I've missed three calls from Frannie, so I call her on my way into the garage.

"You're going to flip," she says. I can hear the heartbeat of the diner in the background. Dishes hitting the counter and cutlery tossed into a plastic bin.

"Can't wait. What?"

"My parents are leaving the zip code."

I find this very hard to believe. Frannie's parents never leave Beechwood. "Like to go to the Home Depot or what?"

"They've won the Sunbelt National Sweepstakes. A two-week-long vacation in Key West."

"What? That's so fun! I can sort of picture them down there in shirts with flamingos on them." I'm smiling into my phone because I adore Frannie's parents. They have matching green pantsuits for St. Patrick's Day. They once showed up to an important city council meeting in powdered wigs and black robes. My mother referred to them as "that couple with the themes." They are the most enthusiastic people in the world.

Frannie and I weren't good friends growing up, but we

were in the same grade, and everyone knows Mr. and Mrs. Hogan because they're a little eccentric and also because they own the two mainstays of our town—the Hogan Diner and the Beechwood Inn. Frannie and I reconnected after Pete and I left Manhattan and moved back to Beechwood, so I've been watching them to see how they'd age. I wondered if Mr. Hogan would tire of wearing his (now vintage) Beechwood High football jersey to every single home game. Or if they'd stop wearing their Yankees uniforms to the Little League Parade. There's been no sign of a slowdown yet.

"I know," she says. "They've gone completely nuts. My mom cut her hair into a bob an hour ago—she says it's more of a Florida look. They leave Saturday."

"There's going to be a lot of pink. And drinks with umbrellas, I think." I'm backing out of my garage and the sunlight surprises me. My geraniums are blooming nicely in the pots by my front door. I plant them on Mother's Day because they're the exact shade of my mother's lipstick, and they also have her stubborn resilience. Geraniums can handle a hot day much more gracefully than you'd expect. Don't overwater and don't be too fussy about them. Pick off the dead bits and new blooms will come. My eyes catch the coffee stain on my gray sweatpants, which used to be Pete's. I truly can't imagine how she would react to how poorly I've been coping without her.

"You okay?" Frannie asks when I've been quiet for too long.

"I'm fine."

"You let out a little sigh."

"I must be getting old."

"Stop with that, Ali. We're thirty-eight. We could be having babies, starting medical school."

"Why would you pick the two most exhausting things in the world as examples of things we still might get to do?" Frannie actually just had a baby last year, and it doesn't seem to be slowing her down all that much. She handles it all seamlessly while also running the diner. She's a different kind of person than I am, and certainly Marco is a different kind of husband.

"Spill it." I can picture Frannie cradling the phone in her neck and wiping down the diner counters after the lunchtime rush.

"Instagram wore me down, and I bought a bunch of floating aromatherapy candles last night. Do you think I'm a mess?"

"For sure. Tell me what pants you're wearing, and I'll tell you exactly how much of a mess you are."

I laugh. "No comment." Frannie's been trying to get me to start getting dressed since my mom died. I argue that, without my mom's help, I don't really have time for things as frivolous as an outfit. She argues that it takes just as long to put on a pair of jeans and a blouse as it does to pull on sweats and a T-shirt. I say, "For what?" She says, "For you." And we agree to disagree.

I pull into Beechwood Elementary's parking lot and get the last spot. "Okay, gotta go do hard time on the blacktop. Tell your parents congratulations and that I want photos."

As I'm pressing the red button to end the call, she shouts the two words that she truly believes will change my life: "Hard pants!"

Before I get out of the car, I say, "Mom." I rest my hands on the steering wheel, ten and two. "I'm so sick of being stuck. And I know I lean on you a lot, but can you work with me here? Like give me a sign?" She believed in signs more than I do, but I need help, so I ask. She doesn't reply, but I hear her laugh. It's her social laugh. The one that let people know she was amused. Not the body-racking, tear-inducing laugh she reserved for Will Ferrell movies and when Cliffy said "Massa-Cheez-Its" instead of "Massachusetts." Or "baby soup" instead of "bathing suit." She kept a tissue in the sleeve of her sweater in case something truly funny happened. You've got to love a person who leaves the house prepared to laugh.

Iris is on top of the jungle gym in conference with the A-one, top-dog alpha girls of the fifth grade. She's easy to spot in a purple tank top, orange shorts, and her soccer socks pulled up over her knees. Iris has a thousand looks that don't quite work, but she owns them completely. I pretend not to see Greer, who is sitting on a bench scrolling through her phone. She walks over from the middle school every day, to avoid the horror of being picked up by me. On the first day of sixth grade, I pulled up in front of the school, put down my window, and waved at her in front of her friends. So we don't do that anymore.

I stand in front of the kindergarten exit to wait for Cliffy. His teacher is outside already talking with the other parents, but I'm not concerned. He's always the last one out of the building. When he finally comes out, backpack secure over his SpongeBob T-shirt, he gives me the smile of a six-year-old boy who hasn't seen his mom in over six hours. This smile could power a small city, and every day I wonder when it will end. I wonder when he'll walk out of school, give me a nod, and then run off with his friends. I have never seen a forty-year-old man look at his mother this way.

Cliffy throws his arms around my waist and starts telling me about possums just as the clouds lower and the sky darkens. The girls spot us, and everyone runs for their cars. I grab Iris by the hand and laugh as the heavy drops of rain pelt my face. When we're in the car, I take a moment behind the steering wheel and smile at the rain pummeling my windshield. This is the sign I was asking for. A storm is a new beginning, and I want to stay in this moment. Greer, Iris, Cliffy, and me, cocooned in this car with the sound of rain filling our ears. We're all together, we're safe, and we're going to be fine. I really do feel ten percent better today. Maybe it was the cookies, maybe it was the forward motion of throwing out one garbage bag of old food. Maybe it's just time. Greer looks up from her phone and I can see a hint of the girl she was before things started to unravel.

My phone rings and Iris hands it to me with her I'm-still-eleven-and-don't-hate-you-yet goodness. "It's Dad," she says.

"Hi, Pete," I say with my phone to my ear. I never take Pete's calls on speaker in front of the kids because I don't want them to hear how casual he sounds when he cancels plans. "It's pouring."

"Yeah, I can see that. Listen, I didn't want to text you. I mean, it's been a year. I think we should go ahead and file for divorce."

I guess Pete does remember special dates.

I say, in my most chipper voice, "Great! Text me the details!" as if he's just invited me to a party.

When I hang up, Greer asks, "Why are you smiling?"

Because now I feel fifteen percent better. I'm going to make a real break from Pete. I'm going to figure out how to make my own money. I know exactly how many boxes of cornstarch I have now. "Fancy keeps sending me signs. We're going to have a champagne summer."

© Alison Rodilosso Photography 2024

Annabel Monaghan is the *USA Today* bestselling and LibraryReads Hall of Fame author of *Summer Romance, Same Time Next Summer,* and *Nora Goes Off Script,* as well as two young adult novels and *Does This Volvo Make My Butt Look Big?,* a selection of laugh-out-loud columns that appeared in *The Huffington Post, The Week,* and *The Rye Record.* She lives in Connecticut with her family.

VISIT ANNABEL MONAGHAN ONLINE

annabelmonaghan.com
⊙ AnnabelMonaghan
f AnnabelMonaghan